Praise for *Landscape*

"The fifty-page climax of the book is one of the most exhilarating stretches of suspense writing I've read in ages."

—John Lehman, *BookReview.com*

"If you can put this book down before you find out what happens next, you have a tighter rein on your curiosity than most people."

—*New Mystery Reader*

"Riveting."

—*Midwest Book Review*

"In her auspicious debut novel, the author proves herself an extraordinarily gifted storyteller, delivering a waiting-to-exhale work of suspense that doesn't let go until the very last pages."

—Joyce Lain Kennedy, Syndicated Columnist

"Absorbing reading. Fast-paced and intense, a fascinating window into the world of medical technology and the environment."

—Judith Michael, *New York Times* Best-Selling Author

"The book rollicks along into thickets of complexity and rising action and double entendre, hitting all its marks but never taking itself too seriously, and then sorts itself out with a beatific smile that reminds you of a Shakespearean ending."

—Peter Brown, author of *The Fugitive Wife*

Novels by DONNA COUSINS
Landscape
Waiting for Bones

—Waiting for Bones—

Donna Cousins

iUniverse, Inc.
Bloomington

Waiting for Bones

Excerpt from *The Shadow of the Sun* by Ryszard Kapuscinski, translated from the Polish by Klara Glowczewska. New York: Random House/Vintage Books, 2001.

Excerpt from *The Tiger* by William Blake, ed. Arthur Quiller-Couch. *The Oxford Book of English Verse: 1250–1900.* Oxford: Oxford University Press, 1919.

iUniverse books may be ordered through booksellers or by contacting:

iUniverse
1663 Liberty Drive
Bloomington, IN 47403
www.iuniverse.com
1-800-Authors (1-800-288-4677)

ISBN: 978-1-4620-6159-4 (sc)
ISBN: 978-1-4620-6160-0 (hc)
ISBN: 978-1-4620-6161-7 (e)

Library of Congress Control Number: 2011918825

Printed in the United States of America

iUniverse rev. date: 11/4/2011

For kindred travelers
Trisha, Dave, Sandy, Brian,
Dan, and in loving memory, Kristen

Africans believe that a mysterious energy circulates through the world, ebbing and flowing, and if it draws near and fills us up, it will give us the strength to set time into motion—something will start to happen. Until this occurs, however, one must wait; any other behavior is delusional and quixotic.

—Ryszard Kapuscinski, *The Shadow of the Sun*

If the wind will not serve, take to the oars.

—Proverb

CHAPTER 1

"WAIT HERE," the guide said.

Then he stepped down from the Land Cruiser and set off on a path so sketchy it might not have been a path at all. The four passengers, seated two-by-two in ascending rows behind the front seat, watched puffs of dust explode behind his boots as he stalked away. Bones, the guide, had never left them alone out there—not for a minute.

They were parked beneath a colossal baobab tree that thrust itself up from parched sub-Saharan earth. The sun had only moments before breached the horizon and begun its assault on the cold morning air. Sitting in the roofless, wide-open vehicle in zipped-up jackets they would soon fling away, they stared at their leader's back, alert for any clue to his unexplained departure.

The land around them appeared spare and endless. Random clusters of flat-topped vegetation measured a foot in height—or twenty—and stood a few yards away—or a mile—perspective being the first casualty of a vast, alien wilderness. To gaze into the distant dawn was to feel as small as an insect. Yet a short drive in any direction could change the landscape entirely, from wide open bushveld to dense, riverine woodland or muddy, croc-infested delta.

"He's going for a smoke," Todd said, squinting into the middle range. He was leaning forward, with his kneecaps hard against the back of the vacated driver's seat. "Bones smokes, you know."

Abby was resting her hand on the plank of Todd's thigh, one variation of the bodily contact that was as characteristic of this pair as their fair-haired good looks. They were always touching, if not like this then with Todd's arm around Abby or her head tilted against his shoulder, as though physical contact formed the bond that made them a couple. But as she watched Bones

1

shrink into the landscape, Abby's fingers gripped more forcefully than before the rock-hard quadriceps of the man she would most likely marry.

"No, I think he wants a better look, up there," she said. She released Todd's thigh to point a crescent of varnished fingernail at a rise spiked with termite mounds the size of tepees. "See? He's walking that way."

In her other hand Abby cradled a pair of binoculars so powerful she could spot the ticks on a distant rhino. She held the lenses against her cheekbones and dialed down on a bouncing black cavern that turned out to be the barrel of the rifle slung over Bones's shoulder. Bones took the rifle? She hadn't noticed until now.

A glance across the seat in front of her confirmed that the gun rack was indeed empty—a long, dark void. Bones's canteen was still there, so old and battered it might have watered Ernest Hemingway on his way to shoot a lion. The ignition held a key attached to a fob that hung in the air like a spider lowering itself for a glance at Bones's guide books: *The Birds of Southern Africa*, *Reptile Encyclopedia*. Next to the books sat Bones's journal, a rain-swelled volume with curling ivory pages.

"I've seen him smoke," Todd insisted, nodding his head. "More than once." He had watched Bones light up after dinner, the flame of the matchstick a tiny comet next to the campfire that warmed them each night under a bright swath of stars. The guide had stood unblinking in the amber glow of the fire, exhaling tusks of smoke that curled upward and vanished into the night. A man who had seen everything.

Abby rubbed the lenses of her binoculars with a silken square, then folded the cloth in a neat rectangle and tucked it inside her multi-pocketed travel vest. Simple tasks that tidied and organized steadied her in untamed surroundings. A careful traveler, she looked for adventure modified by first-class provisions for comfort and safety. She would go almost anywhere with a guide as capable as Bones, and she planned and packed with attention to the smallest detail, ticking from a list the clothes, hardware, and pharmaceuticals suggested for every possible contingency.

"He took the rifle," she announced, in case anyone had failed to notice. "And the radio."

Behind Abby and Todd their friends Nina and Griff occupied the uppermost seat and a marginally superior vantage point for taking in the great sweep of the African bush. At the moment no parts of Nina and Griff happened to be pressed together, but the two shared the nearly telepathic bandwidth that comes with almost three decades of marriage. Now they exchanged a bewildered look that said, *Bones is walking away?*

None of them needed reminding that Bones was more than their driver. He was a bush-savvy scout, navigator, and tracker—the unquestioned leader. Safari guides interpreted roars, snorts, and cackles. They were repositories of essential wilderness skills and lifesaving wisdom. Most of all, they stood between the tourists perched high in unenclosed safari vehicles and the harsh realities of the African bush.

In the middle seat Todd shifted his legs to a new acute angle. His tall, angular body appeared devoid of fat, and he had recently worked his storkish stride the entire length of the Chicago marathon. Immobility chafed at him like a tether. Hands that spanned two and a half octaves on the piano now fingered a riff across the tops of his khaki-clad thighs. As he watched Bones stride away, his head bobbed on his long neck as if keeping time to music, and the toes of his shoes rose and fell against the metal floorboard. He was the image of uncontained energy, a man who had spent a lifetime fidgeting and training, every muscle primed for the long haul.

He visored his hand to stare at Bones's retreating form, hoping to prove his own astute grasp of the situation. "He's probably got a Dunhill going already."

"Why couldn't he smoke right here?" Abby wanted to know. "We wouldn't report him or anything." Her voice had grown testy. She needed the wide, reassuring moat formed by expert guides and camp staffs who kept luxury inside and everything that was harsh and dangerous out. For her, Bones's departure changed everything.

"He doesn't know that," Todd answered. "And he's not going to break a rule in front of us."

"Leaving us here isn't breaking a rule?" She lifted her binoculars. "Look how far he's gone." She paused, watching. "Maybe he wants to see what's behind that hill."

"You mean the dagga boy?" A hint of a smile played on Todd's lips.

Abby twirled the focus. "A buffalo?" The pitch of her voice had risen. "There's no buffalo."

Bones had warned them about dagga boys, the bachelor Cape buffalos infamous for aggression. Ornery and persevering, a dagga boy would charge any intruder, even stalk a person on foot for miles.

"Maybe he wants to shoot our supper," Griff said, joking, hoping to ease her discomfort. "Buffalo burgers."

Nina gave him a look. "Bones would rather shoot a poacher than almost any animal. Whatever he's doing, he'll be right back." She said this with her usual unshakable assurance. It suited Nina to believe that life was controllable and that she was in charge of her own roomy universe, but of course this was as untrue for her as it was for everyone else.

She tipped her face to search the forked thicket of baobab that canopied above their heads and wondered uneasily what wild creatures might be attracted to that stout, sheltering leviathan of a tree. Without guidance from Bones, she was not sure exactly what to look at or listen for. Now every twig and mote, every toot and whistle seemed equally significant. She picked out the network of veins in a translucent leaf. A tiny gecko stared back at her. The natural world seemed to be projecting itself with unusual clarity.

Todd locked his fingers and placed both hands flat on top of his head. He twisted around to look at Griff. "This is fun. Just sitting here."

"Relax, Todd," Griff said. "Watch for birds."

Abby pointed at a small one poised like a jewel on the tip of a thistle. "Look. A lilac-breasted roller."

Todd looked, unimpressed. He was okay during game drives, when the excitement of the hunt sucked up every joule of excess energy. Stopped dead under a tree, however, the urge to move tormented him like an itch. Now he squirmed, drummed his fingers, and eyed their guide's diminishing backside.

Abby, too, was watching Bones. He had walked past the termite mounds, hurried right past them. "Now where's he going?" she said, exasperated.

Todd stood and reached for the side rail. "I'll go find out."

"You're not serious." The expression on Abby's face said she knew he was.

"Forget it, Todd," Griff said. "He's only been out there a few minutes."

"Less than ten," Nina put in.

"Less than ten? Who's wearing a watch?" Todd's eyes traveled from wrist to wrist.

Griff reached over and tugged on Todd's sleeve. "Sit. Please. No one walks around here unarmed. He'll come back any minute."

The expression on Todd's face said, *You are so lame.* But before he could shape his disgust into words, the jarring *yak yak yak* of a frantic baboon rang across the grassland. *Yak! Yak! Yak!* An unmistakable warning to head for the trees.

CHAPTER 2

BONES HAD become a mere speck against the dust-colored plain. Todd sat sullen and fidgety in the Cruiser while the others scanned their surroundings for whatever baboon enemy the alarm call signaled. The sharp bark of a baboon usually warned of an approaching lion, leopard, or spotted hyena—ferocious hunters that pose an ever-present danger on the open plain.

Bones had assured them that predators are not interested in people who sit quietly in vehicles. (They had taken note of the word "quietly," and on game drives, if they talked at all, kept their voices low.) Predators view vehicles as bloodless, bad-smelling intrusions, Bones had said. "Not of interest for feeding, fighting, or, uh, reproduction."

But he also warned that a person on foot presents a far more interesting profile—meat on the hoof—or, equally perilous for the person, a threat, particularly if that person should step between a mother and her offspring or inadvertently startle a creature whose natural reflex would be to strike. If Bones, on foot in the open, had heard the baboon sentry minutes earlier, he would be extremely wary now.

Griff was keeping a close eye on Todd, who had folded his long body back into the seat next to Abby and sat with one arm across her shoulders, rapping a knuckle against the backrest. The alarm call would settle him down for a little while at least.

He estimated that Bones had been away about fifteen minutes. Like the others, he had left his wristwatch back in camp. Keeping track of the hour had seemed irrelevant when a guide was in charge, but in the wake of Bones's departure the lack of a timepiece unnerved him. He felt unprepared and jittery, as though he had acquired the burden of knowing all essential facts—the weight of survival itself.

6

It came to him that he had no idea where they were, no concept of the way back to camp or what hazards might lurk in any direction. He cast a squint at the plain behind the vehicle. Even land they had covered that morning looked unfamiliar and confusing.

No wonder. Bones had driven over a route as erratic and incomprehensible as the flight of a bee. They had crossed flats and hills, sudden tilting dune slopes, water, brambles, logs, and rocks. Shifting seasonal floods wiped out vehicle tracks before they became permanent, Bones had said, explaining the blank slate, road-wise, over which they traveled each day. Apparently, one road, somewhere, led to faraway civilization. He told them this while gesturing vaguely toward the rising sun as if to dismiss the idea of road travel altogether.

Clearly, roads were not required, at least not by Bones. The guide's driving, tracking, and navigational skills were phenomenal. He seemed to divine through superhuman sensory receptors the precise location of any animal within a mile. The smallest sign—a crushed blade of grass or a crumb of fresh scat—could cause him to yank the wheel in a new direction. He drove fast, dauntless, playing every gear. It had not taken long for the tracking itself, the thrill of a lusty hunt, to become as absorbing to Griff and the others hanging on in back as it appeared to be for Bones.

"How will he get a better look down there?" Abby's voice broke through the silence. "Do you think he heard the baboon?"

Bones had skirted a grove of marula trees and was about to sink out of sight into a gully or other sweeping declivity. The distance he had put between himself and the Cruiser struck Griff as irresponsible, no matter what he was up to.

Abby had leaned into the crook of Todd's shoulder. He was staring after Bones too. The heel of his shoe tapped against the floorboard, causing his knee to bounce and on top of it, the fingers of his splayed and rapping hand. Nina, by way of contrast, sat very still. Her hands lay limp on her lap, and her head was tilted back.

Griff suppressed a smile. Agitation in the people around her turned Nina's kinetic motors way down so that her movements slowed to speeds suitable for a coronation. His wife possessed a capacious mind stocked with two foreign languages and an abundant supply of deeply held opinions. Her composure when others came unglued projected either reassuring calm or an utter lack of sympathy, depending on the sensibilities of the agitated. Griff doubted that Todd would notice.

"He's going to the loo, Abby," he said. He was careful to use a doctorly tone he had long ago perfected—authoritative yet soothing; part commandant, part nightclub crooner.

For delicacy's sake, he had kept this theory to himself, but he guessed that Bones required a few minutes alone to accommodate the exigencies of his bowels, a commonly pressing matter in a part of the world where single-cell opportunists colonize every kitchen. The idea of a routine, if urgent, comfort stop reassured him that the guide's absence would be brief—even though in his judgment Bones had walked farther away than necessary.

Griff looked at Abby and added, "That's why he left without explanation and in such a big hurry."

He watched Abby let her binoculars fall on their strap while she registered and seemed to accept this new possibility. An agreeable sense of order and mastery washed over him. Inductive reasoning was a cornerstone of clinical diagnosis, a subject he enjoyed discussing with the residents who rotated through orthopedics, his specialty. He liked to point out that Sherlock Holmes used induction too, thinking retrospectively from available clues back to the likely identity of the perpetrator, from effect to cause, even though Holmes's equally fine powers of deduction had gotten most of the attention.

Now he stared at the horizon, asking himself whether there might be another, more arcane explanation for Bones's departure—something other than a call from nature. He shifted in his seat. Thinking broadly could be stimulating, but in the end Ockham got it right: the simplest explanation was the one most likely to be correct. Common things are common. Medical students learn the principle of Ockham's Razor during their first year of training. *One common cause usually explains all the symptoms. Do not multiply entities needlessly. When you hear hoofbeats think of horses, not zebras.* A smile formed on his lips. Maybe in Africa it was best to think of zebras.

CHAPTER 3

THE GAME drive had begun before dawn and was intended to end around lunchtime at an airstrip scratched in the dirt somewhere to the north. There a light plane would meet the travelers for their flight to another well-appointed encampment about a hundred miles away. Luggage had been sent ahead and might have reached the next camp already, although (as Bones had reminded them more than once) guests could arrive whenever they jolly well pleased.

Like all first-rate safari guides, Bones never hurried clients away from a captivating tableau or abandoned fresh tracks merely to show up on time for something else. Nature's clocks and rhythms determined the flow of each day, and everyone involved in the handling of Bones's charges complied with highly elastic scheduling.

Now, with no sign of a predator slinking their way and no further warning from the baboon, Griff was relieved to see everyone relax a little. Abby dug in a pocket for her sunblock. Todd leaned forward to stretch his long torso. Nina gestured toward the branches above their heads. "There's a hornbill in the baobab."

Griff followed her gaze to a white moon of bird eye. Below the eye, a crescent of yellow beak poked out like a ripe banana. Griff almost reflexively raised his camera and felt the rush of heightened awareness that precedes a great shot. Could a person become addicted to wonderment? Wildlife photography out there was almost too easy.

Todd had jackknifed a knee against his chest and was fiddling with a dime-sized dial sunk in the heel of his infinitely adjustable running shoe. He looked up and announced to no one in particular, "I'm going to jog over there and take a look."

Abby spun toward him. "No way."

"We can't sit here forever, darlin'." His overly loud voice was intended for Griff and Nina too.

"A few minutes ago a baboon went berserk out there, remember?" Nina said, pointing. She used her entire hand, docent-style, correct in any culture. "You know, the lookout?"

Todd half-stood and rocked forward on the balls of his feet, testing the flex of his state-of-the-art shoes. "That baboon probably saw Bones on foot with a rifle."

Griff gripped Todd's elbow with fingers that had snapped more than a few joints into place. "Don't go, Todd. Give him some space."

He claimed more than a decade on Todd in the older and frequently wiser direction. The two of them and Nina and Abby had met years earlier in the Rocky Mountains at a conference on sports medicine where Griff was the lead speaker. Todd, who held degrees in engineering and physiology, owned the patents on a handful of gizmos and technical tweaks that jacked up the performance of high-end athletic footwear. He and Griff found common ground in their professional interests while their age difference spawned the kind of affectionate friendship known to fortunate uncles and their grown-up nephews.

Now Griff watched Todd adjust the properties of his shoes for the stupidest run of his life.

"Let's all sing 'Bulldog, Bulldog, Bow-Wow-Wow,'" Nina said in a voice that managed to convey humor and ridicule at the same time.

At a party marking the conclusion of the conference, Todd had commandeered a piano and flirted with Griff's wife, Nina, a Yale graduate, by hammering out an impromptu rendition of her alma mater's fight song, "Bulldog, Bulldog, Bow-Wow-Wow." A contingent from Michigan got him started on Big Ten tunes and then realized he actually knew them all and begged him to stop.

Todd's encyclopedic knowledge of collegiate pep songs was old news to Abby, of course. She, like Nina, had accompanied her man west for the skiing, and the two women formed a friendship on the lifts and runs of Ajax Mountain. By the evening of the farewell party, Nina and Abby had exchanged favorite authors, electronic coordinates, and promises to stay in touch.

Now Todd aimed a withering glance at Griff, who reluctantly removed his hand from Todd's elbow.

"No, let's sing 'Roar, Lion, Roar,'" Abby put in, visibly cheered by the implication that Todd's idea to run off might be too absurd to take seriously. "You know, like the big hungry cats out there in the grass." She lifted her binoculars. "I think I see one now."

"Did he go to Columbia?" Todd sneered, pulling up his socks and eyeing the vacant grassland. A breeze stirred the faint break in vegetation that marked Bones's route across the plain. Subsets of air had begun to knit the parted grasses, and soon the trail would disappear altogether.

"We could honk the horn," Griff suggested. "Though I doubt he's forgotten we're here."

Most of the time, Griff admired Todd's bias toward action, a trait that served the younger man well on the competitive edge of technical innovation. But in a primitive wilderness where personal safety rested on a tenuous noncompete bargain with bigger, stronger animals and thousands of smaller ones equipped with lethal fangs and fluids, all of which could out-sprint, out-climb, out-fly, or out-swim any human, restraint very often trumped action as the wisest course.

While Todd sat back and appeared to reconsider his plan, Griff watched Abby raise a water bottle to her lips and drink thirstily, as if reviving herself from a near-death experience. The thought that Todd might chase after Bones clearly rattled her. Griff wondered whether she had endured his recklessness before, and whether her indulgence might be wearing thin.

A sunbeam gilded a wisp of hair that had escaped her hat and twined against the delicate curve of her neck. He endured a rush of feeling that was not desire or even yearning, but something he would place between admiration and nostalgia. Abby's beauty moved him in a deeply satisfying way, he realized, even as his thoughts turned over not-so-distant memories of more acute reactions to feminine charm.

He had learned professional detachment, of course—the deliberate ramping back of romantic feelings and sexual desire required for unfettered access to an attractive woman's bone structure (without putting in the requisite time, tenderness, and dimly lit dinners!). Not such a difficult thing, really. Buddhists studied skeletons to remind themselves of beauty's fleeting nature.

It came to him that his current, almost curatorial appreciation of feminine attractiveness seemed at once more cerebral and more nourishing than the edgier impulses he remembered from his youth. He felt mildly shocked by this idea, even as he recognized the new sensibility as one of the dubious gifts of advancing age.

At the moment Todd seemed to be moving fast in the other direction, age-wise. Griff eyed his young colleague warily. Would he stay put? Or would his restlessness combined with the impulse to show off in front of Abby override his common sense? Every bone-headed scheme had a sexual accelerator, and Todd was unlikely to hold a foot on the brake in the presence of a pretty and hyper-vigilant female admirer.

He leaned forward to check the dashboard for a horn. At the same moment Todd rose, shrugged loose of his jacket, and vaulted over the side rail. Griff reached out to grab his arm and instead clamped on a slack and empty sleeve.

"Todd, come back." His voice was a hammer.

Abby sucked up air and slid into the dent on the seat cushion left by Todd's whittled hips. Nina canted her body across Griff's. All three leaned sideways to stare down at their companion who had sprung lightly to earth and was stretching like a cheetah on a bare patch of dirt.

Todd snatched a glance upward. "You worry too much," he said, pressing a push-up against the baobab. "People live in the bush—families with children. They spend their whole lives here without trucks to cart them around." He nodded his head in the general direction Bones had gone. "I'm just going to run over there and see what our guy is up to."

Griff rose, dropped his camera on the seat, and descended the metal steps that zigzagged down the dark green flank of the Cruiser. Standing eye to eye with Todd, he labored to keep his voice even and friendly.

"Think about it, Todd. This is way too dangerous. Bones has been gone, what? Fifteen minutes? If he isn't back in a while, we'll drive to find him."

A flash of annoyance preceded Todd's familiar, easy smile. "You want to come too? Fine with me." He paused. "Bones exaggerates, you know. To keep his little flock under control."

Griff glared at the cocky, grinning face, forerunner to the frightened, grimacing ones he had seen hundreds of times staring up from a gurney, attached to a broken young body. Risky behavior on playing fields, ski slopes, and bike trails was common among his orthopedic patients. Most of them lived to tell the tale. But in a country teeming with wildlife, where mortality was a central drama of the food chain, foolhardy risk really could mean death. A person who left the audience to stand on center stage would be lucky to exit alive.

Without warning, a breezy *whoosh whoosh whoosh* split the air above Griff's head. "What the ...?"

Already on edge, his body taut, he overreacted and dropped hard to the dirt. He broke the impact of his fall with open palms that took the full weight of his body. A stab of pain pierced his left hand, and he saw that he had landed on a jagged length of thorn branch that transected the path of his fall. A second later he looked up to see the hornbill lift to the sky, circle, and drift out of sight. When he scrambled to his feet, Todd was already gone.

CHAPTER 4

TODD PUSHED through the shoulder-high grass without looking back. His limbs stirred gusts of cool and warm air that teased the skin on his face and sent particles of dust shooting up his nose. The muscles that propelled him forward pulsed with energy and a sudden infusion of rich, oxygenated blood. He knew that Abby was watching him, probably Griff and Nina too. His shoes pounded on the dirt, and his spirits began to rise.

Sitting in the Cruiser, he had sunk through every level of inertia to its deadly, leaden pit. Another ten minutes and his muscles would have petrified. He didn't know how Griff and the women could stand being stuck there, parked and abandoned under a tree.

The blood hummed in his ears. He pressed forward, riding the adrenal rush through a head-high stand of elephant grass and out again onto a shoal of hardpan. His footfall beat fast for a dozen or more strides before the plant life rose up again to grapple at his legs. A pair of scarlet-chested sunbirds flew out from the underbrush, and as he passed a copse of trees, he got a close-up view of a weaver nest the size of a bushel basket. He slowed to study the nest's fine construction, a miracle of avian architecture.

Africa's abundant bird life interested him much more when he was on the move than when he had to sit, wait, and watch. He turned to follow the sunbirds as they wheeled and dipped. Too bad the others are missing this, he thought. Their efforts to deter him only proved how ridiculous they'd become, how submissive and helpless they were as Bones led them by the nose through the African bush. Not one of them possessed a map or a watch. He himself hardly knew what day it was.

The degree to which they had surrendered their independence and accepted every rule and limitation Bones laid on revolted him. All of them had become more passive and incapacitated with every passing hour. Now they were parked smack in the middle of the incomparable wilderness they had traveled thousands of miles to experience, and they were supposed to molder in the truck like cargo?

A grin parted his lips. The hornbill was one fine genius of a bird. Hadn't he played that diversion well? He would have loved to see Abby's face, Griff's and Nina's too, when he spotted his opening and took off without a moment's hesitation. The whole rigmarole out there, the conditioning against quick thinking and decisive action, had made those three as passive and compliant as inmates.

Looking around at the unfamiliar world he had so hastily taken on, he had to admit that his split-second reaction, the speed with which he launched himself on foot into rough territory, startled even him. He wouldn't have minded a few more minutes to prepare himself by stretching and gearing up. But that was the thing about taking action: the conditions were never perfect.

He vaulted through a faint V-shaped break in the grass, hoping Griff wouldn't split a gut. Abrupt changes in plan nettled his friend, a brilliant physician whose thinking proceeded in cautious little increments. Careful judgment was an excellent characteristic in a surgeon, he supposed. But really, how dangerous could it be to run a short distance on a wide open, clearly vacant plain in broad daylight?

It confounded him the way Griff could take a scalpel to another human being day after day yet prove so plodding and risk-averse in other parts of his life. No one can function on protocol alone, he thought, scaling a sand slope in three long strides. A man needs the ability to feint, thrust, and parry when life pokes him in the gut.

A tiny wavelet of guilt lapped up into his throat and dampened the euphoria he always felt when he worked his body hard. He knew that by abandoning Griff's strictly defined safety zone, he had caused his friend more than a little distress. Abby would fret too. She tended to fret, but her worry always seemed to heighten her relief and gratitude when everything turned out all right. *Hakuna matata*, Abby!

He was running well, settling into a rhythm. His breaths came even and deep. Exercise stimulated his best thinking, even now as dust tickled his airways and pooled the liquid in his eyes. Blood was rushing like a drug to his brain. He blinked away tears and realized he felt unaccountably happy.

There was a time when he wouldn't have imagined a woman like Abby would look at him twice. He had been a first-class teenage dweeb, a high school nerd who won obscure science prizes for semi-successful aeronautic experiments and still took piano lessons in the tenth grade.

Fortunately, he didn't meet Abby until years later when he was a full-grown, abundantly educated, marathon-running man. By that time he had matured, of course, and gained a few needed pounds along with new confidence as he discovered that the world embraced restless young men with his skills and abilities. But the embarrassment-rich milieu of adolescence with its harsh judgments and deeply ingrained self-images had left a mark. When Abby fell for him more than a decade beyond those awkward years, he couldn't believe his good luck.

Thinking about Abby still gave him the charge he remembered from their initial encounter. The first time he saw her, at the gym where they both worked out, he tried not to stare at the striking topography of her body, its lovely slopes and alluring, spandex-covered furrows. She had an amazingly symmetrical face and skin so fine it appeared to lack the usual outlets for oil and sweat. Her fair hair produced its own highlights (she told him later), and she possessed the most captivating kneecaps he had ever seen, neat little ovals that sat up on the long, lustrous plains of her legs. He had added two sets of lifts to his normal routine while he watched her surreptitiously, guessing she was a model or a former NFL cheerleader.

When they finally met, she deflated the blimp of his preconceived ideas by telling him she was a middle-school math teacher who in her spare time tutored executive MBA candidates needing to brush up on their calculus. She loved the elegance and exactitude of numbers, she told him somewhat defensively, and asked, was he by any chance familiar with Pascal's Triangle?

Todd still remembered the change in her face when he said that yes, he was familiar with Pascal's Triangle, that he found binomial progressions fascinating too—and would she please marry him and bear his children?

They hadn't gotten around to children yet or even to marriage. But for more than a year they had lived together, sharing the white hot urges of their bodies and the cool, dispassionate routines of daily life. Abby somewhat ruefully gave up her regular teaching job so that she could accompany him on his more exotic travels for business and pleasure. She also enlarged her tutoring practice to include a dozen feverish teenagers headed for elite colleges. The job, Todd assumed, gave her professional fulfillment as well as ample opportunity to expound upon the wonders of Pascal's Triangle.

These sweet eddies of thought both heightened his adrenal rush and cooled the engine that powered his legs. Trotting more slowly now, with a vibrant current thrumming through his veins, he stifled a sneeze and looked around. The bushveld at ground level was a new and disorienting world. He hadn't realized how high he had sat in the Land Cruiser or how drastically even a slight decrease in elevation could skew a person's perspective. With his feet on the earth, the landscape seemed to surge and engulfed him, and the once-distinct break in the grass that marked Bones's departure had all but vanished.

He had agreed to go to Africa with Abby in part because he knew that an extravagant, ramped-up adventure carried high potential for enhancing his status as her protector. She could be fearful, but she had an insatiable curiosity about the world combined with an adventurous streak he was glad to encourage for this very reason. He did not mind admitting that he liked his role as her guardian. He complemented this delicate, accomplished woman. And he believed that travel, especially adventure travel, helped cement his position in their still-unofficial partnership.

He breast-stroked through a stand of brush while keeping watch on the tall knob of termite mound that stood to the left of his destination. The chunky turf had slowed his stride to a halting gait, and he wondered what the others might be making of his awkward gallop across the plain.

An unusual ping made itself felt in his right knee. He shortened his stride and felt nothing out of the ordinary, so he lengthened it again. Antelopes communicate by clicking the cartilage in their joints, Bones had said. Fortunately, his own cartilage remained mostly mute.

Talons of vegetation scratched his hands and face. The air was thick with insects. Some kind of raptor was tracing a spiral above the ravine that had swallowed Bones. He pushed forward to an open space where the soles of his shoes beat against hard, cracked earth.

He was approaching the termite mounds, almost even with them, when his eyes fell on a round indentation pressed in the powdery soil. He nearly stepped on the print, a blunder he knew, after days in the bush observing

Bones tiptoe around spoor. Tracks were important signposts that led you where you wanted to go. Just in time, he dodged left and landed on a relatively blank stretch of dirt. Resting his hands on his knees, he stared at the imprint and listened to his breath settle.

An elephant, he was pretty sure. What else could leave a print the size of a hubcap? The markings webbed across the track were faint and worn, a sign that the animal was old as well as huge. A similar print was visible several yards ahead, but most of the earth around him was a scrabbled mess of ruts and dents, as indecipherable to him as a tablet engraved in Setswana.

He turned to look at his companions in the distant Land Cruiser, stretching tall to view their pea-size heads over the sea of grass. Griff had returned to his seat up on the vehicle, naturally. Abby and Nina were both looking through binoculars, though not in his direction. He shook his head. They had lost him already.

A pair of plump brown birds with red beaks was bathing in the dust a few yards away. They stirred a gray cloud that drifted low over his shoes. He noted the direction of the wind, a reading Bones seemed to know at all times, but at the moment he couldn't come up with a useful application for this information. He cast a parting look at his marooned companions and turned his attention to the job of finding their guide.

Stepping carefully, he scanned the ground for human footprints or any other sign of Bones. Gifted trackers could read a whole scenario from a broken branch, yet here every growing thing seemed twisted and trammeled. Even the huge prints he had seen moments earlier had melted into nothingness. Sweat braided down his neck, and he wished he had thought to bring a bottle of water. It occurred to him that his key provisions, including hat and sunglasses, remained stowed in the pockets of the jacket he had left behind.

With a sudden crackling rush, some dark thing detached itself from the grass under his feet and lifted into the air. *Krraae krraae krraae!* "What the …?" His heart leapt into his throat. It was a bird, a francolin. Its flapping wings waggled inches from his wide-open eyes and fanned a slipstream of sand into his face.

Tears distorted the scene before him. He lurched to a halt. Where had *that* come from? The pheasant-like fowl fluttered toward a thicket a few yards away, waddled into the underbrush, and disappeared.

He blinked and sniffed and detected the metallic scent of his own rising sweat. The sun-bleached grass betrayed no sign of the bird that had rushed into it moments before. The concealing properties of the vegetation gave him something new and troubling to think about. He looked uneasily around, standing on one foot while he rubbed the back of his calf with the other.

A battalion of predatory insects had discovered the long corridor that opened beneath the hem of his pant leg. He scratched and slapped and, still blinking like a barn owl, did his best to seal the thoroughfare by tucking the cuffs of his khakis into the ribs of his socks. The sun had risen to a blinding blob. Through his squinting eyes, the heat-shirred earth appeared to lift and waver, and he was beginning to truly miss his hat.

He cast a wary look at the clutter of plants that enveloped the francolin and started to run again. Gulping air, he stepped up the pace. The day would only become hotter and more suffocating. This little foray by Bones was beginning to irk him. Had he cut out just for a smoke? He could have smoked a whole pack by now and still had time to sing the national anthem. *Where was he?*

CHAPTER 5

ABBY SLUMPED in her seat, scanning the plain that had sucked up Bones and now Todd. Todd had been gone, what? Ten minutes? She missed the watch that she, like the others, had left behind. A knot of hunger clenched her stomach, or was that tension? She uncapped her water bottle and took another swallow. Already the liquid tasted tepid and stale.

A few yards from the Land Cruiser, a waxbill shot out of a scrubby bush. She hardly noticed the bird as she dug in a pocket for her sunblock and squeezed a white pearl onto the tip of her finger. She tried to be diligent about applying protective potions to her fair skin at regular intervals, tipping back the brim of her canvas hat, adjusting her polarized Oakleys. Based on avid consumption of travel advice and cautionary tales, she believed a person could not be too careful in a vehicle open to every sub-Saharan particle, vector, and ultraviolet ray.

Working the lotion into the easily scorched skin on the ridge of her nose, she fixed her gaze on the break in the grass that marked Todd's route into the bush. She could kill him; she really could.

What was he thinking? Running away like that into open season on fresh meat? It was just plain idiotic. Her anger almost eclipsed her fear, she realized, sitting taller while she assessed the complicated undercurrents Todd always managed to stir up.

She pocketed the tube of lotion and lifted her binoculars. The barrels quivered in her hands. She focused on a line of parted grasses that might have marked a person's path across the plain, but saw that the vegetation on either side of the break looked equally disturbed. Little squalls of wind were opening and closing similar routes in every direction. She had lost him already.

He had pulled this more than once, long before they came to Africa. He would steam off on some ill-considered, possibly life-threatening mission without a thought for the consequences while she stayed behind to hyperventilate with worry and the crushing thought of a future without him.

So far he had always returned, of course. He would reappear wearing the high-wattage grin that showed off his beautiful teeth, moving his long body in her direction with the loose-limbed stride that melted the starch right out of her. She couldn't seem to stay mad at him long enough for her anger to impress him at all.

One hot summer night, he had taken off in pursuit of a mugger who had snatched her shoulder bag on the run and disappeared into an alley. She stood alone on the sidewalk for what seemed like forever, staring at the black crevice that had swallowed both men while she listened for the sound of the gunshot that would end Todd's life, or the cry that meant he had been knifed. When he jogged into view under a streetlamp down the block, his golden hair tousled and shining and his chest as taut as a tree trunk, her leather bag was slung diagonally from his shoulder to his hip. He possessed the look and carriage of a man who had slain a wooly mammoth, a male so primal and fine he took her breath away.

That and her relief at the sight of him had seemed to liquefy her joints. To hold herself steady she had needed to rest a hand on top of the wrought-iron fence next to the spot where she stood. As glad as she felt to be reunited with Todd and the carefully curated contents of her handbag, the terrible risk he had taken shook her to the core. His talent for the unexpected, for courting danger, created in her a chronic sense of foreboding that had become a subtext of their otherwise congenial life together.

She knew she had aligned herself with a human force field that even now, well into her third decade, drew her like gravity. Todd's appetite for risk occupied a space as central to his being as his charm and personal magnetism. This was the bargain she supposed she had struck—her orderly, predictable existence revved up with physical passion, world travel, and high, pulsing drama in return for her forbearance, no matter what impetuous, goofball thing he got it in his head to do.

Now, in the seat behind her, Nina and Griff took turns trying to reassure her that Todd would be all right, that he really did need the exercise and would return very soon. Abby could tell they were worried, though. Griff was furious too, although he tried to hide it from her. She glimpsed a look he intended for Nina alone, the deep parallel creases between his eyes, the tight knit of his lips. Nina nodded almost imperceptibly and placed a hand on his knee.

The two of them could do that, she noticed—communicate without sound, like elephants. They seemed to read each other effortlessly. Sometimes, sitting side by side, they gave the impression of one organism gazing out at the world through four eyes, their individual selves united inside a seamless integument of memory, sexual partnering, and common experience. They had been married twenty-seven years.

Observing Nina and Griff together, so comfy and in tune, she wondered whether physical passion and serial globe-trotting could possibly sustain her relationship with Todd. Did a long and happy life as a couple really come down to companionship, affection, and mind reading? She doubted that Todd had the slightest idea what went on inside her head most of the time.

Something in the distance caught her attention. She lifted her binoculars. A zebra trotted into focus, then another. They were cropping grass, and in the bright morning sunlight they looked as sleek and groomed as a string of prize-winning fillies.

"A dazzle of zebras," said Nina, who had spotted the herd too and seemed to know a vivid collective noun for every species. "The zigs and zags in their stripes confuse predators."

The zebras stood in pairs, nose to tail, swatting flies from each other's heads while keeping an eye out fore and aft. Across the distance Abby heard the faint sound of contented whistle-chuffing. About a dozen small birds pecked in the dirt among the zebras' hooves, and as if to complete the composition, a pair of giraffes ambled onto the scene.

Lowering her binoculars, she took in the big, gorgeous picture—the orderly zebras, the somnambulant giraffes, the sprinkling of industrious birds. Surely nothing disastrous could occur in a place where disparate animals coexisted so peacefully, she thought, knowing at the same time what wishful thinking this was. Bones had told them that zebras frequently grazed near browsing giraffes because the sixteen-footers' superior sight lines made them excellent lookouts. Should a hunting carnivore slink into range, the giraffes would be the first to know—unless a sharp-eyed baboon occupied a taller tree, that is. She had not forgotten the alarm call. She turned to Nina and Griff. "At least we've heard nothing more from that baboon."

"Yes, whatever bothered it must have gone away," Nina said.

"All's quiet on the Western Front." Griff used just enough muscle to form a small smile. "Those giraffes will keep guard on things over there." He swept an arm in a wide arc that included the general region that had swallowed the two absent men.

Abby doubted that the giraffes could view even half the territory Griff indicated, and "guard" was hardly the function served by a lookout that would lope away at the first whiff of danger. She felt a wave of affection for the kind doctor, a giant in his field, whose trust and friendship Todd treated so cavalierly. Beads of sweat had formed on his upper lip, and she noticed an ugly red swelling on the meaty part of his palm.

"What happened to your hand?"

He upturned the palm and frowned at the injured flesh as though presented with a puzzling foreign object. "Oh. It happened down there," he said, gesturing toward the spot where the hornbill had flattened him. A thin trickle of blood had meandered unchecked to the cuff of his shirt.

She rummaged in a pocket for a tissue and handed it over. "There must be a first aid kit somewhere," she murmured, folding her body to peer under her seat. The space was occupied by a half-dozen rolled-up ponchos. Her own carefully packed medi-kit currently sat, useless, in the travel bag she had sent ahead with the rest of the luggage.

Nina lowered her binoculars to inspect Griff's hand. Concern tugged at the corners of her mouth. "The first aid kit's probably in back," she said, looking at Abby.

Nina had been paying close attention to their surroundings, Abby noticed, glad that someone was. Every species needs a vigilant lookout. "Try these." She handed up her higher-powered lenses. "If you spot Todd, please shoot him." Her own words startled her. She glanced at Nina, whose unchanging expression suggested that shooting Todd was a perfectly reasonable idea.

Was Todd right in thinking that guides exaggerate dangers to keep their clients passive and obedient? Surely a hike in the bush was not the death sentence Bones had implied.

She stole another look at Nina and Griff and wondered whether Todd had been correct, that they were too gullible and overly compliant. Three or four über-obedient students in her classes came to mind, kids who never seemed to entertain an original thought or impulse. They secretly bored her a little.

She felt for the lens cloth and got busy polishing her already immaculate sunglasses. Even as she reconsidered Todd's view of the situation, it struck her that she was afraid to get out of the vehicle—something hard for her to admit, even to herself.

Griff dabbed absently at his hand. He seemed less interested in searching for first aid supplies than in watching the horizon, as if he expected to spy the men any minute.

"Would you like some water for that?" She jiggled her bottle in his direction.

"Yes, I suppose I would." He frowned at the bloody tissue. "But first, let's have a look in back. We'll be safe if we stay near the vehicle."

In other circumstances Abby would have been eager to step out of the Cruiser. Under Bones's protection she had enjoyed their stops for midmorning cups of tea and, later, for drinks in the peachy glow of sunset. Every day at the correct hour for these libations, Bones steered up a slope, crested a hill, and parked in a spot with a new and spectacular view: a river churning with hippos or a pair of rhinos jousting on a distant stretch of plain. His timing was uncanny, and the scenes never failed to thrill.

Whatever location Bones chose, he always patrolled the vicinity on foot, rifle in hand, before anyone else was allowed to touch ground. No one got out of the vehicle until Bones said they could. In matters of safety, Abby trusted him completely. His surveillance secured the area in her mind as effectively as a fifty-foot electric fence.

But even then, when Bones had signaled the all-clear and she had set foot on the ancient soil, she felt a great disjunction between the African bush and the fragile humans who ventured there. White humans in particular, with their delicate pale skin, sun-squinty eyes, and sweat-plastered hair. People like her who reeked of repellants and shrank from every insect. Who thought themselves educated yet recoiled from every reptile and arachnid, every innocent microbe, nearly every living thing.

And now, as she followed Griff around to the back, she realized that in the protective bubble of a guided safari her thoughts tended to range far more boldly than her actual person. She could muse at length about the ridiculous frailty of her species compared to just about every other creature she saw. She knew herself to be captivated by a controlled proximity to wildness and danger. Yet standing behind the Cruiser on unsecured African turf without the oversight of a guide, she felt something new and unsettling—a shriveling fear that tightened her muscles and made every movement feel awkward and unnatural.

She glanced at Griff, hoping he wouldn't notice. He looked intent on the contents of the hold, and when he leaned in to retrieve the camp box, she stood behind him and tried to relax by rotating her shoulders and dangling her arms. When she finally stepped forward, she zeroed in on the provisions with the zeal of a customs inspector, a strategy that did little to block out the intimidating world behind her.

In the camp box she found tea bags, sugar, and thermoses of coffee, hot water, and milk. Tucked beside these were a tin of cookies and the brightly woven kente cloth she had watched Bones spread across the table that folded down from the front grill.

She had hoped for more—extra water, for instance. But a quick and focused search of the vehicle turned up only Bones's canteen on the front seat. Apparently, their guide considered emergency food and water superfluous.

She supposed that Bones knew what he was about, given that the two daily game drives lasted only four or five hours apiece and always included the refreshments he packed. Many guests also carried their own water bottles. She certainly did. And she topped off her supply at midday when they returned to camp for the customary brunch followed by three or four languid hours at leisure during the day's peak heat.

Abby had loved safari life from the first day. The time-honored rituals of life in a spectacularly outfitted camp combined with forays to untamed reaches of the earth appealed to her sense of order as well as her appetite for adventure. It shamed her a little to suspect that she could appreciate the African bush only in the cushiest of circumstances. Yet standing in the scrubby grass at the back of the Cruiser with no guide and a fresh understanding of the limited supplies available to them, she felt the cords in her stomach knot.

The buzz of insects swelled and faded, and the early morning sun had begun to cook up a stew of vegetable scents. She tried not to think about the minutes ticking by, the cool of dawn melting away with no sign of Bones or Todd. Neither of the men was carrying water as far as she knew. Her own mouth had turned pasty with thirst. The day was just beginning to crank up the heat. She leaned against the reassuringly solid chassis of the Cruiser and told herself to breathe, breathe, breathe.

CHAPTER 6

NINA RAISED Abby's high-powered binoculars and willed Todd's cretinous blond head to show itself over the fringe of grass. Even for an irrepressible extrovert like Todd, running into the African bush was stunningly rash behavior. She would relish the spectacle of him trying to charm his way back into their good graces when he rejoined the party—if he rejoined the party.

The notion that he might not return came to her sharp and unbidden, like the sting of an insect. Just as quickly, she brushed that thought aside. Todd was impetuous, but he was also a superbly conditioned runner with a young man's hearing, vision, and reflexes. Of course he would return.

She tightened her grip on the barrels and took a long look at the countryside, paying special attention to the shadows trailing from every tree, bush, and rock. Although the sun still sat low on the horizon, heat was beginning to distort the view across the savanna, and each patch of shade had darkened to a black, impenetrable pool. The day was warming up, and soon the big cats would be looking for a cool place to rest.

Normally she viewed a lion sighting as a welcome event, even when the drowsy creatures were sacked out and senseless, as they often were during the day. From the safety of the Cruiser all lions seemed thrilling and accessible— the frisky cubs calling *awuuh awuuh awuuh*; their canny mothers, all sinew and stealth; and the ferocious, widely yawning males with shoulders hunched like loaded springs. While two men wandered around on foot, however, the last thing she wanted to see was a lion.

She had paused to examine the damage to Griff's hand, a troubling injury for a surgeon, and decided not to interfere. Griff would submit graciously to Abby's attentions, she knew, and Abby herself could benefit from the relief of action versus free-floating anxiety. Providing first aid gave her something to do, at least, while the minutes dragged on.

Abby was one of Nina's youngest friends, a person she found refreshingly outward-looking, with interests and curiosity that bridged the divide in their ages. She had a head for numbers and a lifelong love of reading, a combination Nina thought admirable and particularly treasured in a teacher. Abby's age placed her on the connecting isthmus between Nina and her own adult children, another undeniable attraction that made her helpful from time to time as a sort of intergenerational lookout with a view in both directions.

Interestingly, it seemed to Nina, Abby appeared unaware of her own beauty, an indifference that did not preclude a somewhat comic compulsion to tend to her person. She was a dedicated self-slatherer, mirrors not required, with access to personal care unguents at all times. Her frequent applications of lotions and balms seemed almost unconscious, a self-protective gesture that laid bare a fearful and compulsive nature.

Nina shifted in her seat. The absence of Bones and Todd was beginning to irritate her, not just because they were gone but because she had no way of knowing how long they had been gone. Without her watch she had lost a defining characteristic of her life—a knowable, linear structure that provided rigor, certainty, and deadlines. If a person said "wait here" and was gone fifteen minutes, one could reasonably wait a little longer. But what if half an hour went by, and that person still had not returned?

She squinted into the sun. Nature's timepiece still hung in the lowest quadrant of the sky, but it told her nothing useful. All she knew for sure was that minutes were passing, and time had begun to feel freighted with worry.

She swept the binoculars across the horizon, hoping to spot both Bones and Todd. At this point she would settle for just one bobbing head atop the shoulders of a man whose relaxed demeanor told her he was bringing an unremarkable report about the other. She wanted news, any crumb of information that would move all of them out of the current insupportable status quo.

Through the lenses two spindle-legged foals came into view, high-stepping to join the grazing zebras. In the spotlight of the sun, the striped animals stuck out as vividly as an old chain gang laboring on a rural road. She moved her sights to the nearby giraffe. It seemed to blink its long eyelashes at her between bites of foliage torn from a treetop. Occasionally she glimpsed a foot or so of prehensile tongue.

She panned to the shadows and studied each black depth for a shape or movement out of synch with its surroundings. Zebras and giraffes were favorite lion foods, she knew, although a giraffe was difficult to bring down unless the lion caught it splay-legged at the edge of a water hole. Zebra foals, however, were relatively easy prey. Bush groceries, Bones called them.

At one time she might have found the scene before her dull, a swath of undistinguished wasteland bereft of cultivation, refinement, or any sign of higher intelligence. But she knew that such an attitude revealed more about the viewer than the view. Time and again on her travels with Griff, a knowledgeable guide had shown them how to see a place differently, with greater understanding and appreciation. This was a goal of her own work as an architectural docent.

She could identify hundreds of buildings by ownership, architect, building materials, and style. Equally important, she understood the habitual inattention of human beings, a peculiarity that fueled demand for her walking tours. Even lifetime residents of Chicago, her home city, who walked its most notable streets every day required guidance to really see and understand the extraordinary buildings all around them.

It was not lost on her that Bones supplied similar insight to the African bush. Under his guidance she had come to experience the bush through more enlightened senses and to recognize in it a realm as complex and fascinating as any on earth.

Bones knew animals, plants, rocks, and more birds than she thought existed. Ask, "What's that insect?" and he would know. Inquire about an herb, and his reply might wander to indigenous medicines. He could name constellations in the night sky, fish in the river, the spoor of a hundred creatures. Best of all, Bones possessed an engaging ability to parlay every subtlety of nature into an enchanting drama.

At first she had taken his erudition with a big dose of skepticism. Had he really mastered, just for starters, the correct common and scientific names for every living thing? She was well aware that he could easily invent to fill in the blanks.

"Look! A rare, white-bellied Cessna!" He had said this shortly after their arrival as they watched the small plane that had delivered them circle and fly out of sight. The joke had given her pause.

But Bones had won her over almost immediately. He showed a profound respect for the natural world and an ease of functioning in it that could come only from long, richly informed experience. The details he doled out at judiciously spaced intervals, occasionally with the help of a reference book, seemed logical as well as fascinating, and she had days earlier suspended her disbelief just as she would when reading an engaging work of fiction.

"Let me remind you what to do when an animal comes too close." He had said this during their first game drive, his soft, polite voice melting into the natural world as smoothly as his earth-toned clothing. The syllables marched out evenly spaced, like goslings headed for the river. "You do not wish an animal to feel threatened," he had said. "Therefore, should one approach, please remain calm. Do not move or make a sound. If you are on foot, you may back away slowly, but you must not fall down."

"What happens if you fall down?" Abby had asked, wide-eyed, knowing the answer.

"Then you become eaten."

Someone had commented that the bush was the ideal place in which to commit murder because within hours all the evidence including the corpse and its boots would be dragged away, shredded, or consumed. The remark had been made innocently, but thoughts of infamous human behavior on the continent had caused a moment of uncomfortable silence. Even the land they explored each day hosted criminal violence, they all knew. The ongoing duel between game poachers and conservationists had more than once resulted in a vanished person.

"I think the patient will live." Abby's voice pulled Nina back to the little universe of their parked vehicle. She was walking around from the rear holding a thermos and one of the metal coffee mugs that fit into the camp box like pieces of a puzzle. "Would you like a half cup of coffee? We're rationing."

"Yes, I'll come down," Nina replied, detecting the willpower behind Abby's cheerful tone.

With her feet on the ground, she stretched luxuriantly, enjoying the deep massage of kneading muscles. She bent double to touch the toes of her shoes and watched a millipede trace a circle in the dirt.

"Let me know if you want more," Abby said, pouring a thin stream into a mug.

Griff joined them, carrying the tin of cookies. His free hand was swathed in a patchwork of taped gauze squares. He raised this construction like a witness taking an oath. "We found a first aid kit in back," he said, looking at Nina. "Abby fixed me up."

"Mm-hmm," Nina murmured, noting bruised puffiness around the edges of the dressing. The wound would need more care soon to prevent a nasty infection. She knew Griff was thinking this too.

Abby took Griff's hand in hers and gently flattened the corners of the bandage. "I could have done a better job with soap and water and my own first aid supplies." Exasperation colored every word.

"Yes, and opened a clinic too," Nina said with a smile. Preparedness was the raft that kept Abby afloat.

She watched her friend tend Griff's patiently extended hand. It occurred to her that Abby might be nursing a crush on her husband. She turned the idea over in her mind not with alarm or jealousy but with detached consideration. Infatuation can be harmless, even beneficial, she believed, when the parties involved keep the sparks under control. Sexual attraction adds a frisson of energy to group dynamics, a *je ne sais quoi* that she actually preferred to the rigid awe Griff seemed to evoke in most people familiar with his rarified status in the world of medicine. Abby, on the other hand, had always appeared charmingly at ease around both of them, a quality that helped draw them together as friends.

Nina sipped the rich brew and cast a long look across the plain. She was not one to dwell on disquieting thoughts or to turn neutral observations into something sinister. Very correct people often possess unrestrained imaginations regarding the sexual lives of others, and she liked to think that she was different in this regard—a realist. Griff was quite a dish, actually, and it did not surprise her at all that other women might flirt with the good doctor. In fact she rather expected it.

She took another swallow. The coffee tasted delicious, as did all of the impossibly elegant food and drink that emerged from bush kitchens on the outskirts of their camps. A twinge of hunger twisted inside her.

The previous night's dinner, served on a long table lit by candles under a brilliant night sky, had been the usual three-course miracle. Carrot ginger soup, roast lamb with couscous and grilled vegetables, lemon cake as velvety as the evening air.

The sensual pleasure of the outdoors heightens every experience, she reflected, savoring the memory of the food and wine followed by a torch-lit walk with Griff back to their tent. She had lingered under a hot shower, soaping herself with fragrant lather on a slab of granite not thirty yards from a pod of honking hippos. And then came the deep comfort of the spectacularly netted bed with Griff's warm body close beside her.

She glanced at him. Away from the demands of his practice, he redirected forgotten energy to their bedroom, a stirring place in itself when the walls were canvas and the night music a symphony of frog croaks, hippo snorts, and the occasional roar of a not-so-distant lion.

Griff was a little like Abby, she realized, in that he didn't begin to fathom his own appeal. His flirt detector was shockingly weak, and she was quite sure he saw nothing out of the ordinary in Abby's solicitous behavior. His innocence in this regard had at one time annoyed her. *Wake up, Griff!* But with time and the understanding that she had nothing to fear, she had come to view her husband's naiveté as part of his charm. Now she leaned into his chest and planted a kiss on the nascent stubble that roughened his cheek.

He looked abashed and responded by waving the biscuit tin in her direction. Griff wasn't much for spontaneous displays of affection, a trait she had learned to accept, even admire. In the end, her husband was a still-waters-run-deep kind of man. His innate goodness and constancy, she knew, would outlast all the stormier and more strenuously demonstrative varieties of love and romance.

She selected a fat wedge of shortbread. The pastry was dense and crumbly, baked in the early hours before their departure from camp that morning. Griff and Abby each took one too. They fell silent while they ate, standing in a row by the truck. The absence of Bones and Todd pressed down like a lid. No one was prepared to voice a plan of action that suggested the men would not return soon.

Griff cleared his throat. "Our supply of water could become an issue."

"You've taken inventory?" Nina looked at Abby, guessing she would have numbers.

"Mm-hmm." Abby swallowed. "We used about half the hot water to clean Griff's hand. Bones's two-quart canteen is full. My water bottle is down to ten

ounces or so. We have a cup of milk. The coffee thermos holds about a quart."
She raised the container in her hand. "That's roughly, um … a hundred and
thirty ounces."

Nina and Griff shared a look.

"A little more than three cups per person. For the five of us."

Nina peered into the mug she was holding. "Coffee isn't the same as
water."

"Water is best for rehydration, yes." Griff's brows had pushed the creases
between his eyes into a pair of dark ravines. "Neither of the men has water
with him, and they're both going to want plenty when they get back here. All
of us will need more before long."

He threw a glance toward the blaze of sun that had just cleared the
treetops. "There will be lunch and a cooler at the plane. Does anyone know
how far we are from the airstrip?"

Nina glanced at Abby, who returned a blank expression. They both looked
at Griff. None of them had any idea where they were.

CHAPTER 7

GRIFF'S HAND had begun to throb. He didn't want to worry Nina, but he was sure that the wound under the makeshift dressing harbored infectious contaminants, possibly fungal spores from the thorn punctures in addition to whatever microbes lived in the soil. Abby had rubbed the dirt-caked mess with a tissue while he trickled warm water over it. He had used an antiseptic wipe too. But with little water and no soap, the job had been sketchy at best.

His tetanus prophylaxis was up-to-date, at least. When they got to the next camp, he would do a thorough job of debriding and bandaging the wound using the medical supplies he carried in his luggage. He would start a course of antibiotics too.

It had never occurred to him to bring a first aid kit on a game drive, not aboard a heavy-duty Land Cruiser captained by an operative at the elite end of the wilderness travel business. Of course, he hadn't anticipated that the captain would abandon ship, that Todd would run off like a fool, or that he would be felled by a hornbill and land on a thorn branch, either.

While Abby and Nina returned the camp box to the rear hold, he had climbed back to his seat in the Cruiser. Now he made a nest of his good hand and rested the hurting one on top.

"Do you think it would be all right to walk around the tree?" Nina stood on the ground near him, looking at the baobab as if already planning her route. "I'd like to see the whole thing."

He regarded her with alarm. *Certainly not.* But he held back the impulse to say no. Questions like these from Nina were not really questions; they were Nina thinking out loud. She would make up her own mind, whatever he said.

"Well," he answered, choosing his words. "The safest choice would be to stay right here." He watched her study the tree. She was not a big risk-taker, and he wondered whether Todd's disdain for caution had infected her too.

"The animals must be giving us a wide berth by now," she said. "You know, to them the Cruiser reeks." She smiled up at him. "I'll just go take a look."

He intended to smile and nod, but she turned to go before his lips or head actually moved. He fixed a stare on her back as she picked her way over the network of baobab roots. It wasn't easy to quash the impulse to shout warnings. *Go slowly! Be careful!*

"Don't worry, Griff," she called over her shoulder. "I'll go slowly and be careful."

To his surprise, Abby fell in behind her, like something stuck to her back. He guessed that Abby needed to urinate, and he almost smiled at the girl's modesty, even now. She looked to be suffering an inner fit, as though following Nina around the tree was as awful a choice as peeing near the vehicle or wetting her pants.

Abby tended to be fearful, Griff had noticed. Jumpy. Especially around Todd, whose unpredictable behavior would rattle anyone's nerves. But with Bones in charge she had relaxed a little. The guide's protection had felt unwavering and secure, even to him. That's what guides were for, after all.

And now their protector had abandoned them. Yes, he had to admit, he was beginning to feel abandoned even if Bones's intention had been to spare the rest of them an unpleasant gastric emergency. He glared across the forbidding terrain. *Get back here right now, Bones, and we won't tell anyone you left us alone, defenseless, and lost in the African bush.*

He slipped off his hat and dropped the dusty thing into one of the metal troughs used for stashing gear. The hat settled next to the camera that had given him pleasure that very morning but now seemed extraneous to their current, increasingly acute needs. Tension and thirst were giving him a headache. He used all ten fingers to massage the crown of his head.

Photography suddenly struck him as a presumptuous pursuit—arrogant, even, to sit high above the ground taking pictures of creatures eating, drinking, and struggling to protect themselves and their young, as if those biological imperatives were somehow strange or entertaining and not applicable to himself. At the moment he felt less than superior to any animal that could thrive in a place that might so easily defeat him. Although the tasks of life here seemed elemental and clean, they were way beyond his sphere of competence.

The spiked branch that had clawed into his hand sat on the ground near the Cruiser. He got out and stepped back to take in its full measure. About thirty inches long and the diameter of a broomstick, it resembled a disciplinary tool from some primitive dungeon. He found a safe place to grab the branch and lifted it from the dirt. Ragged fibers jutted from either end. The section had been ripped from a larger limb and then broken again, possibly by an elephant foraging for a pleasant addition to its high-fiber diet.

The black bark bore no resemblance to the gray exterior of the baobab. How that piece of tree had ended up in this location, he could only guess. Hooked on the hair or hide of the elephant, perhaps, or tumbled about by the wind. He placed the branch under the top seat in the Land Cruiser as a precaution. If he did develop an unusual infection, the lab might be interested in its source.

Nina and Abby had moved out of sight. They had been careful in their movements, he was glad to see. Both of them had paused to look and listen before every few steps forward, the way Bones had done when he scouted out a new area. Unlike Todd, the women had learned the value of caution in the African bush.

Griff guessed that the baobab was at least a hundred years old. The species was the world's largest succulent plant, and this tree's multiple trunks had thickened at their common base to a circumference of seventy-five feet or more. The growth rose up from the ground like a fortress. A dozen fat branches grew from the top, and each of those upper limbs was the size of a more conventional tree. The limbs pointed skyward, subdivided, and tapered off at swaying, drunken angles. "The upside down tree," it was called because the crown resembled inverted roots.

Animals had stripped away wide patches of bark near the bottom, but this abuse didn't seem to have harmed the big galoot at all. About nine feet up, a slender fig tree grew out of a fold of bark where an airborne seed had long ago taken hold. On the fig's branches sat a gathering of twittery black-necked birds whose name he didn't remember.

He decided that the women had had more than enough time alone. "Nina? Everything okay?" he called with sufficient volume for her to hear, he hoped, but not loud enough to disturb the wildlife. Would a human voice out there disturb the wildlife? He did not know. He ventured a few steps into the maze of baobab roots. "Nina! Everything okay?"

There was a quickness in his breathing as he moved deeper into the shadows, away from the refuge of the vehicle. Nina and Abby might not hear him, he realized, glancing up at the chirping birds. And he might not hear them. Instead of waiting and worrying, he decided to take a few steps around the tree.

He moved counter to the direction they had gone, hoping to meet them coming his way. Bugs whined in his ears, and a yard or so ahead a small, deft creature scooted into the underbrush. He kept his eyes moving from the ground in front of his boots to the gradually emerging world beyond the ancient tree trunk, ready to freeze or bolt should an inconvenient animal turn up.

Each step added another slice of bushveld to his view—a strip of sunny grassland, a wind-whipped thorn tree, the soaring acrobatics of two bateleur eagles that climbed, looped, and flew out of sight. The surface of the baobab itself drew his attention as he moved around its convoluted footprint and discovered a sequence of hefty bulges and folds that looked more like muscles than wood.

He had covered less than a quarter of the tree's girth when something grabbed his right leg, the one extended behind him mid-stride. His pant leg tugged against his shin as if gripped in the incisors of a tenacious animal. He teetered and did his best to balance with all of his weight on his forward foot. The toe of his right foot remained rooted to the ground behind him. He felt the push of his lungs against the skin of his shirt. Holding both arms close he tried to keep his torso immobile while he turned his head for a look at his attacker.

A sharp, three-cornered thistle had snared his pants. The prongs were sunk like fangs into the woof and warp of the cloth. The thistle grew from a stem that bowed toward him and was pulling back with unrelenting force. A trout on a hook would have a better chance of wiggling free, he thought, crouching to examine the spines that held him.

Although he felt vastly relieved not to be facing the jaws of an African animal, the injury to his hand was more than enough reminder to respect the powers of African foliage. Plants too had developed strategies for survival and procreation—impenetrable armor, noxious juices, savagely spiked and serrated weaponry. Even the tiny hairs of the buffalo bean would cause horrific welts on a person's skin after the slightest contact. Bones had told them that, and of course, he thought with grudging admiration, Bones knew everything.

The thistle was no buffalo bean, but a promiscuous little hitchhiker that attached itself to passersby in an indiscriminate lust for fertile ground. Griff knelt on one knee and with his good hand gingerly fingered the seed pod, tilting his head to look through the magnifying portion of his bifocal sunglasses. The thistle held a firm grip on the fibers in his pants. Detaching the prongs from the cloth would require some kind of instrument, cutting forceps maybe, or the staple remover in his desk.

A squadron of low-flying insects whizzed past his bare head, and with every breath he drew in a peppering of dust. He wanted nothing more than to stand up and get out of there, with or without the thistle as a passenger, so he yanked the stem to disconnect the thorn flower from its moorings. A tangle of interlocking flora two feet away shimmied and shook and gave him such a fright that he sprang up and stumbled backward. A bee the size of a hummingbird rose from the foliage. With one swift kick he freed himself and stepped away, trailing a length of stem from the thistle stuck to his pants.

Four rapid strides took him to the crest of an extruded root, one of dozens that snaked out from the base of the tree before nosing into the earth. He stopped there a moment to compose himself and scratch an itch high up near his hairline.

"Nina! Everything okay?"

Now he truly doubted that she could hear him. The baobab was immense, surely one of the largest living things on earth and a formidable barrier to the wavelengths generated by his puny human vocal cords. The tree seemed to both gather and muffle the ambient sounds of the bush—the shush of the breeze in the grass, the constant buzz of insects, the tapping and chirping of birds that became one with the ever-present undercurrent of the audible. For a man to speak or even shout into this churning river of noise was to fling a droplet into the Zambezi.

The next turn in the tree resembled the profile of a tall, stout woman emerging through the bark. Griff hurried around the apparition, feeling increasingly uneasy about his separation from Nina and Abby. With every step, tiny thistle points brushed against the skin of his calf.

He skirted another bulbous outgrowth and spied an impala in the grass about a hundred yards away. A herd of ten or fifteen impalas was spread out on the flatland between the baobab and a cluster of acacia trees. They were slender, graceful animals the gold-brown color of autumn leaves. Each individual stood stock still with its neck stretched tall and stiff below a dainty head turned to look directly at him.

He recognized the posture. Impalas were unusually alert to possible dangers and gave early warning to other animals in their vicinity. This bunch probably held Nina and Abby in their sights too. He watched two or three flag their white tails and turn away or nibble grass, but only for a moment. As long as they detected humans on their turf, they would remain sensitive to every move.

He inched forward, taking care to watch where he stepped. A superbly disciplined army of ants marched single file up and over the next root in his path. The pulsing black line circled a seed pod and exited beneath a fringe of bracken. A tiny lizard was flattened on the wall of the baobab as if shot from a cannon. Some kind of falcon hovered over the grass beyond the tree. The bird dove earthward and rose up with a fat, squirming rodent hung from its beak.

He had walked at least halfway around the tree. Still he saw no sign of Nina and Abby, who, he realized, must have gone back the other way. This would be comical if he felt like laughing. He did not. The sun was on him now, and though it had barely cleared the treetops, heat pressed against his face like a flat iron. He was glad for his sunglasses and couldn't believe how shortsighted he had been to leave his hat in the vehicle.

Out of the corner of an eye, he caught a disturbance, nothing more than a flash in the grass. The impalas exploded in a confusion of kicking and leaping. Their whizzing alarm calls roused a pair of frisky spring hares from their hiding place.

A dark, sloped silhouette cut through the underbrush, and a moment later, Griff witnessed the panicked thrashing of a small white-bellied yearling. He backed against the tree and hastily side-stepped around its broad curves, retracing his route back to the Cruiser. He tripped on a root and caught himself against the trunk. The lizard he had seen earlier dashed off to a new, safer location. Griff managed to move out of sight, but not out of earshot. Even as he backtracked, the baobab could not blunt the sound of the ill-fated impala's frantic shrieks.

CHAPTER 8

"Is THIS whole thing one tree?"

Abby was behind Nina, following so closely her voice could have come from an earbud. From time to time, Nina felt warm breath on the side of her neck. When she stopped suddenly, which she did often as she picked her way over and around the roots of the baobab, Abby bumped into her.

"I think it's the kind that can grow multiple trunks. The trunks fuse together, and sometimes the center is hollow," Nina said over her shoulder, positioning a foot carefully. "I'd like to find an opening."

"I thought you had to pick a flower." Safari code for take a pee. "And I didn't want you to wander off alone."

Nina stopped and turned. "Very thoughtful. But no. I wanted to see the rest of the tree."

She had read that African tribes had once used hollow baobab trees as post offices, prisons, and even water tanks with spigots sticking through the trunk. The idea intrigued her, and she decided that a cautious, hypervigilant exploration of the tree's perimeter would be a low-risk venture. She hadn't counted on the added worry of Abby trailing along behind her.

But now Abby was there, and so far she had behaved admirably. While they advanced around the tree's great belly, Nina stayed in the lead, watching where they stepped. Both women had on lightweight pants, tall socks, and sturdy boots. Abby had zipped up the travel vest she wore over her long-sleeved shirt and then spritzed her own and Nina's cuffs and collar with insect repellant, a precaution Nina usually reserved for late afternoon when the mosquitoes began to rise. She had quashed a flare of impatience and then succumbed silently to the spray, knowing that Abby drew comfort from small, practical measures that held at least the illusion of control.

The immense tree by their side offered a sense of protection too, a barrier to put between themselves and danger should a frightening species amble into view. Nina wasn't about to mention it, but at present the biggest dangers were probably from snakes, dehydration, and the snare of Abby's own disabling fear—threats the baobab did nothing to minimize.

She stopped for a moment, balancing on a woody ridge to look back at her friend, whose skin was slick with sunblock and pale with apprehension. "Trees are comforting, don't you think?"

Abby looked at her, dubious.

"When you were a girl, did you read *A Tree Grows in Brooklyn?*"

"Uh-huh."

"A tree that withstood every hardship, like the people?"

Nina had done this with her children, cited literature to enlarge or redirect their thinking. Before long, her sons and daughter had perfected the technique themselves. "I'm just trying to help enlarge and redirect your thinking, Mom," they would say after quoting a rebellious or anarchistic author. It was a brainy brand of talking back they knew delighted her.

Abby wore a look that said, *What am I, a moron?* But she played along, her voice turning creepy. "Yeah, but don't forget *The Message in the Hollow Oak.*"

"What was the message in the hollow oak?"

"I have no idea." Her glistening lips parted in a grin.

Nina hadn't seen her smile since Bones walked away, and the sight raised her spirits too. The morning had been particularly unnerving for Abby, a worrier with a vivid imagination who found herself with no guide, no guy, and no gear. So far, Nina thought, she was holding up pretty well.

"How about *Tree Women?* Louisa May Alcott?"

A glint in Abby's eye said she was game. "You mean, *Little Trees?* I loved it. Almost as much as *A Tale of Two Trees.*" She laid a hand on the baobab. "It was the best of trees, it was the worst of trees …" Her chortle ended in a snort that could have come from a warthog, and this made both of them laugh. Her cheeks had flooded with color.

"*Moby Tree.* Call me Baobab!" Nina shot back.

Nina had once suggested to Griff that he write prescriptions for laughter along with the medications he prescribed. "A cartoon with every pill," she had said, liking the idea. He had replied gravely that he required scientific proof that laughter was efficacious.

They had now walked around a sizable fraction of the melded trunks, but Nina could not tell exactly how big the baobab was or what unexpected wings and additions might jut out beyond their line of sight. The full face of the sun hung well above the distant foliage, casting its bright light on her and Abby and everything they touched. Penetrating rays reached deep into nooks and crevices on the baobab's gnarled exterior.

She placed a hand on a rounded column skinned of its bark and thought how unlike a plant the immense tree seemed. A curb-like root led to another columnar growth and then to what she had been hoping to find. Even so, its sudden appearance brought her up short.

The tree had long ago split apart and opened to reveal a circular interior space the size of a small room or apse. The cavity was tall enough for a giraffe, the walls as smooth as the inside of a gourd. At that hour the sun floated at the precise angle required to illuminate most of the chamber. The enclosure glowed with a woody, almost golden hue. It smelled of pencil shavings mingled with the damp scent of ancient plant life.

Nina leaned in for a look. She heard the faint sound of Griff's voice somewhere around the perimeter. "Nina? Everything okay?"

Griff had left the vehicle? She felt a constriction in her chest, a combination of concern for Griff and annoyance at the ill-timed interruption. *Of course we're okay. Now I have to worry about you too?* She stepped back from the opening and said, "We're fine," as loudly as she dared. "Come and see what we found."

She peered cautiously through the split, wary of creatures that might reside inside the natural shelter. Abby was at her back, whispering exclamations.

The pointed archway over their heads would not be out of place in a medieval cathedral. She moved a few inches forward, just far enough in to look up and inspect the higher reaches of the interior. Like a clerestory, the upper story appeared to receive additional sunlight through a break in the trunk well above the floor. The area around her feet was littered with leaves and other, unidentifiable organic debris. With Abby close behind, she stood for a moment in the embrace of the living tree and felt a reverence as profound as any she had ever experienced.

Abby gripped her elbow. "Nina, look outside."

The fright in Abby's voice gave her a chill. She drew in her arms to rotate within the tight space and stretched tall to take in the view over Abby's shoulder. Not twenty feet from their position stood a spotted hyena.

At close range the animal's bone-cracking jaws appeared exceptionally threatening, a razor sharp set of teeth attached to ears, legs, and a tail. The slope-backed, powerfully built predator was poised in the grass with erect posture, pricked ears, and at that moment, intense concentration on something other than herself and Abby.

"Don't move," Nina murmured unnecessarily.

They stood only a foot or so inside the split in the tree in full sunlit view of the hyena should it care to look at them. Apparently it did not. The spotted hyena, Nina knew, was a cowardly, opportunistic scavenger—a stalker of the old, the injured, and the newborn. This hyper-alert individual probably held its next meal in its sight. A thought struck her like a body blow.

At the same moment Abby whispered, "Griff."

The hyena's jaws had parted. Drool dripped from the moist slab of its tongue. Nina sucked in air. Before she had time to gather her thoughts, Abby launched herself away from the tree, stomping her feet, cycloning her arms, and shouting in a powerful voice that seemed to have flown in from a different person entirely. "Scram! Go away! Go!"

The hyena swiveled its pointy skull to face her. For interminable seconds the animal fixed an expressionless stare on Abby. A rumble sounded deep in its throat.

Nina felt the blood drain from her face. Moments passed before the creature dipped its already drooping head, turned, and slunk into the brush. The grasses closed behind its scrawny hindquarters as if it had never been there.

Abby turned, hollow-eyed, to face her.

"Did you just do what I think you did?" Nina placed a hand on her shoulder, a move that propped up both of them. "My god, Abby."

CHAPTER 9

THE SUN had cleared the treetops, and the day opened up to pour its saturating light on every clod of clay and stem-choked cul de sac. Todd's socks were wooly with burrs. Innocent-looking twigs had grabbed and nicked his neck. Sweat stung his eyes. His calves itched. Even his running shoes, the model designed for maximum performance on multiple surfaces, had begun to weigh on his feet. As he pounded over the cratered earth, he was feeling more thirsty and aggravated by the minute, and still he hadn't seen the merest trace of Bones.

If he turned to look behind him, he could spot the towering crown of the baobab tree that marked the location of the Land Cruiser and his companions. But his interest in looking back had ebbed as soon as he realized the others were no longer watching him. He was pretty sure they had lost sight of him mere minutes after he took off. Even Abby's superb binoculars could not pick out a man in the bush if the binoculars were pointed in the wrong direction. The thought made him shake his head at a white-browed robin-chat perched on a mess of thornbush. For a smart woman, Abby could be hopeless.

He was learning to discern faint breaks in the elephant grass and to follow the path of least resistance, as he imagined Bones had done when he came this way. Four-legged creatures must have preceded him through the shoulder-high mazes too, and he wondered uneasily where those animals might be now. Every footfall raised a swarm of high-jumping grasshoppers. A turtle dove swerved overhead, calling, "Drink lager, drink lager." *Twist my arm*, he thought, looking up. His tongue felt gummed to the roof of his mouth.

A banded mongoose trotted into his field of vision. It poked its pointy head right and left in search of food or females. What else was there in the life of a mongoose?

Todd followed the scratching animal to the edge of a clearing and paused to look for an extended mongoose family, not remembering whether this species foraged alone or in a pack. Some runty little thing darted into a shadow several yards to the side, but he couldn't make out what it was. A moment later, the mongoose slipped away too.

Beyond the clearing the terrain tilted down to a wide riverbed. Braided bands of darkness indicated moisture near the edges of the rutted thoroughfare. A modest stream flowed through a central channel shadowed by a smattering of date palms. During the rainy season, the river would look very different. For now, animals had worn a network of paths to the water on a slope thick with caper bushes and across the muddy flats.

He picked his way down the grade with mounting excitement. This had to be the depression into which Bones had sunk while he and the others watched so attentively from the vehicle—unlike the easily distracted crew back there now, he thought with a trace of disappointment.

Every dozen or so paces, he stopped to slap insects from his face and search the landscape for signs of a man on foot. He was aware that the environmentally attuned colors of Bones's clothing worked against easy detection, as did his own khaki slacks and shirt. When he reached the bottom of the river bank, he took a moment to slick back his sweat-soaked hair and rub his itchy calves. He looked around and considered where Bones might have gone from there.

Then he saw it. Not a man but a giant, solitary Cape buffalo. He knew about this animal, the most aggressive and unpredictable creature in Africa. Separated from the herd by age and loss of rank, a bachelor bull seethes with fury and the torment of social isolation. Skittish, stubborn, and easily enflamed, the animal can rev his body to speeds of thirty-five miles an hour and charge with the force of an avalanche. Bones had said that Cape buffaloes cause more human deaths than any other big game animal.

The bull was ripping grass from the ground with his teeth under a copse of corkwood trees about twenty yards from Todd's position, facing away. In the shadow of the trees, the dark girders of the animal's hips looked more mineral than animal, a deception that had delayed Todd's awareness until he stood way too close for any thinking man to be. Even now he had to blink a few times before he was sure of what he saw: a black granite muscle machine caked with dried mud from a recent, lonely wallow. This was a dagga boy, aptly named for a building material, dagga, and the mud-plastered youths who mixed it.

The moment he registered *dagga boy*, he became exquisitely aware of his own body's protective circuitry, the urgent codes that power up and race from ganglia to cortex. Glands fired; hormones pumped. In one tick of time, the entire, elegant chemistry of the fear reflex flashed through his mind like a PowerPoint presentation. He knew that his bloodstream was flooding with fuel for strength and endurance and that other chemicals had crossed the blood-brain barrier to stimulate the wetware up there. His perception and cognition would never be sharper. He would die on full alert.

In an instant he understood with utter clarity that he was too close to the bull and too far from safety to turn and run. The air feathering his face told him the wind direction was favorable, and this would buy him time. He recalled in full Bones's story about the enraged dagga boy that had sent a man who startled him climbing like a monkey up a tree and then hung around for days, snorting and hoofing the ground while he waited for the defenseless captive to fall or surrender. Todd even gave a fleeting thought to West Texas A&M's fight song, "On, On Buffaloes," guessing that the university's students would embrace this terrifying African version of their mascot. All of this plus a calculation of the odds for and against his silent, undetected retreat up the river bank raced through his mind while he looked right and left for Plan B—the nearest decent climbing tree.

A spreading leadwood stood a few yards uphill, separated from the path by a thicket of thigh-high caper bushes. The tree's lowest branch was at least twelve feet above the ground—not the optimal configuration for easy climbing. But unlike the greased poles of the nearby date palms, the leadwood offered a trunk that was cracked along deep longitudinal and transverse furrows. Bark with traction.

He crouched to lower his profile and tried a tentative step backward, keeping his sights on the bull's massive haunches. Could he creep silently all the way up the bank and out of sight? He was going to try. The tree floated in his peripheral vision. Plan B.

Another duck step in reverse. With every footfall, the bottom face of his running shoe pressed against a fickle, crinkling mat of vegetation pasted together by mud and decay. He realized that he had walked quite normally down that very path moments earlier without disturbing the buffalo, and this gave him courage. Toe, heel. Toe, heel. As light as a cat he went, backward.

He had never felt so exquisitely attuned to the qualities of his footwear, the grip and the grab, the messages that his shoes were or were not sending back from the earth beneath his feet. He felt the hug of the elastic power band that locked his foot in place so that appendage and shoe seemed a single unit connected by tendons, vessels, and nerves. He willed those living parts to breach the manmade components for cushion and traction, to sensitize the insulating barrier of the sole that pleased him as a runner but deadened sensory input to an alarming degree on a strewn path where a misstep could mean catastrophe. It took all of his self-control not to turn around and run like hell.

Something crispy crackled under his weight. The bull lifted his giant skull, chewing, but did not turn to look in Todd's direction. Todd had no idea how well Cape buffalos could hear, see, or smell. A pungent odor he associated with cattle filled his nostrils. Geese in flight honked above the riverbed. *Geese mate for life*, he remembered. He had the presence of mind to think this an oddly timed reflection. The sun felt like the coils of a broiler on the back of his neck.

He moved steadily uphill, one cautious step at a time, until he drew even with the leadwood tree that stood near the path. He estimated that he could reach the trunk in three lunges. So far, though, Plan A was working well. He had made progress up the slope, the buffalo seemed none the wiser, and although every subsequent move would take him farther from rather than closer to the safety of the tree, retreat from the riverbed remained the most desirable outcome by far.

His quads knit and strained as he crouch-stepped past a small burrow and over a berm of displaced dirt. A thick-bodied snake with coloring like gravel bellied onto the path a few inches in front of his toe. An involuntary gasp escaped his lips.

Bones had identified this species: a "two-step" snake. After they bite, you take two steps and die.

CHAPTER 10

A JARRING dissonance of high-pitched animal calls filled the air. Abby looked across the grassland to witness a dozen or more impalas fleeing in all directions. A moment later a singular scream pierced the air and flattened every other sound, and she knew the hyena had attacked and felled one of the herd.

She stood in place, balanced on a baobab root, and endured the cry of the doomed impala while she assessed the toll exacted by her own confrontation with the predator that was now devouring a living creature. Other hyenas would arrive soon to churn the feed into a mass of roiling fur. Within hours, every speck of the fallen animal, even its bones, would be crushed and consumed.

She had always believed that fear is not merely notional but as real as a riptide and with equal potential to debilitate or even kill. Would her body exact a price? So far her legs felt strong and steady. Her heart was pumping hard, just fast enough to make her feel vigorous and alert. Her hands didn't shake when she held them open in front of her.

In fact she was struck by how ordinary she felt, as though she had chased away a rabbit instead of a powerful, predatory carnivore. If the hyena had not spotted a more substantial meal nearby, what might it have done when it saw her violating the oft-repeated rule to freeze or back away slowly? Shouldn't she be on the brink of collapse from some sort of posttraumatic stress?

Nina wrapped an arm around her shoulders. "Thank you, Abby. What you did was very brave."

Brave? Abby squirmed under the combined weight of Nina's arm and what seemed a dubiously earned accolade. "We were lucky the hyena decided to leave us alone."

"Maybe. But you didn't know it was stalking an impala. You acted to protect Griff, and for that I am deeply grateful."

Abby felt the heat of a blush rise in her face.

"Are you okay?"

She said that yes, she was okay. In fact, she felt next to nothing. Was numbness the same as courage? She brushed a tiny green caterpillar from her sleeve. The wall of grass near the baobab revealed no sign of the hyena. It was as though she had imagined the entire encounter.

"Really, Nina. I'm fine." For some reason, embarrassment was the only emotion she could identify. She watched Nina run her tongue over her teeth, creating the impression that a small animal was trying to escape from inside her head.

As she spoke, Nina's lips barely moved. "Does your mouth feel like glue?"

Abby nodded. Her mouth did feel like glue. That part of her, at least, was functioning as expected.

"Let's go find Griff. And have a drink," Nina said.

They hurried over the obstacle course formed by the protruding roots. A few more bends in the baobab brought them within sight of the Cruiser and Griff, who stood at the rear, brushing dust from his hat as if getting ready to set out again. His hair spiked out at crazy angles, and a long twine of plant life trailed from the leg of his trousers.

"Where have you been?" he called, looking vastly relieved to see them. "Did you hear the kill?" His face was a circle of sweat and worry.

"We saw the killer," Nina said. "Close enough to catch fleas. Abby thought the hyena might be interested in you, so she shooed it away."

Still absorbing this new information about herself, Abby shrugged. She glanced sideways at Griff, waiting for his reaction.

He looked back and forth between them while Nina recounted the details. As he took in the facts, including news of his own proximity to a drooling, stalking predator, Abby could see that he was torn between gratitude and horrified disapproval. Her attempt to scare off an aggressive creature on foot without a weapon could have been catastrophic.

But the ongoing cries of the dying impala kept the present moment sharply in focus. With the baobab positioned between them and the frenzy on the plain, they stood next to the Cruiser and endured the harsh, elemental sounds of animal predation. Nina handed around a water bottle, and each in turn swallowed a sip. Like a sacrament, Abby thought. No one said another word until the death rasps faded and finally ceased.

Abby grabbed the side rail and hoisted herself up to the middle seat, where she collapsed in the relative cool of the shade. The sun was rolling higher and hotter now. The scent of baking soil rose in waves. She watched a worm curl and fry on a sunlit corner of the metal hood. She felt hungry enough to eat that worm. A vulture appeared in the sky beyond the baobab and was soon joined by several more. They funneled down, flying in ever-smaller circles to the feast on the plain.

Nina and Griff climbed past her to their usual spots on the upper seat. No one had chosen to sit in Bones's vacant place in front. Some kind of fixed-wing insect came in for a landing on the cover of Bones's journal. For a few moments a silence almost like sleep fell upon them.

Nina was the first to speak again. "Do you know how to drive a stick shift?"

Abby felt her stomach heave. She had been afraid this would come. "Todd does," she dodged, swallowing. With dread she eyed the shiny worn face of the clutch pedal and the knob-topped gear selector rising in the middle of the floor. The notion that one of them would pilot the Land Cruiser seemed almost inconceivable, a critical and frightening redistribution of responsibility. Apparently, Nina, at least, was ready to give up on their guide.

Abby had driven a stick shift once, with Todd, on the German autobahn. She had worked the gears up to fifth and kept them there for as many kilometers as possible. When they reached an exit or a slower stretch requiring more complicated driving, her attempt to downshift usually resulted in a cringe-worthy grinding of gears, if not a dead engine. "I'm really no good at it," she said.

"Well, me neither," Nina said. "The automatics parked in our garage backed that goal right off my list—although I've always thought this is a life skill every person ought to learn."

Along with decent manners and juggling (literally, with three balls), Abby recalled with a hint of a smile. The Ivy League, polylingual, ass-kicking downhill athlete, Nina, took a definite and quirky view of personal achievement. Yellowing academic credentials impressed her less than what a person learned last week. "A new magic trick always trumps a decades-old doctorate," she had once said, only half in jest.

Nina intimidated Abby a little. She seemed so decisive and opinionated. These were qualities Abby wouldn't mind emulating even though her own natural habitat existed closer to the middle of the road. She was a mollifier and an arbitrator, not a stirrer-upper. She worried that seeing both sides of a question without holding a strong opinion one way or another might be seen as a weakness. Or would that indicate a nimble and nuanced mind? She really couldn't decide. At the moment she simply hoped that Nina didn't think less of her for her failure to master the stick shift.

Griff brushed dust from his hat and smoothed back his scrambled hair. The careful way he held and used his wounded hand suggested that the injury to his palm bothered him more than a little. "Well, I guess that leaves me," he said. He flexed his fingers, testing the give and pull of the gauze bandage.

"Can you manage it?" Nina asked, solicitous and brisk at the same time.

"Probably." His tone suggested otherwise.

"We have to go find them, you know."

Abby said nothing. She picked up her binoculars and scanned the grassland, clinging to the hope that Bones and Todd would simply reappear. She loathed the thought of leaving the place where she had last seen them. She loathed even more the idea of driving around without a guide—without a map, even, or a compass.

Griff was surveying the open plain too, and his face looked pale and drawn, like a man stunned by recent events. Abby understood how he felt. Who would have guessed when they woke up that morning in a luxuriously appointed, extravagantly serviced bush camp that they would end up fending for themselves with no guide and minimal supplies in the heart of the African bush?

"They might come back after we're gone," Griff finally said. "And they're going to need water."

Nina was already reaching for her hat. "We'll hang Bones's canteen on the tree. And leave a note."

"A note?" Griff's eyebrows shot up. "Telling them what—'be back in an hour'? Can we even find our way back here?"

"The baobab will be visible from a long way off, Griff." Nina's voice had hardened. "And we won't have to drive far to catch up with two men on foot. If we lose sight of the tree, we'll mark our route. Draw a map. You could photograph landmarks along the way."

She touched Griff's knee in what struck Abby as a fine example of advanced wifemanship, an inspired blend of determination and cajolery. All of them, including Griff, Abby suspected, knew that his reservations were not meant to quash the plan altogether. They served as brakes to slow a headlong rush forward, like the traditional timeout in the OR before the surgeon makes the first cut.

"Let's write in the note that if we don't find them, we'll come back here." Nina hesitated. "Before sunset."

They fell silent, stricken by the thought that darkness could arrive before they found help. Nighttime came early in the bush, and fast. Around six o'clock the light drained from the sky, and night chill fell as if dumped from an ice melt high in the heavens. In minutes the world went dark. The temperature dropped thirty degrees or more, and diurnal, heat-loving animals fled for shelter as a crowd of restless, nocturnal hunters was just waking up. Africa's mightiest predators would rule the black, churning bush until dawn.

Griff rubbed his forehead, leaned back in his seat, and turned a steely visage toward the sun, as if gauging how many hours they had left to live. Abby buffed the lenses of her sunglasses while she bare-eyed the distant horizon. Nina sat as motionless as marble.

CHAPTER 11

STILL CROUCHING on the path, Todd stared into the blunt-eyed gaze of the puff adder stretched across the dirt in front of him. The snake darted its tongue in the air, and for one horrible moment Todd thought it was about to strike. Instead, the deadly creature turned its triangular snout toward the underbrush and took its sweet time to slither out of sight.

For several seconds Todd remained frozen in place with his eyes locked on the concealing foliage. He had no idea where the snake had gone once it left the path. The dagga boy still faced away from him, chewing, and the sound of grinding molars pulsed through the air.

He took one tentative duck-step backward. Then another. The bull did not react. There was no sign of the snake. He was giving serious thought to turning and sprinting up the path when a stick snapped beneath the heel of his shoe, and the crack rang out like a gunshot.

The buffalo swung around the great box of his head. The flat little eyes found him at once and seized upon his crouching form. Ratty, cone-shaped ears cupped toward him, alert. Above the ears sat a terrifying casque of horn with side-thrusting, U-shaped hooks that spanned at least three feet between points as sharp as ice picks.

Todd quickly sized up the distances between the buffalo, himself, and the leadwood tree, figuring his chances. The bull turned his body sideways, still looking at Todd as if to advertise his own great size and muscular development, and then swung around to face him squarely. The broadside display, the hooking horns, and the way the animal tossed his head and arched his tail told Todd it was time for Plan B.

Still squatting on the path, he turned and braced his feet for a solid push-off toward the tree. The bull grunted, hoofed the ground, and horned the dirt.

Todd's throat felt constricted. Clearly, this goliath was not going to let him run up the hill and out of the ravine.

Like a sprinter at the sound of the starting gun, he lifted his face and sprang into the brush with the full force of his legs, knowing that only luck would save him from a fatal step on the snake. He hurdled over a caper bush and reached the tree in three long strides. A vervet monkey perched on a branch overhead screamed a warning. Panting, Todd hid himself behind the trunk. Then he dared to peer around.

The dagga boy had advanced two or three body lengths and stopped, huffing. He was poised with his front legs wide apart, looking for the trespasser. Todd drew back. Pressed against the tree, he wondered if he could outlast the tenacious animal. Would a dagga boy simply lose interest and go away? He was pretty sure he knew the answer, and it terrified him.

A frisky ground squirrel dashed into the open. The squirrel stopped for a moment to stare in Todd's direction, then darted past the tree and out of sight. In a few seconds Todd heard a new sound. *Waaa waaa waaa*, like the cry of an infant.

He looked in time to see the little rodent poised between the bull's front legs, flicking its tail a few feet below the great black snout. The buffalo shied and bucked, calling, *Waaa waaa waaa*. His eyes bulged white with alarm. The thousand-pound animal feinted and dodged and then, amazingly, turned and headed up the riverbank in a pounding gallop. Todd watched in disbelief as the bull rounded a bend and disappeared.

He blinked and swallowed and blinked again. Had that just happened? He sank against the leadwood tree and stared upriver, willing his pulse to slow.

Minutes passed while he sat at high alert, moving his eyes back and forth between the riverbed and the knotted carpet of plant material under his feet. The buffalo did not reappear. The adder was not in sight either, but he pulled his legs in closer, just in case. Whole kingdoms live on the sly next to the earth, he reminded himself, armies of the quick and the deadly.

It wasn't lost on him that twice that day a small creature had popped out of nowhere and intervened on his behalf—first the hornbill and now a squirrel. He sniffed at the cartoony image that flashed through his mind. The Cape buffalo was not at all funny.

For some time he kept watch upstream in case the bull decided to circle back and have another go at him. Dagga boys were known for their perseverance, and what else would a lonesome outcast have to do today?

But as the minutes passed with no sign of the buffalo or the snake, his breathing slowly settled and with it, his fear. Innate optimism rose in him, and as he eyed the placid, light-dappled woodland, he had to admit that so far he had handled things quite well, quite well indeed. His only mistake had been to advance down the path to the river without first stopping to study the entire area, to really see it, with sharp and discerning attention. Constant vigilance out there was essential, he told himself. That and a long, sturdy stick for flushing venomous reptiles from the brush in front of him.

Yes, he thought as his courage blossomed, he could learn from this episode and go forward at least a little farther. Thirst might turn him back before long, but the rest of it he could handle. He had been sure that he would spot Bones in the ravine, and he wasn't ready to give up yet.

A small flock of blacksmith plovers was pecking invertebrates from the mud recently disturbed by the buffalo's sucking hoofs. Every action by one species precipitates a reaction by another, he thought, watching the birds pluck and feed. The sun's strengthening rays had penetrated to the bottom of the riverbed and scented its still, impacted air with an earthy perfume. Looking beyond the birds, he studied every shape and shadow and detected nothing resembling a buffalo.

He was certain Bones had come this way. If the bull had managed to tree him, surely he would have made his presence known by now. He scanned the tops of the trees lined up along the river bank. His gaze fell upon the parasol-shaped crown of a rain tree some distance south. It had a wide trunk and thick, nearly horizontal lower branches. A species without thorns, he remembered—by all measures, the ideal climbing tree. He noted the lowest limb, straight as a bench about eight feet up, and looked away. Then something made him look again.

CHAPTER 12

BONES'S JOURNAL was thick and worn, the pages clamped between front and back covers so discolored and cracked they resembled the hide of an old rhinoceros. Next to the spine Abby found a pencil tied with string attached to the binding by a fat wad of tape. On the first page Bones had neatly printed his given name, Bongani Baas, an unexpectedly endearing touch that reminded her of her former middle school math students.

Plenty of blank pages were available for tearing out at the back. She intended to remove a sheet for the note they would leave at the baobab tree with Bones's canteen, but she couldn't help glancing through the journal's densely written earlier sections—the lists and drawings and jotted marginalia. She had seen Bones write on those pages as recently as yesterday. The entries dated back several years and displayed a great variety of leads and inks—which would explain the string around the pencil. Misplaced writing implements must be a common phenomenon in the bush, she reflected, appreciating the frustration of a writer without a pen.

Bones wrote in a largish, outgoing hand with a forward right slant and a confidently ascending baseline. He wasn't too particular about dotting i's or crossing t's, she noticed. The overly wide left margin signified something, but she couldn't remember what. Fleeing the past?

One summer she had taken a graphology course at a community college taught by an expert who worked in criminal investigations. He presented handwritten statements gathered from suspects whose penmanship pointed toward their guilt or innocence. The information was not admissible in court, he told the class, but it was useful for directing inquiries toward the likeliest suspects until admissible evidence could be found.

Spacing was always a big giveaway. An extra wide break before the lie, for example. Recurring, secretive loops and stabs inside the ovals. Every mark and margin held a meaning, and for months after the class she could barely write her own name without thoughts about what her penmanship suggested.

Would the journal contain something, a hint or revelatory passage about Bones that might explain his abrupt departure? She glanced at Nina. *The Secret in the Hide-Bound Journal.*

Nina had retrieved Bones's canteen and carried it to the side of the baobab tree, where she looked to be experimenting with ways to hook the shoulder strap onto the trunk. Griff had moved to the front and installed himself in the driver's seat. Abby noticed that he was still keeping watch on the horizon, no doubt hoping to spot their actual driver. He tapped a foot against the clutch pedal and pressed a tentative grip on the knob atop the gearshift. Both Nina and Griff had shed their jackets in the rising heat.

Puffs of warm breeze played on her hair. She swept a strand behind her ear. Her vest was beginning to feel too warm, but she liked the sense of protection it gave her. She swatted a fly from her face and returned her attention to the journal.

There were many lists. Bones had told them that he maintained a count of the animals he saw and where he saw them. She turned to a typical day:

Cape buffalo herd, Little Serengeti
8 ♀ lions (Asanu Pride) Threeflat Rocks
4 juveniles (Asanu Pride) Threeflat Rocks
3 ♂ lions, brothers, east of Threeflat Rocks
9+ elephants, Cliffside View
pair of giraffes, Grassy Reach
6+ zebras, Grassy Reach
crocs/springbok kill, Hippo Pool
troop of chacma baboons, Six Mounds
impala/tsessebe/kudu, Jackal Pan
cheetah, Thorn Fence
black spitting cobra, Gianni's Gap
wildebeest carcass, Sausage Tree Circle
leopard tracks, Round Bend
9 wild dogs/warthog kill, RIP Gulch

An abundance of animal viewings was not unusual on game drives. What struck her most about the list were the number and variety of place names. To her the bush seemed a vast, uncharted territory, but to a guide like Bones its flats and rises were familiar neighborhoods where every tree, bush, and rock read as instructively as a sign post. Bones had mentioned that one road, somewhere, led to people and civilization. But even without roads or conventional maps, the guides knew where they were at all times and in more specific terms than she had imagined.

She paged to the most recent entries. Had he recorded sightings that very morning? Sightings with place names that could lead them back to the camp they had just left? Her pulse quickened at the thought of a fast drive to the safety and amenities of camp, to people who would know how and where to find Bones and Todd.

But her hopes crumbled as soon as she saw the previous day's date on the final entry. Equally discouraging, the place names from their last game drives were not vividly descriptive, as they would have to be for anyone to track down the landmarks by sight. There were no notes with the specificity of "Threeflat Rocks" or "Six Mounds." Instead, Bones had noted "New Trail," "Big Loop," and "Harper's Dawn." She sighed, knowing too that Bones had driven in a different general direction that morning, toward the airstrip, and his confusing, circuitous route had covered many miles of unrecorded territory.

Had he made a map? She fanned through the journal looking for hand-drawn cartography. A dark sketch of a crescent caught her eye. The caption read, "A scorpion hole is flat and shaped like a half-moon to make room for the pincers when the scorpion backs into it."

The illustration appeared among the earliest entries, perhaps from Bones's training as a guide. The dozen or so pages at the beginning of the journal were full of random pointers for life in the bush. Stuck among them was a stained pamphlet that looked to be a retired beer coaster. Apparently, Bones had moved beyond "Bush Basics" some time earlier—unlike her, she thought, peeling open the pages. An entry caught her eye: "If you see a snake, back off. If the snake is within striking distance, remain motionless until it withdraws. Do not blink. Snakes have poor eyesight and strike at movement." A shiver shuddered through her, and she rapidly turned the page.

"When you are short of water, do not eat food. Digestion requires moisture and will steal it from elsewhere in the body." The shortbread she had savored felt suddenly like a stone in her stomach. She had found no map, and nothing she read shed light on Bones's disappearance.

An exasperated sigh escaped her lips, a gesture that had more to do with Todd than with the contents of the journal. Where was her man when she really needed him? Out making a bad situation worse.

With more force than required, she yanked a blank page from its binding. On it she wrote,

Bones and Todd:

We have driven to find you. If we are not successful, we will return to this spot before dark. The water in the canteen is for you.

Abby, Nina, and Griff

She thought the wording admirably restrained. She could have written, "We have driven to find you two idiots." A few more choice phrases came to mind, especially for Todd, but she would deliver those later, in person.

Nina had hung the canteen from a nodular outgrowth on the tree trunk. Abby joined her there and tucked the note under the canvas strap so that a few inches of ivory paper were visible. "Should I leave Todd's jacket too?" She ran her hand over a likely hook, considering.

"No. He won't need it before dark, and by then we will have found him." Nina's certainty was a force unto itself. "But we should leave something eye-catching, maybe the tablecloth, as a flag. Otherwise, if they see from a distance that we're gone, they might not come back here."

Abby regarded her friend, so brisk and confident, galvanized by resolve. You can't know the measure of a person until you see them manage a crisis, she thought, watching Nina dig into the camp box. A predicament unmasks the higher powers, for better or worse—judgment, wisdom, courage: strengths you don't necessarily see when everyone is drifting along in comfort.

"I'm not planning to come back here at all," Nina added, snapping the cloth in the air. "We'll pick up the men wherever they've gone and drive straight to the airstrip. Bones can retrieve his canteen on his own time."

As opposed to what, our time? thought Abby. The idea that Bones might be obliged to take direction from them came as a jolt, a revelation. Rarely had she felt so willingly subordinate to another person.

"Are you two ready?" Griff sat in the driver's seat with both hands on the wheel. He had returned his hat to his head and leashed the hat's rear brim to the back of his collar with a clip on a cord. He wore sunglasses attached to a string that hung back there too, along with binocular and camera straps that encircled his neck.

Abby regarded him fondly. A belt and suspenders man, Todd would say. So unlike himself. The notion cast a shadow on her thoughts, and she frowned at the distant horizon that had claimed her partner. She knew herself to find comfort in predictability, something Todd could never give her.

Nina slid in left of Griff on the front passenger seat. Abby stepped up to the bench behind them and sat in the middle. Delving into a compartment on her vest, she quickly applied fresh layers of sunblock and lip balm. Her skin felt like an oil slick. She pulled on her canvas hat and wrap-around sunglasses. The vest was too hot now, but she merely unzipped it a few inches. What fool removed her armor before the battle?

CHAPTER 13

GRIFF TURNED the key in the ignition. The fob on Bones's key ring traced a circle in the air. The engine fired and settled to a rumble. Abby planted her feet on the floor and gripped the rails with both hands.

Griff looked to be trying to push the gear selector left and forward into first gear without pressing too hard on the raw nerves in his palm. His efforts were painful to watch. He grimaced and pushed again. Each time, the lever sprang back into neutral.

Nina tried to help by manipulating the gearshift from her side while he worked the clutch pedal. Their failure to coordinate these functions marked the first time Abby had seen them so out of synch. The gears rasped like a drill. The chassis bucked. Everyone bounced on their seats. The engine died.

He turned the key again and this time managed to push the gearshift in place himself using the heel of his hand, but Abby saw another grimace distort his face. Nina was watching him closely, and her expression darkened. The vehicle lurched forward.

Griff's bandaged hand rested limp on his knee, palm skyward, and Abby wondered how he could possibly use that hand to manipulate the stick through an entire shift pattern. She had watched Bones work those gears with the ease of a chef stirring porridge. When he drove up and down hills, across gullies, and back and forth over logs, mud, and rocks, his grip remained firm on the stick and nearly always in motion. Up, back, across, down. The classic H pattern. Stir, stir, stir.

Griff managed to get out of first, at least. He pulled the handle straight back using the tips of his fingers, simultaneously releasing the clutch pedal with minimal imbalance and jerkiness. Abby relaxed a little but kept both hands on the guard rail in front of her, just in case.

They were moving now, fast enough to stay the course and maybe even complete their mission without having to accelerate into a higher gear. A wrecked transmission would be someone else's problem as soon as they located Bones, Abby told herself, willing the vehicle to withstand the abuse at least until they located their guide.

As they pushed through underbrush, they raised a nimbus of dust and a chittering flock of red-billed quelea. The birds lifted and landed a safe distance away. Abby watched Griff lean forward in his seat, driving as carefully as a farmer hauling ostrich eggs. The knuckles of his good hand shone white against the wheel. Vegetation shushed so slowly past the side rails that she could make out the markings on beetles that weighed down the tallest blades of grass.

They had passed the metropolis of termite mounds when the deep vegetation gave way to a stretch of chalky hardpan. Griff nosed the vehicle into the open. A kestrel cruising overhead cast a shadow on the white earth. Nina pointed to an unusually large weaver nest suspended within a stand of currently leafless marula trees.

Up close the jagged tree limbs clawed the sky. The branches that arched over their heads were tinted innumerable values of brown and gray. Bark and wood and shadow became almost indistinguishable. Todd had been near this location when she last saw him, Abby realized. She sat stiff and watchful, barely aware that her binoculars were bouncing hard against her chest with every bump and pitch of the Cruiser.

As Griff nosed among the trees, a forked trunk deep within the woods swayed and fell. Brush in the foreground trembled, and a cloud of white tit-babblers rose into the air. The gray palette of the woods took on shape, size, movement. Abby sat with her eyes fixed on the commotion. Then, just a few yards from the vehicle, she spotted two gleaming arcs of tusk and above them the square head and wide, flapping ears of an elephant.

Griff turned the wheel, attempted to shift, and killed the engine. Abby pressed back in her seat, looking up at a pair of extravagantly lashed eyes and a potentially lethal, unfurled trunk. The mountainous animal raised its head and let out a growl Abby wouldn't have associated with elephants. One of the tusks was cracked at its tip, she registered, trembling. A molar the size of a baby's head flashed into view.

The earth's largest terrestrial creature towered above her. It projected both awesome majesty and casual power, a combination that held her attention like nothing she had ever seen or felt. The great, gray bulk seemed to pull energy from everything around it, to absorb and concentrate light itself.

Now the trunk wanded toward her, sniffing, sensing, taking her measure. The giant placed an eerily silent foot forward and then another. My god, was it going to touch her? If she stood up, she could grab a tusk. The trunk waved inches from her face.

"Griff, back up," she managed to croak, as if he didn't know. The front grill was almost touching the trunk of a fat marula tree. "Back up now!"

CHAPTER 14

WITH A long, cautious look up river, Todd stepped out from behind the leadwood tree. The plovers barely paused in their excavations for mussels in the mud. All that remained to mark the dagga boy's departure was a trail of hoof prints rapidly filling with tea-colored water.

His throat felt clotted with thirst. He would love to suck up a mouthful of almost anything wet—but not the tainted liquid oozing into the depressions in the riverbed. Bilharzia juice, Bones had called it, after the nasty parasitic worms that commonly inhabit local waters. Unless he found Bones soon, thirst would compel him to surrender and head back.

He turned to study the rain tree that had caught his attention earlier. The tree grew a few hundred yards down river, near the middle of the ravine. It was likely to be growing on an elevation that would become an island during the rainy season when high waters braided around each side. He cursed his failure to grab binoculars before his hurried exit from the Land Cruiser. The tree's lowest limb looked oddly misshapen. Too fat. There were definite bumps in its profile and maybe something hanging down too.

A leopard? He tried cupping his hands around his eyes to concentrate the view. Leopards recline on tree branches, he knew. They are notoriously elusive creatures, and the few times Bones had spotted one, you would have thought he had found the lost shrine of Akbah.

"The prince of stealth," Bones called this cat, a silent and infinitely patient stalker that could creep within a few yards of unsuspecting prey before pouncing.

Todd tried to make out the characteristic black rosettes that distinguished a leopard's coat. At this distance he couldn't say for sure what color the thing was. Tan? Gray? Spotted? His pulse quickened when he realized he could not rule out the neutral tones of Bones's clothing.

But if Bones was, literally, up a tree, what had sent him there? The buffalo? Surely Bones would have used his rifle. And if he himself could spot something unusual on the tree branch, couldn't whatever was there see him too, standing in plain sight? He cast a nervous glance around and then waved at the tree, unsure about the wisdom of making himself conspicuous.

The mystery of it, the slightest chance that the figure in the tree might be Bones, presented a challenge he could not resist. Maybe the guide had fled from the buffalo and was keeping watch from the higher elevation. He imagined himself rescuing Bones. Sweet! Abby and Griff would have nothing to complain about then.

On the other hand, he could picture the looks on their faces—on Nina's too—if he returned with little more to show for his mission than burrs and insect bites and a vague impression of something in a tree. No, he wasn't ready to admit defeat quite yet.

His itchy ankles required a minute's attention. With a quick look behind him, he put a wide trunk between himself and the rain tree, jittery about what might be watching him. The burrs clung to the ribs of his socks, but he managed to rip away the worst of them and retuck his pant legs, all the while keeping watch on the thick mat of organic matter pressed beneath his shoes. He needed to find a long, sturdy stick to tap in front of him like the blind man he was—blind to the mincing, slithering denizens of the world underfoot.

Not far away, he spied a pair of yellow frogs poised on a dark patch of moss, clutched in copulation. What, no champagne and candlelight? He watched for a moment and detected not a scintilla of movement. The mating of amphibians couldn't titillate a sex addict, he thought, aware that two pairs of shiny black eyes were staring back at him. Sex among animals in the bush wasn't particularly sexy, now that he thought about it.

On game drives they had witnessed abundant couplings, most often among the chacma baboons and their wildly promiscuous cousins, the vervet monkeys. Even during the most brazen displays, Bones had been adept at whipping up scientific rather than salacious interest. Strategies for mating, reproduction, and the protection of infants took on a measure of gravity when a guide such as Bones laid them out in the context of an elemental struggle for survival.

But now Todd preferred to imagine the yellow frogs having a jolly good time of it. They had chosen the wrong spot for their assignation, though, if they relied on camouflage to keep themselves safe. Clutched together against the moss they stood out like a halogen headlight.

The compulsion to mate must be mighty indeed when it entices two bright mortals into such a vulnerable state, he thought, glancing about for frog-eating birds and reptiles. The mental leap to himself and Abby seemed more than obvious: two other bright mortals buzzed with sexual chemistry— and susceptible to a marriage that could eat them alive.

The notion of matrimony sent a cloud scudding across his normally untroubled consciousness. Usually he managed to avoid thinking about commitment and was quite happy to go from day to day with the glorious, unwed, so-far-compliant Abby by his side. When the topic of marriage did come up, he found himself grappling with uncomfortable thoughts about the death of novelty and the reigning in of freedom and possibility. Could his life with Abby survive those transitions? The question itself, the fact that he asked it, made him squirm.

Yet if Abby ever did demand a Plan B (the thought knotted ropes in his gut), he knew that he would agree rather than lose her.

With his socks reasonably burr-free and his pant legs bunched inside them, he unfolded his body and turned to survey the wide ravine. He decided to make his way toward the rain tree through the sheltering scrim of trees on the river's edge. That way he could move forward to a position with a closer view of the tree and still be hidden from a certain large, horned bovid that might be looking for him in the ravine. Hidden from a possible reclining leopard too, he hoped.

He tested several walking sticks before settling on a silvery shaft of driftwood. It took some practice to remember to poke the ground before every step. And way more patience than he could maintain. As he followed the river bank, he fell into a routine of stabbing the ground as far ahead as he could reach, then taking several strides forward all at once. These exertions yielded nothing more than a few rocketing grasshoppers, and very soon he gave up and let the stick simply stump along by his side.

He tried to step lightly from tree to tree but failed to avoid the crackle of dried foliage. His shoes seemed to find every crispy leaf. A bat-eared fox danced into view, snapping the air for winged ants. It spotted him, froze, and then ran out of sight. Some kind of boomerang-shaped swift knifed across the airspace above the ravine. A pod dropped from a sausage tree a few yards ahead and landed with a thump that gave him a start.

He stopped to study the tree's heavily laden branches, looking for a fruit-hurling monkey or baboon, but saw only thick, elongated pods suspended like the sausages in a deli. Except for its potential to land a twenty-pound Krakowska on his head, the tree looked like the perfect cover from which to study the ravine. He crept forward as stealthily as he could.

At the tree he knelt to minimize his profile before leaning out to take a look. The rain tree stood in the riverbed about ten yards downstream. But the viewpoint he had chosen disappointed him. The crown of the tree was denser than he had anticipated—a teasing, lacey skirt of leaves. In the breeze the leaves swayed and lifted, but they offered mere glimpses of the limbs underneath.

He was able to discern that whatever occupied the horizontal branch was lighter in color than the tree bark and clearly monochromatic. He cupped his hands around his eyes. Through breaks in the foliage he made out winking fragments of beige. Gold? He did not see a single black spot or rosette and concluded with some relief that the shape on the branch was not a reclining leopard.

He looked again and drew in a lungful. Were those human limbs and a torso? A well-muscled arm or leg dangling limp in the air?

What came into view on the ground below the branch alarmed him even more. Three or four spotted hyenas had materialized and were sniffling and scratching at the base of the trunk. He recoiled at the sight of the disgusting creatures. The slinking, yowling devourers of the dead were pointing their dripping snouts directly at the branch above their heads.

CHAPTER 15

"BACK UP now!" Abby's fingers dug into his shoulder.

"Keep your voice down," Griff whispered. The elephant stood next to the Cruiser, so close that he could lean over the side and touch its wrinkled skin. They had never driven this close to any animal, certainly not an elephant. "Just sit still."

Although his own hide was prickly with tension, Griff recognized the overriding sense of control that possessed him now, an adrenaline-fueled state of function familiar from the operating room. He made a quick assessment of the animal that loomed above them and saw none of the usual warning signs.

The ears were gently flapping, legs at ease. The trunk waved at a casual pace back and forth above their heads.

"It looks very calm," he said quietly, stretching out the words. "Not bothered by us at all."

On the other hand, he knew that stiff ears, wide spread front legs, and a rapidly tossing head were signals to crank the motor and get out of there. Depending on the axis of the vehicle, retreat could mean backing up, a sign of submission, or going forward. Imperfect knowledge about animal behavior made these judgments difficult, though. Even Bones, who understood so much about the creatures they saw, conceded that wild species could be unpredictable.

"Don't worry," he murmured. "We're leaving."

He flicked the engine and used two hands on the stick to jigger for reverse—three when Nina tried to help. They found their mark, but he rushed the release of the clutch. The ensuing two or three backward bounces sent

Abby flying into the handrail behind his head. Her lungs expelled air with the force of a bellows, and the engine died.

The silence that followed seemed absolute. The elephant had stepped back a few feet and then stopped to watch them. For his ineptitude behind the wheel, Griff felt annoyance and frustration in equal measure, and his hand was throbbing painfully. But still he did not feel overly worried about the animal hovering less than its body length away. Every instinct told him that this individual was not a threat.

The slow fanning of the ears resumed. The tail hung languid and swishing. Most interestingly, the trunk seemed extended toward them not merely to sniff but (was he imagining this?) to extend a greeting.

The impression would evoke snickers from his colleagues. He himself was not given to anthropomorphism or romantic notions in general, and he held no illusions about the capacity of this animal to flatten the Cruiser and dispatch any of the occupants with a single swipe of the trunk. But the elephant's demeanor suggested something other than mere relaxation. Its quiet gesturing brought to mind curiosity or, heaven help him, friendliness.

He heard Abby ease slowly back into her seat. "Sorry," he said in a soft voice. "Are you okay?" He knew that she was struggling with fear. But the pluck she had shown in the face of the spotted hyena shed new light on her capacity to function in frightening situations. He suspected that beneath that fragile exterior beat a sturdy heart.

She reminded him a little of his daughter, actually, who had passed through a skittish stage before becoming as imperturbable as Nina. The fleeting thought of his youngest child, grown now and with a busy life of her own, produced an unexpected stab of pain. The years had gone too fast.

"Uh, I guess so," Abby answered.

He sat with one hand on the ignition, ready to try again. At the same time he found himself captivated by the creature standing next to them. The elephant appeared to hesitate, as if uncertain about moving closer. Like other herbivores with eyes toward the sides of the head, elephants have difficulty judging distances. Griff watched it lower the mitten-like tip of its trunk, probe the grass, and grasp a bundle of dried ground cover with remarkable delicacy. It furled the plants back to its open mouth and masticated twice before letting the food fall out again.

"This is mock feeding, Abby," he said quietly. "Testing behavior that says, 'I'm not paying attention to you. What will you do now?'"

A quick, sampling glance at Nina told him that unlike Abby, she was thrilled by their close encounter with the planet's largest land mammal. She sat forward with her fists on her knees, inspecting the elephant as if to memorize every fold of skin. She slid her gaze to Griff's face and smiled with such rapture that he fingered his camera. But he decided just to appreciate the view.

"Let's stay another minute," he said over his shoulder. "Bones would." He hoped this was true.

Abby did not respond, but the sounds of the bush gradually reasserted themselves—tiny rustlings and crepitations, the squawk of a bird, and a gurgling that puzzled Griff until he realized it came from digestion deep within the elephant's broad belly.

It was a female, he saw, with two swollen mammary glands side by side up front, not unlike human mammaries. She stood at least ten feet tall. Her great size, impressive tusks, and forward position suggested age and seniority. One tusk was cracked at the tip as if put to frequent hard use. She raised her head and pointed her trunk at him, vacuumed up his scent, batted her heavy eyelashes.

He was feeling something akin to an undergraduate crush when a small, hairy calf trundled out from the trees and rushed to the shelter of the female's great body. The calf was small enough to stand between her two front legs. The cow curled her trunk under to nuzzle the calf, but she never turned her attention completely away from the visitors in the vehicle.

Griff noticed movement in the stand of marulas from which the calf had come, movement that bore little relation to the morning's gentle breeze. Leaves shivered on random branches, and dusky forms took shape. Almost noiselessly, the rest of the herd appeared, moving as a unit. Behind him, Abby gasped.

He counted eight adult females, four young, and two infant calves. The animals seemed wary but not particularly agitated. Fingering the ignition key, he considered whether to try again.

The elephants took up position in tight formation behind the matriarch, facing the Cruiser and the arcing sun. The infants peeped out from sheltering columns of legs, and again Griff would have liked to snap a photo but opted to keep his hands on the wheel and the ignition instead.

Some of the elephants had begun to feed for real, a positive sign, he thought. He watched one of them use its trunk to grip and uproot a sizeable mopane bush. Then it lifted a massive front foot and daintily tapped the roots against its toes to dislodge the dirt.

It occurred to Griff that this herd was too calm to have recently encountered Bones or Todd. Many African elephants carry memories of the blood baths wrought by ivory hunters armed with AK-47s who slaughtered their species by the thousands for tusks and meat. The ivory trade had become illegal when elephant populations shrank to endangered levels, but an underground industry continued to flourish.

Bones had pointed out that elephant poachers were still active in the region. They tended to shun noisy vehicles and instead stalked their prey as quietly as possible, on foot. Griff wasn't surprised to learn that when a person walking through the bush encounters a herd of elephants (animals that truly do not forget), one of two things is likely to happen. Either the herd turns and lumbers away in terror, or it charges, spears, tosses, and kicks the person to death.

"Okay," Nina murmured, touching his knee. "Let's not press our luck."

"Right," he said.

He fired the engine and felt his wounded hand burn with pain. The earlier backward bounce had opened enough space to carve a tight circle going forward. The matriarch stood in place as the Cruiser rolled ahead. But then another elephant stepped from the woods not ten feet in front of the grill. Griff flattened the brake, popped the clutch, and killed the engine. Agitation simmered in the herd behind him. The matriarch voiced a rumble.

The newcomer was male, a big tusker with deeply notched ears that told of more than one violent encounter with sharp thorns or combative claws and teeth. The bull stopped, affronted, facing the Cruiser dead on. His battle-scarred ears stuck straight out. A pair of thickly veined eyes locked on Griff. Runny secretions streaked and darkened the indented temples. The trunk curled tight and then unfurled like a party noisemaker. With a threatening stomp that fanned up dust, insects, and a few startled birds, the elephant lifted his head and sounded a trumpet that told Griff in no uncertain terms to get out of there.

CHAPTER 16

IN THE seat next to Griff, Nina caught her breath. The big, randy bull stood ahead of them like the face of a cliff and equally impossible to breach. Temporal secretions indicated musth, a state of heightened aggression. Either the elephant or the Cruiser would have to yield very soon, and she was quite sure this male would not back down.

She eyed the space between herself and Griff, the books in the center console, the stick shift. Could she take over at the wheel then and there? The idea energized her even as it sucked oxygen from her airspace. She braced herself and pulled in a deep, ragged breath.

After his dramatic appearance the bull appeared to be waiting for their next move. He loitered like a mugger in the shade of the trees, voicing a continuous, pulsing rumble. A mock charge, she knew, sent an unequivocal warning to scram. With a herd of skittish females shifting to and fro on the other side of the vehicle, the current situation felt worse than tenuous.

"Griff, let me drive."

He looked at her. A bead of sweat rolled down his cheek. "You don't know how."

"Yes, I do." Her voice was low and urgent. "I know the shift pattern. I know about synching the pedals. I've watched you; I can do this. Please. Move over now."

She wished she felt as confident as she sounded. But for too long she had watched Griff endure the pain and humiliation of driving with an inflamed hand. He had done pretty well, considering. Now, stopped dead in the path of a riled-up elephant, even her own theoretical skill seemed more secure than his tortured fumbling.

Without further discussion she scooted over, half stood, and swung a leg across his lap, forcing him to slide under her into the passenger seat.

Behind them Abby hissed, "Can we hurry, please?"

Nina settled into driving position with her attention locked on the elephant, as if staring down the animal could prevent a deadly charge. The bull swung his head from side to side, brushed the ground with the hook of his trunk, and stirred up a mess of dust.

The herd shifted uneasily. The two infant calves had fallen back into a sheltering circle of females. The alpha cow turned her great body to face the intruder and sounded a long, unfriendly protest call. She was not in the mood for romance, apparently. The actions of this matriarch would determine the behavior of the entire herd.

But Nina wasn't counting on an elephant to control the situation. Her palms felt clammy. Swallowing hard, she turned the key in the ignition. The bull curled and thrust his trunk.

She steeled herself to work methodically, one step at a time, well aware that rushing the clutch was the fastest way to kill the engine. The stick shimmied like a living thing under the tight knot of her fist, and she wondered how Griff had managed to subdue it at all. She gripped the knob with force and muscled the lever across and down into reverse.

The bull's trunk unfurled a foot in front of the hood. Willing herself to stay calm, she eased up on the clutch and slowly depressed the gas pedal. The chassis jerked and bounced, but to her immense relief, the engine did not die. She released the clutch, and the Cruiser shot backward into the grass.

The vehicle bounced violently over the cratered terrain. With every jolt she strained to hold her foot steady on the accelerator. The sun produced a dazzle in the side mirror, and even wearing sunglasses, she was forced to squint to catch a glimpse of where they were going.

At the moment she was more interested in where they had been, in the rapidly opening gulf between the Cruiser and the elephant's swinging bludgeon of trunk. Apparently their submission was sufficient victory for the bull. He stood in place with his legs planted wide, watching the vehicle speed away.

Still, she intended to back up a good distance before trying to shift again. She hung an elbow over the side and leaned out for a better look aft. The rising banks of seats behind her blocked much of her view.

Abby had moved to the upper bench and was facing the rear to guide her. "Coming to a dip."

The axels rocked down into the depression and up again. Hoping that nothing more substantial stood in their way, Nina sped half-blindly in reverse through the brush, hanging over the side, pressing her lips together. Grasses whipped against her chin. A turquoise butterfly flashed up and out of sight.

"Termite mound, two o'clock," Abby called out.

With one hand on the wheel, she steered around the mound, a wide one, and put it between the vehicle and the elephant. A sounder of warthogs sprang from nowhere and trotted off in single-file formation. Normally the sight of seven wiry black tails bobbing straight up through the grass would have delighted her. This time she barely noticed.

Behind the mound she brought the Cruiser to a halt more abruptly than she intended. With the idea of pausing to reconnoiter, she unintentionally stalled the engine instead of turning it off on purpose, but she was quite happy with the result. She had put at least thirty yards between the vehicle and the musth bull. She reached for her binoculars.

The herd was already moving south with the matriarch and her calf in the lead. Browsing time was over, apparently. The animals appeared to be making haste for some new destination far from the marula grove. Nina guessed they were headed for water and a cooler afternoon location. She panned to the woods and spotted the big male's backside receding into the shadows.

"He's lost interest," said Griff, who had raised his binoculars too.

Feeling almost light-headed with relief, Nina turned and shared a look with Abby who appeared to have weathered the ride in decent shape. The flaps of her hat had blown upward, and a strand of hair was stuck to the gloss on her lips. She grinned at Nina and silently signaled two thumbs up.

Griff placed his good hand on her knee. "Nice job, Neener."

She smiled, grateful for a husband who could surrender the driver's seat with his ego intact. The knob at the top of the shifter had darkened a circle on his bloodied bandage, she noticed, and vowed to redo the dressing at the first opportunity.

"Don't forget, we still have to go forward," she said, unworried, guessing that forward must be the easier drill.

But her maiden voyage in first gear did not come easily. She started, killed, and restarted the engine several times and with each attempt bucked the Cruiser and everyone in it only a neck-snapping yard or two. Working the gear selector and the clutch pedal reminded her of a dance class in which simple repetition teaches the steps, but more advanced skills are required to coordinate the moves with an unfamiliar partner. She glanced at Griff and appreciated anew his trial behind the wheel. It wasn't easy to mesh stick and pedals in a fluid waltz with such a cantankerous date.

By the time she achieved sustained forward motion, the sun had risen at least three quarters of the way to noon. Griff and Abby sat silent and dull in their seats while the heat pressed down like a weight. Months without rain had cooked the moisture out of the bushveld. Grasses that brushed against the vehicle rattled with drought.

She chose a route well away from the male elephant, a loop that circled the woodland farther north than the path the men had taken. Once she had put a good distance between the Cruiser and the trees, she planned to angle over to the rift or gulch or whatever it was that had drawn in Bones. Then, she reasoned, finding the men should be a straightforward matter of following the gully south.

Griff pointed toward a tall, gray-necked ostrich poised like a post on the grassland. Nina did what Bones would have done: slowed and shifted into neutral for a brief look at the bird. She was getting the hang of the transmission, even finding pleasure in the coordination that shifting required—the timing and the touch. To declare mastery would be premature, but already she felt the sense of accomplishment that comes with learning something new.

The ostrich held itself rigid and unmoving. Nothing matches the stillness of wild animals, she reflected, the coiled energy, the crafty, time-bombish quality of creatures with the ability to spring instantly to action. This great bird, the fastest thing on two legs, appeared to think they couldn't see its fat black torso and flagpole neck standing high above the grass. "Crafty" was not the best word for an ostrich.

"Nina." Abby cut short her reverie. "I smell smoke."

Nina leaned out. Wisps of white curled around the rear tire. "It's under us!" Her voice was a shriek. Even in the grip of panic, she experienced an instant of mortification for abandoning the low tones of acceptable bush-savvy vocalization. She shut off the engine and leapt to the ground. Griff and Abby scrambled to their feet.

At the back of the vehicle, she knelt in deep grass and parted the curtain of straw. The space under the chassis was clouded with smoke. Fumes stung her eyes and made her cough. She reached a bare hand past the axle and pulled out a handful of smoldering grass. Choking on heat and a rising sense of alarm, she gagged and coughed and frantically ripped out bunch after bunch of charred and smoking vegetation.

Griff and Abby fell to their knees at port and starboard while she worked the back. They labored feverishly, clawing out handfuls of combustible clumps that had snagged and stuck to the undercarriage. Nina extracted a small bundle wedged against the exhaust pipe. It glowed red, a breath away from flames. She beat the embers against a patch of dirt, ignoring the pain in her fingers, blinking tears from her smoke-stung eyes.

Through the space she had cleared, she saw Abby's chin almost touch the ground while her hands tore at the grass. She seemed oblivious to the harsh treatment she was inflicting on her carefully tended nails and skin. Nina felt a wave of affection for her friend whose newfound courage plumbed the deepest pockets of fortitude. She doubted that Abby herself had known how bravely she could meet a crisis.

"Back away," Griff shouted.

He had retrieved the thorn branch that had caused his injury and with carefully positioned fingers was using the spiked stick with some success to hook and clean smoking straw from the center of the undercarriage. Nina hurried to his side to extinguish the smoldering material he extracted before the surrounding brush caught fire too. Abby joined her there, waving off a cloud of insects that rose against the smoke. They worked their feet fast, stomping out the tiny embers until Griff fell back and declared the job done.

Nina had never felt so hot and parched. She ground a final ash into the dirt and thought about heatstroke. The sun on the open plain burned with terrifying intensity. The top of her hat felt like a griddle.

"We need to drive through a puddle," Abby said cheerfully, shuffling through an already well-pummeled pile of char.

"A puddle would be very welcome." Nina almost smiled. She glanced at the tiny cuts and burns that stung her fingers. Sweat salted the corners of her mouth. The sun was nearing its zenith, and heat clamped down with suffocating force.

She was glad to see Griff carrying the camp box and first aid kit around from the back. With only three people riding in the Cruiser, there was plenty of room now to stow both items more conveniently between the seats. They passed around sips of water and shared an antiseptic wipe to clean their hands.

But no one wanted to linger for long in the sun. Griff secured the boxes on the floor while Nina knelt for a last look below the vehicle. Even in the midday heat, she could feel hotter air radiate from the ticking, pinging hardware beneath the floorboards. Until they reached deep shade or were lucky enough to find a "puddle" to drive through, she planned to stop at frequent intervals to clear any accumulated tinder.

They climbed aboard. Griff yielded the driver's seat without comment. Abby stepped up to the highest, rear bench, saying that she hoped to catch a cool breath of air. Nina steered the Cruiser toward the deep shade of the tree-lined embankment and noticed that the ostrich had vanished.

CHAPTER 17

TODD WATCHED the hyenas below the rain tree circle and pace. The grimy little morticians disgusted him. Hyenas were acutely sensitive to the smell of death, and they wasted no time in gathering under a branch loaded with another animal's fresh kill. To lick up blood and fight over scraps. Fend off vultures. Wait for bones.

Leopards stow their prey up in trees, he knew. Then they retreat to the cover of brush and return at intervals to climb up and feed until the flesh is fully consumed. It sickened him to remember that Bones had said a leopard can pull down and clamp a stranglehold on a subadult wildebeest, abduct a human without a sound, and drag more than twice its body weight up a tree trunk.

He shivered, blinked, and strained to connect the puzzle pieces visible through the leaves. Surely the corpse in the tree was that of a baboon. A big, unlucky baboon. The golden coloring was accurate. The size and configuration, what he could make of them, were about right. And, he thought with rising certitude, a fallen baboon would explain the alarm calls he and the others had heard earlier.

He squinted for evidence to confirm this theory—wished for evidence—knowing that he was not fully convinced of what he saw. It came to him that his mission to locate Bones required that he find out what was in that tree, if only to eliminate a horrible possibility.

On hands and knees he crept slowly forward. The brush provided cover from the hyenas, and he needed to go only a yard or two for a better view of the branch in question. Insects simmered around his face. A pod dropped with a thud from the sausage tree behind him, and he turned to glance at the offending noisemaker. What he saw was worse—much worse.

The dagga boy stood twenty feet away with his eyes fixed on him. The bull snorted and rocked his heavy head, slinging saliva like a rodeo rope. The lethal headgear dipped and scooped.

Without a second thought Todd scrambled out of view behind the tree and mounted a buttressed root. He planted a toe on a ridge in the bark and felt for a handhold. The nearest branch was still several feet above his head but accessible via a knobby growth in full view of the buffalo. He reached for it.

With flared nostrils and a bloodcurdling bellow, the bull lowered his horns into ramming position and charged. Just in time, Todd pulled up his feet. The buffalo horned the trunk a yard below the branch Todd straddled. Leaves shimmied and shook, and another pod fell to the ground. The bull reared back and then head-butted the trunk so forcefully the tree swayed.

Todd yanked one of the sausage-shaped fruits from its stem. The pod was nearly two feet long and heavy, at least fifteen pounds. He braced his feet against the trunk and used both hands to lift the missile above his head. Taking aim, he thrust it down and scored a direct hit on the square, snorting snout directly below him. The bull shied and backed away, crying, *Waaa waaa!* But he did not turn and run.

Todd plucked another pod from the laden branches and took aim again. This time he missed but came close enough to back up the bull another few feet. The animal snorted, hoofed the ground, and kept his distance. The raggedy ears twitched against the screeching of the hyenas.

It took four more bombs, including two direct hits, to persuade the buffalo to surrender. After enduring another blow between the eyes, the animal half-turned and lowered his head, chin out, as if to reconsider his aggressive stance. The yowling of the hyenas had reached a frightful pitch. That might have played a part too, Todd suspected, as he watched the bull wheel and trot away. But he preferred to think that this time at least, he himself had fended off Africa's most tenacious adversary.

The moment the bull moved out of sight, Todd dropped from the tree, picked up his walking stick, and ran.

A man can outrun almost any animal over a long distance. This and other heartening bits of intelligence pulsed between his temples as he raced into the heat of the plain, darting quick looks behind him. A body cooled by sweating has superior endurance to a body cooled by panting. A very fit man can outrun a horse in a marathon, especially in hot weather. Fortunately, at the moment he did not appear to be running from an animal.

Sweat poured down his forehead, breached the berms of his eyebrows, and stung his eyes. He was intrigued by the idea that endurance running might have enabled primitive humans to add meat to their diet. Early hunters would search the sky for scavenging birds, the theory went, and then run a long distance to steal fresh kill from whatever carnivore had brought it down. Like hyenas, he realized with a jolt, glancing back at the rapidly receding tree line.

He couldn't get away from the ravine fast enough. A pack of riled-up hyenas, a leopard, a dagga boy, and who-knew-how-many puff adders twisting through the riverbed were enough to turn anyone away. He couldn't believe that Bones had walked straight into that seething pit. Surely he knew that dangers increased near water, especially during the dry season (a realization that had just come to Todd). Even with a rifle and a radio, what was Bones trying to prove?

Admiration, incredulity, and resentment occupied adjacent chambers in his overheated mind. He assumed that Bones was capable of handling himself in the bush. This unexplained foray while clients sat and waited, however, was over-the-top risk taking, show-offy, and totally irresponsible.

His umbrage took a poke when he asked himself if he might have miscalculated the guide's destination. Perhaps Bones had not dropped into the ravine at all but instead concealed himself in the tall grasses for whatever purpose took him there. Griff had thought Bones wanted to relieve himself in private. That required little more than a screen of vegetation, and khaki-colored clothing would make the man almost invisible.

The thought gave him pause. It also opened the not unpleasant possibility that his own little run might turn out to be more daring and adventuresome than the foray by their guide, wherever Bones was now. The theory helped ease his battered sense of competence and not incidentally appealed to the competitive streak that ran through him like marbling in meat.

He pushed forward through the grass and felt an agreeable awareness of his toes. He pictured them working inside his shoes, pushing, flexing, gripping. Each big toe lined up in a neat little row with its four stubby neighbors, not divergent as in apes and chimpanzees or so long that they reduced the efficiency of the foot. Short, straight toes evolved over millennia for the purpose of pushing off fast.

He demonstrated this interesting fact by vaulting neatly through a break in the brush. Thirst hadn't depleted him too much. He was running well, appreciating the strength and spring of bipedal mechanics. Built for distance! Born to run!

An unusual trio of big, boxy rocks claimed his attention. The weirdly branched top of the baobab tree poked up beyond one of the rocks some distance across the plain. The thought of shade and water spurred him on, even as he dreaded the moment when he would have to deliver his rather uninformative report to the others.

Unless Bones had already returned to the vehicle. The notion hit him all at once. This was possible, even likely, he realized, feeling a surge of excitement. With their leader safely aboard, Abby would focus her lovely furrowed brow on the sole missing man: him. Grinning, he used his free hand to wipe sweat from his face and slick back his hair. The prospect of a full house on hand to greet him back at the Cruiser cheered him immeasurably.

But his diversion to inspect the rain tree had rerouted him several hundred yards south, downriver, and now he found himself headed toward the baobab on a longer, chunkier path across the plain. In the vicinity of the table-topped boulders, the underbrush was mined with smaller rocks and dense with serrated grasses that lashed across his face and ears.

He swung the driftwood spear wide to open a path through a tangle of straw. How well evolved, this man with straight toes! Already, a tool! He grinned at a clutch of helmeted guinea fowl that exploded into the air. Even with dehydration at work in his body, he felt strong and capable. On the whole, the run to the ravine had done him good.

Trotting at a reasonable clip, not paying close attention to the surface ahead, he failed to spot the burrow until too late. The toe of his shoe rammed deep into the hole, and his long body slammed forward onto hard, brown dirt. A bright and twirling constellation spun across his field of vision while the foot pinned in the ground throbbed almost as painfully as the ankle above it.

How long he lay there, he couldn't say. The next thing he knew, he was opening the crusted slits of his eyelids to observe a beetle rolling a ball of dung the size of a golf ball in a wide detour around his aching face. The sun had advanced several degrees. Heat pressed down like a blanket. His mouth felt furry with thirst. His ankle screamed with pain. Abrasions oozed on the palms of his hands, and a formation of whining insects had flown in for a look.

He wedged his forearms under his chest and raised both shoulders a few inches off the ground. His neck still supported his head, but the rotating function felt rusty and stiff. Blinking, he looked around.

He had fallen onto a patch of crabbed earth not much larger than a yoga mat. Clumpy, straw-colored grass grew all around him, tall enough to curtain his view in every direction except straight up. The sky had turned a deep, brooding blue. A pair of hawks hung on the thermal current directly above him and then drifted out of sight.

Chapter 18

Abby rolled up her sleeves, untucked her shirt, and unbuttoned three top buttons and two bottom buttons. Then she bunched and tied the shirt in a fat knot well above her belt, at the solar plexus—for the prevention of solar apoplexy, she thought, feeling a little cooler already in spite of the noonish UV rays that played on her newly bared arms, throat, and midriff.

Her vest with its cargo of miniature toiletries sat neatly folded on the seat next to her. She removed her hat, placed it on top of the vest, and used both hands to smooth her sweat-mangled hair. The hot wind felt almost cool on her rapidly drying scalp. Seated high on the rear bench looking down at Nina's and Griff's bobbing hats, she breathed in the sage-scented air and felt something close to exhilaration.

For one thing, they were following a direct route to the blessed cover of trees. For another, the depression beyond the trees most likely held water, a stream at least or maybe a full-fledged river. She felt a tingle of excitement at the prospect of exploring new terrain. Bones and Todd would be there too, she was certain, a short distance south, if they hadn't already walked back to the baobab.

The thought gave her a start. She turned to look across the grassland. Only the splayed base of the baobab tree had sunk out of view. The brightly printed cloth Nina had attached higher up was still visible. She did not see the men.

She retrieved her binoculars and brought into focus the canteen suspended next to the cloth. Certainly anyone who had returned to the tree would have wanted a drink right away. The container hung where she and Nina had left it, and the folded note was still tucked in place.

Relieved, she let the binoculars drop. At this point simply noticing Bones and Todd under the tree would seem crushingly anticlimactic. Farcical even, after what she, Griff, and Nina had been through to get this far.

The realization that she didn't want to find the men quite so easily required some thought. She shifted in her seat. What about all the bad things that could happen to Todd on foot in the bush? To Bones? And don't forget, she told herself, Griff's hand needs medical attention. Yes, she thought, actually nodding her head, it is very important to find the missing men as soon as possible.

But even with effort she could not make herself worry too much. The anxiety that had hung over her like a net seemed to have lifted or at least loosened its power to constrain her. She felt freer, more open to whatever happened next. Most surprisingly, she could not drum up a shred of guilt for this new and relatively relaxed attitude about the absent men.

Todd was out on an adventure; why shouldn't she have one too? Both Bones and Todd had gone off voluntarily, she reminded herself. Bones was an expert bushman armed with rifle and radio. He could take care of himself. She felt sure that both men would turn up sooner or later.

Then their reunited group would drive to the airstrip as planned, tend to their wounds, continue their journey, and go back home. An audible sigh escaped her lips.

In truth, she was finding the unexpected turns and twists of that day more than a little exciting. She leaned forward and let the breeze rake back her hair. Riding high through the African bush with a challenge at every bend felt new and affirming.

She would never forget her face-to-face encounter with the female elephant, the close-up view of the jagged fissure in the tusk, the trunk sampling the air an arm's length from her nose. Thinking about that elephant, the way she had looked her in the eye, evoked a powerful sense of connection—and wonder.

Then there was the smoldering undercarriage that could have turned into a catastrophic fire. She had been the first to detect the smoke, she remembered with a glimmer of pride. She glanced at the scratches on her open palms. They would heal, she knew, even without the anxious scrubbing and applications of salve she normally would have undertaken. What mattered now was to pay attention, to apprehend and appreciate all that this great swath of Africa served up. It occurred to her that random anxiety has no place in a world where life and death realities keep a person sharply focused at all times.

She looked at Nina in the driver's seat, operating a manual transmission for the first time, and at Griff beside her, so reassuringly solid in his measured approach to every situation. He was maintaining vigilant watch on their surroundings, she noticed. Without a guide, more was required of all of them, and more had been forthcoming.

The sun was a blast furnace now, spewing heat. She gathered her ponytail and twirled it up off her neck. She had found a porcupine quill in the smoldering grass, a beautiful thing as long as a chopstick and smooth as polished ivory. With practiced skill she poked the quill through the bun at the back of her head, pinning it securely.

A bowerbird flit past her carrying a sheaf of tiny blue flowers. The sight brought a smile to her face. Bones had explained that male bowerbirds create elaborate displays of pebbles, nuts, and blooms for the sole purpose of attracting females. The effort and creativity that go into a hookup! That night Todd had placed a pretty striated rock, a peanut, and a purple sprig of sage on her pillow.

About halfway to the trees, Nina pulled onto a grass-free patch of hard pan and turned off the engine. "Let's check underneath," she said, climbing out.

Abby joined her at the rear while Griff knelt on the side next to the front passenger seat. They pulled away a few handfuls of grass but nothing like the accumulation that had stuck and smoldered there earlier. Nina was using a stick to clear a clutter of seeds from the exhaust pipe when Griff's voice rang out.

"Get in the vehicle, now!"

The rhinoceros looked like a craggy rock formation with calla lilies for ears. Griff had spotted the animal grazing in thick grass about fifty feet away on a forward trajectory aimed directly at the Land Cruiser. As they scrambled to their seats, Abby noted how adept the three of them had become at responding quickly to new situations. She leveled her binoculars on the saw-toothed point of the rhino's forward medial horn. A broken horn, she knew, was a sign of a fighter.

But this animal seemed content to graze and chew. Occasionally it lifted its heavy head to gaze myopically toward the vehicle. Bones had said that a rhino's ability to raise its ponderous snout was so limited that a three-ton adult could drown in a shallow pool of water. A wide, weighty head was useful for mowing grass, though, and this individual was going at it with gusto.

Nina settled quickly in the driver's seat and turned the key in the ignition. The engine cranked and fell silent. Abby drew in a breath. This time Nina had rushed the clutch, with predictable results.

The rhino was moving steadily toward them, its head swinging right and left while the square lips clipped grass like a machine. Rhinos possess weak eyesight but decent hearing and a keen sense of smell, Abby remembered. No doubt the animal had sensed their presence already. It did not comfort her to know that a rhino's sensory attributes accompany a brain so small that it might have forgotten, for example, that a Land Cruiser was not a playmate.

Nina flicked the ignition and failed again.

"Take a breath, Nina. Slow down," Abby murmured, keeping her eyes on the rhino.

It had drawn parallel to the vehicle less than a Cruiser's length away. In height and heft it resembled another parked truck. A half-dozen red-billed oxpeckers were perched on its rear flank, drilling for insects in the folds of bulky genitalia. With a blast of throaty squawks, the birds flew off, far less relaxed than their host about drifting so close to humans.

The sound of the bull's placid chewing and an occasional gusty breath did not broadcast imminent threat. But Abby knew that this male could easily spin and roll the Cruiser and even with a broken horn skewer a human like satay.

While Nina collected herself for another go at the engine, the bull executed a surprisingly agile right-hand turn and fetched his great mass around to position himself directly in front of the vehicle. Abby felt a shimmy and registered that they had just been thumped by a couple of tons of wild rhino. With a snort the bull leaned the barrel of his body into the grill. He appeared to find the contact agreeable. Thoughts of grazing apparently vanished as he turned his attention to some deep and needy itch.

When a rhinoceros tends an itch, the project is nothing like the scratching of a household pet. Skin resembling vulcanized rubber more than two inches thick requires serious grinding against an immovable surface. Bones had explained this while pointing out rhino tracks next to the toppled rubble of a formerly concrete-hard termite mound.

Abby gripped the rails and hung on while the creature went to work. The Cruiser rocked and bucked. Rhythmic exhalations gave way to lusty panting. The rubbing increased in speed and intensity. With a loud twang a heavy gauge fastener snapped from the abuse, and a portion of the front grill folded like paper.

In the low front seat, Nina and Griff sat at eye level with the bull's lethal horns. One crisp turn to the right and the rhino could easily poke his snout in Nina's face. Her shoulder was touching Griff's as they both leaned toward center.

Abby questioned the wisdom of sitting quietly while this goliath had his way with the Cruiser. Clearly the rhino was not interested in any of them and possibly not even aware that humans were there. But what if he wrecked their vehicle?

The damage to the front grill had created a protrusion of jagged edges that would shred human skin but seemed only to increase the rapture of the scratching rhino. He was moaning now, rubbing harder, causing the Land Cruiser to buck violently from side to side. Abby held on, not knowing whether to laugh or cry. The bull made a groan that sounded almost human, and she felt herself blush. How should one respond to the erotic pleasure of a rhinoceros?

"He wants to mate," she said with a choking sound that might have been a chuckle if she were, say, watching a movie instead of rocking in synch with an actual, revved-up rhino.

Another section of grill, the one that folded down into a table, crumpled with a crunch not unlike the report of a violent auto accident. Now a metallic screech accompanied every thrust and grind.

Finally, Nina had had enough. She turned the key and this time succeeded in starting the engine. The rhino snorted and stepped away, fixing his expressionless button eyes on the crumpled metal. Nina yanked the stick into reverse and backed off, bouncing the heavy chassis through ruts and divots until they were well away from the rhino and could turn away going forward.

Griff pointed a finger. Abby looked. Binoculars were not required to see that the great bull had, indeed, been ready to mate. He stood quite still, seemingly stupefied, while he watched his heartless patootie recede to a blur. Nina steered a wide circle around the animal. Long after they were back on course and headed for the trees, the spurned bull remained in place gazing at the vacant clearing with his head hopefully raised.

CHAPTER 19

THE DUNG beetle walked backward on its front legs, head down, while its hind legs rolled a perfectly round sphere of excrement past Todd's throbbing jaw. Through the half-closed lids of his eyes, he watched the insect labor in the hot patch of sun. It was a scarab, the symbol of rebirth and regeneration.

The beetle's destination would be soft soil where it would dig a hole, roll the dung ball into the depression, and lay eggs on top. Before long the hatching larvae would burrow into their edible nursery and feast until it was time to clamber from the earth fully grown. An elegant system of sanitation, nutrient recycling, and soil enrichment—not to mention infant care.

Todd blinked. His own aching body would enrich the diet of a passing carnivore soon if he didn't pull himself together and get up. Heat, dehydration, and the pain shooting from his ankle had worn him out. He felt dangerously tempted to lie on the ground, sweltering, in the company of the little beetle until his heavy eyelids dropped and sleep took over.

"When a man's shadow abandons him, he dies," someone had said.

The stare of the sun told him it was at least noon, the time when a man's shadow disappears, and the bush sinks into overheated insensibility. When any thinking person seeks shelter from the punishing rays. He knew that he must stand and drag himself to the safety of the Land Cruiser, to shade and water and the immediate attention of the world-class orthopedist who happened to be on hand under the baobab.

Abby would be sick with worry, he knew. He pictured her seated up in the vehicle scanning the horizon with her high-powered binoculars. He hoped she would be the first to spot him limping across the plain. Would she have the guts to run into the bush to meet him? He doubted it. But he could almost feel her pale hands tending to his wounds and massaging lotion into his parched skin once he reached the Cruiser.

Still lying on his stomach, he extracted the trapped foot from the burrow that had tripped him, trying not to think about the animal that had dug the hole and whether that animal might currently be in residence or coming home from work. He rolled to his side. Pain ripped up his leg. He took a few deep breaths and tried to assess the damage.

A badly sprained ankle and possibly a sprained foot too, he guessed. He hoped the injuries weren't any worse than that. Swelling had tightened the shoe on the aching foot and puffed the flesh beneath the ribs of his sock. He would know more when he tried to put some weight on it. A few scratches had carved up his palms, but they did not look too serious. He waved off a simmer of flies and felt for his walking stick.

A sound made him stop—the faintest intrusion on the hush of the clearing, like the low vibration of distant thunder. He held his breath. The tall grass around him rustled, and the deep rumble grew louder. There was a change of light. He stared into the patch of sky over his little clearing and knew that he was not alone.

A great flap of ear fanned above the grass, so close that he felt a movement of air. The massive crown of an elephant came into view and then the trunk, curved up like a periscope, taking in scent. Through the growth at ground level he made out a gray pillar of leg not five feet from his face.

He drew in his limbs, wrapped his arms around his head, and curled into a ball. One elephantine footfall could kill him, and who knew how many of the giants were out there? He could not think of a thing to do except keep himself small and hope for the best.

The trunk was snuffling through the grass now. From under the crossed struts of his forearms he saw its delicate tip pat around as though looking for the source of the sour odor that was seeping from his terrified, sweating body. The trunk snaked toward him. He smelled a puff of rancid air and then another. He dared to glance up and found himself staring into the liquid gray depths of an elephant's eye.

A tusk swung above him like a scimitar. The ivory was cracked near the tip, he noticed, with the oddly acute sensibility of a man about to die. Elephant sounds surrounded him: rumbling, slurping, sloshing, and the ominous susurrus of a multitude of legs swishing through the grass. But the great head lingered above him. He tucked himself tighter and braced for impact.

Something touched his arm. And again. Tentative and light, the touch of an angel. Was he dead?

He opened the chinks of his eyes to glimpse the fuzzy face and outsized lower lip of a baby elephant. The calf had poked its head through the wall of grass a foot or two above his body and was tracing random, awkward loops through the air with its miniature trunk. Adorable, Abby would say. He would think so too from the safety of the Cruiser. He eyed the little bugger warily. This baby could kick in a man's skull. He froze in place, making the knot of his body as inert and uninteresting as possible.

He remembered Bones's frequent admonitions to stay quiet and immobile around wild animals. You don't want to be perceived as food or a threat or even a curiosity, particularly around mothers and their young. He knew that to an elephant he would never look like food, but he could easily seem a threat and, rolled up on the ground like a pill bug, definitely a curiosity.

The calf's explorations ended abruptly when a super-sized trunk looped around its body and pulled it back into the sheltering brush. Todd watched the little wizened face melt into the grass. He moved his eyes to the gray silhouette that loomed like a guard tower above him—a female, he realized, a mother keeping tight rein on her calf while she stands watch over the oddball curled up in the grass.

A possibility struck him, an idea so out of the realm he wondered if he might be hallucinating. Could the big female be protecting him too? He snatched another look at her huge head and tusks, the flapping ears, the trunk moving over him.

More likely she was suspicious, he guessed—holding him in her sights to make sure he stayed in place while the rest of the herd ambled past. Elephants were cooperative that way. He heard her voice a rumble that sounded like distant thunder.

The earth that pressed against his bones trembled with the weight of the passing herd. The elephants were moving almost over him, each footfall a seismic event. Yet the female with the cracked tusk had not budged except to sniff him and corral her infant. He swallowed. His mouth felt cottony. He knew that if he had any chance of returning to the world beyond the tight, impacted clearing that felt like a grave, he must remain calm, contained, patient. So unlike his normal self.

89

It occurred to him that he had been safer sprawled on the ground when the herd showed up than he might have been walking through the bush or merely standing upright like a hunter. Elephants move with care and are surprisingly agile on their feet. During a herd's normal drift across a plain, none of the animals would be likely to stumble over or step on a man's inert body.

But the crunch of mammoth footfalls within yards of his puny form told him that nothing about his safety was guaranteed. He tightened the tuck of his body and tried to withstand a barely contained sense of terror. Trampled by elephants—what a way to die.

Now all of his energy seemed concentrated in the tiny apparatuses inside his ears. Two sets of hammers, anvils, and stirrups quivered with strange and disturbing vibrations. Elephants tread remarkably quietly for their great size, he noticed. But their bodies seem to continually broadcast the slosh and gurgle of digestion. He listened with hyper-alert fascination. A new sound intruded, as loud as the slurp of a monsoon drain, and he realized that the calf was suckling at its mother's breast just a few feet away.

Moments later, he noticed a subtle shift in the ambient noise. It was movement, like the slow drift of a faraway storm. The light winked above him. He looked up to stare at a blank patch of sky. Had the female moved away?

He strained to hear what was taking place, hardly daring to blink, while the whisper of rattling grasses coalesced somewhere beyond his location. The collective gargle and groan of the elephants grew fainter. He held his breath while he listened for any vibration that might reveal the disposition of the herd. The sounds continued to fade. And then he heard nothing.

He waited for some time (how difficult to gauge the minutes!) to make sure that the herd had passed out of range before he slowly unfolded his stiffened limbs. Even the pain sinking its teeth in his ankle could not diminish the relief that swept over him. To be both safe and free, in charge of his own movements again and not far from the refuge of the Land Cruiser, felt almost euphoric. In the great scheme of things, a sprained ankle didn't seem so dire after all.

He lifted his cramped body up on hands and knees. The scarab beetle and its ball of dung had disappeared. He glanced around, hoping the industrious little insect had survived the cataclysm of footfalls. But he did not see the beetle again.

With the help of the walking stick, he pulled himself up on his good foot, a Lazarus rising to meet the sun. To minimize his profile in the grass, he stayed bent at the waist and leaned hard on the shaft of wood. The swaying backsides of about a dozen elephants were moving steadily away from him, probably bound for a cooler destination. The female with the cracked tusk brought up the rear with her calf trundling along beside her.

He felt a rush of affection for that sensible female, an emotional surge that almost undid him. "Thank you," he whispered, blinking. He swiped a hand across his eyes. Even depleted and weak, he was not a blubberer. At least he didn't think so.

Remorseless, buzzing flies flew circles around his ears and yanked him back to the thoroughly unsentimental reality of his current situation. African flies, he had noticed, thrive on heat. They seem to grow more brazen and annoying with every added degree of temperature.

His sweat-soaked shirt had dried and crisped. His skin felt crusty with salt. He touched his injured foot to the ground and quickly lifted it against excruciating pain. With only one good leg he would have to hop or crawl back to the Cruiser.

The stick helped, although it was too short for a crutch, and its ragged end dug painfully into his underarm. He lowered himself to the grass and unlaced the shoe girdling his swollen foot. The loss of compression was regrettable, he knew, but of lesser importance than moving as quickly as possible to shade and water. He placed the shoe upside down on the top end of the stick where it made a reasonable brace to wedge under his armpit.

The irony of using a state-of-the-art running shoe as part of a crutch for the runner who had fallen while wearing said shoe was not lost on him. He managed a mirthless chuckle. Even for an infinitely adjustable sole designed to accommodate multiple surfaces, a man's armpit was a bit of a stretch.

But the improvised crutch enabled him to stand and move forward a foot or two with each step. He was well past the boxy boulders now, and he could see the crown of the baobab tree above what seemed a solid wall of fever berry scrub. Eyeing the shortest route around the thicket, he pressed on, one awkward step at a time. The elephants had moved well into the distance but not far enough yet to risk yelling for help.

Pain is temporary! Pride forever! He had seen those words on a sign at the eighteen-mile mark of the marathon, a notoriously treacherous stretch in any twenty-six-mile course, where runners hit walls, drop out, and puke by the hundreds. He had made it to the finish, though, fueled as much by mental toughness as by months of rigorous physical training. He knew that he needed every bit of that mental stamina now.

A yellow fluff of seeds rose on a stream of hot air and floated into his mouth. He lacked the saliva to spit. His temples throbbed. Vegetation snagged at the crutch and almost tripped him. He stopped to remove his shirt and wrap the cloth around his head like a turban. Sunburned shoulders or heat stroke? Sunburn.

Keep moving, he told himself. Stick, step. Stick, step. The whisper and scurry of small creatures accompanied his halting progress through the grass. He felt less worried about snakes so far from water, even though he knew that plenty of them like it dry. In the distance he spotted a small herd of wildebeest. A spiral of raptors circled above the far plain. The elephants had become mere specks on the horizon.

He cupped his hands around his mouth. "Abby!" His voice was an unfamiliar, raspy thing. He tried again. "Abby! Griff! Nina! Over here! It's Todd!"

He listened for their voices or, better yet, the sound of the Cruiser firing up. Nothing.

"Here. Beyond the hedge!"

The thicket still obscured most of the baobab, and he wondered if the dense growth might block the sound of his voice. He envisioned the position of the Land Cruiser relative to the tree and knew that he had to go only a few more yards until he spotted the vehicle. Until Abby, Griff, and Nina would see him too.

Stick, step. Stick, step. Buoyed by thoughts of companions and water, he moved a little faster. The termite mounds he had passed on his way out came into view. They were not far from the vehicle, he remembered. His ankle felt on fire, and his quads ached from holding that foot in the air. The shoe was chafing his underarm raw. He was dizzy with thirst. But he had almost reached the finish line.

He stopped, rubbed his eyes, and stared across the shirred landscape. Corrugated air rose up from the earth like the heat from a grill. The baobab appeared to ripple and dance. He took in the tree, the bright cloth attached to it, the canteen. With crashing spirits he saw that they were gone.

CHAPTER 20

AFTER THE heat on the plain, the deep shade of the trees felt like a cold, clammy sheet smacked against his face. Griff slipped off his hat and let the cool air wash over his scalp. They had made it to the tree line, where Nina brought the Cruiser to a halt under a shielding roof of leaves. Now she and Abby were fishing around for drinks and first aid supplies. They all agreed that they needed a few minutes to tend and refresh themselves before following the river south.

The elephants and the rhino had redirected them north of their intended route, on a long downward grade that gradually erased their view of the baobab. When they finally reached the fringe of trees, they discovered dense, intertwining strangler figs that hugged a lush oxbow of river. Floods from an earlier season had eroded the banks to a gentle slope, and on the near side of the water, a sprawling white beach stretched twenty yards wide.

During the rainy season the beach would disappear, Griff surmised. Whole trees lying uprooted at its edge signified a history of raging currents, but at present the relatively shrunken stretch of water flowed at a more sedate rate. A glossy ibis pecked near the shore. A few feet from the ibis a saddle-billed stork pulled a fish from the depths with its long red and black-banded bill. Several species of ducks cruised the open waters. Compared to the dry, unyielding savanna they had just crossed, this was a fertile and rugged paradise.

"See the hippos?" Nina was pointing toward the widest span of river and a congregation of ears twiddling just above the surface. Each pair of ears framed two piggy eyes that were looking directly at them. "The resident pod."

There were about ten of the big, bossy brutes, Griff estimated, watching the almost completely submerged animals watch him back, ears twigging.

One of the hippos yawned, raising a titanic snout out of the water in an impressive display of tooth and tusk. A hippo's jaw could snap a ten-foot crocodile in two, he remembered.

Ears and snouts sank randomly out of sight and reappeared a minute or two later, producing hardly a ripple. Digestion and sleep ruled the day for hippopotamuses. At night the big herbivores piled out to graze on land, but they always returned to the water around dawn, before the sun could broil their tender skin.

Nina gave out sips of water while Abby rummaged through the supplies remaining in the first aid kit. Griff lifted a corner of the bandage on his hand to inspect the damage. He wanted a glimpse before deciding how much to reveal to the women. Nina decided for him.

"Let's have a look," she said, taking his wrist.

She winced when she peeled back the gauze. Not to his surprise, the wound looked as bad as it felt: red, inflamed, and oozing. She slid her eyes from the festering mess to his face. Her expression told him she was more than a little worried about her surgeon husband's gifted mitt.

He waited while she took a minute to clean her own fingers. Then she used a few drops of drinking water to moisten a tissue and gently swab away the dried blood, yellow seepage, and grit that had accumulated during their trip across the plain.

He took up an antiseptic wipe himself, knowing that she would wield it too gently. He tried not to grimace as he massaged the germicide over the punctures and tears. The injury concerned him, but he felt optimistic about rapid healing once his palm received a proper cleansing and he started himself on a course of antibiotics, surely before the end of the day. For now he would do the best he could. His good hand bore minor abrasions from the grass fire, and he used a corner of the wipe to dab at those too.

When he was done, Abby stepped forth holding her freshly washed fingers in the air like one of Griff's colleagues entering the OR. Griff shared an amused look with Nina. Abby had loosened up a bit, even exposed a few inches of skin, he noticed. He couldn't help thinking that in Todd's absence she had relaxed and brightened.

After Abby taped him up again, he went around to the back where he knelt one more time to inspect for snagged grasses. Nina appeared by his side and insisted on clearing the undercarriage herself. "Let's keep your hands as clean as possible, okay?" She patted his arm. "You be management. I'll be labor."

"Spoken like a manager," he said, sitting back on his heels, grateful for the suggestion.

He watched her peer under the frame. He was not unaware that she had both managed and labored without complaint for decades, running their family life almost solo while he devoted himself to his career. She cared for the children; paid the bills; did the shopping, cooking, cleaning, laundry. Wait, did she clean? Do laundry? He knew that she hired help, but he wasn't home enough to know the details. What he did know was that he could always count on an orderly household, decent meals, and an abundant supply of clean, immaculately pressed shirts.

Their children had turned out all right too. The thought of their grown children gave him a pang, a mental flinch he had come to recognize as regret. Increasingly, he found himself ruminating about their three young adults with pride and regret in equal measure. He wished that he felt closer to all of them, even as he understood that this failing was the result of his own choices—the career he had chosen and the way he had almost always let his surgical practice come first. He wondered whether it was too late to do things differently.

Nina was good at staying in touch using midget electronics. Midget words too. "How r u?" She seemed to know what was going on with everybody at all times. But he would feel ridiculous instant messaging or whatever. If he suddenly joined the Twitterati, his sons and daughter would probably text Nina to find out what was up.

While these thoughts occupied him, he almost absentmindedly caressed Nina's back. She was leaning forward, nearly prone on the ground with one arm folded under her chest and the other stretched out to reach under the vehicle. Her dust-colored shirt had darkened with sweat. Faint crenellations of ribcage rippled through the fabric, and those slender, curving bones moved him inexplicably.

When she straightened up to toss away a few strands of straw, he touched her flushed cheek with a tenderness that seemed to startle her. She studied his face as though searching for signs of fever.

Words of affection were forming in his mind when Abby's voice rang out. "There's a crocodile down on the river bank. A big one."

Their eyes met, and Nina smiled. They both knew that the moment had passed. He offered her a hand up. "Let's go have a look."

The croc resembled a decomposing log pressed against the earth. It had darkened with age from green to the color of mud. Camouflage was this animal's meal ticket, Griff could plainly see—that and a powerful jaw capable of locking passersby by in its grip.

"Let's leave him to his sunbath," he said, protecting his hand as he climbed gingerly into the Cruiser, one foot at a time, like a spider creeping into a casement. He glanced through the trees to the dazzle on the open plain. It was already well past noon.

The emerald shade of the canopy that cooled and refreshed them came with entanglements that made forward progress difficult, especially with barbed metal protruding from the front of the vehicle. Nina steered slowly over roots and stumps thick with interlocking vines. More than once she had to stop altogether to unhook a clot of plant life and reconsider which way to go.

"We'd make better progress down on the beach," she concluded, dipping her head in the direction of the white terrain below. "Bones drove through riverbeds, you know."

They were idling in a clutter of growth that faced a wall of wild creepers. Going around to the left meant leaving the shelter of the trees for broiling sunshine. But on their right a gentle, trampled slope gave way to a mostly dry and shady thoroughfare created by the shrunken river. An easy choice, Griff agreed.

He nodded and pointed toward an opening. "This is probably a hippo path, a good place to go in."

Nina swung the wheel and nosed the Cruiser down the grade. A couple of slaty blue bitterns flew up, calling, *Ra ra ra ra ra*. Griff saw a turtle slide from a log into the water. The vehicle rolled smoothly onto the flat strip of beach, and he felt himself relax for the first time in hours.

The corridor ahead appeared free of foliage that could snag and ignite. The trees that leaned over the ravine provided welcome shade, and the gently flowing water by their side lent moisture to the air and at least the illusion of serenity. All they had to do now was follow the riverbed as planned to locate the men. He sat back in his seat with a welcome sense of relief, thinking that he might even take some photos.

"Three o'clock!" Abby called from the rear.

Griff looked. A six-foot-long rock monitor lizard lounged on the opposite bank, a seriously creepy looking reptile. Griff reached for his camera and snapped two or three images before the lizard slithered up the bank and out of sight.

A few minutes later he was focusing on an African spoonbill when the forward motion of the vehicle abruptly stopped. For a moment he thought Nina had applied the brake in consideration of his photographic efforts. The scream of the engine told him otherwise.

"We're in sand," she shouted, stepping on the gas.

"Hey!" Abby yelled.

Griff turned. Sand and muck were shooting up from the spinning front tire and splattering her hair, sunglasses, face, and shirt.

"Nina, stop!" he shouted, grabbing her arm.

Nina stomped on the brake and killed the engine.

"I was *trying* to get us unstuck," she said, prickly, barbing the participle. She followed Griff's gaze to Abby's muddied face and stifled an embarrassed laugh. "Oh, Abby, I'm sorry!"

Abby removed her sunglasses, not smiling. "The instant you lose traction in sand, acceleration is useless. Worse than useless." She spit over the side. "The tires spin, and you sink down even deeper."

Griff looked at Nina, who seemed to be mulling over both the driving tip and its unexpected source. Her smile had become fractionally taut. Stress was having an effect, he could see, and Nina wasn't used to taking lessons from Abby.

"I read it in Bones's journal," Abby added.

"Did Bones's journal say what you *are* supposed to do?"

Abby ignored the mildly sarcastic tone. "Dig out by hand. Put branches under the tires for traction." She jumped to the ground. Sand cascaded from her shirt and pants. She brushed herself off, shook out her hair. "I'll get the shovel," she said, turning away.

Nina climbed out and followed her to the rear. Griff heard her murmur something that sounded contrite and a brief, unintelligible reply from Abby. It occurred to him that Nina rarely apologized, partly because she was a remarkable avoider of faux pas and partly because she expected everyone else to be as tough as she was. Unlike people whose feelings were easily bruised, Nina had the hide of an elephant.

On the rare occasions when she did say she was sorry, she did so sincerely, he thought. And that was the end of it. Regret, guilt, and, worst of all, grudge-holding were to her complete wastes of time and energy. Just get on with it!

It wasn't difficult to shepherd the implications to his own increasingly poignant regrets about their children, although how to "get on with it" where they were concerned eluded him. His medical practice demanded as much time and energy as ever, and he wasn't about to abandon the work of a lifetime. He unstrapped and stowed the camera. Could his photos stimulate a dialogue? Maybe get the kids interested in a family safari?

He stepped onto the unstable footing of the beach and circled the Cruiser, wondering about irrational gestures of the mind. Another safari? What was he thinking? All four tires had sunk to the wheels. No one on earth knew where he and the women were. Their supply of water was dwindling. The bush around them was mined with traps and ambushes. His hand was a seeping mess. Even so, he had to admit he loved the idea of sharing the companionship, the campfires, and the adventure of a safari with his whole family.

His gaze rested on the adjacent, nearly vertical embankment. Exuberant masses of vegetation carpeted the incline. Finding sticks and branches for traction would be no problem here. He actually smiled, imagining his sons and daughter collecting wood. Those three would free the Cruiser in no time.

A new sound caused him to lift his face to the ceiling of leaves. Bees? Cicadas? He listened. It was the faraway burr of an airplane.

"A plane!"

Even as he shouted, he was running past the women, treading with difficulty through the loose sand. How many times in the course of a day did aircraft pass by? He did not recall seeing any planes at all except the one that had brought them there. Someone must be searching for us, he thought with a surge of feeling that combined hope and panic. To be seen, they would have to climb into the open very fast.

The buzzing swelled. He heard the women's rapid footfalls behind him, backtracking to the place where they had driven in. The steep, impenetrable bank that corralled them now seemed endless, the uneven traction agonizing.

The plane was almost overhead when the gentler slope of the hippo path came into view.

He pressed forward, panting with exertion and keeping an eye out for the crocodile. One of the submerged hippos reared up and aqua-planed toward him. *Whee honk honk honk. Whee honk honk honk.*

"Mock charge," Abby gasped as she ran past, taking the lead. She fast-footed her way up the parallel tracks forged at night by the hippos' tidy gait. Left feet here, right feet there.

Griff watched her. He was puffing hard. Racquetball on Saturdays had not prepared him for this. He started up the grade with Nina at his heels. Abby would get there in time, he hoped.

Up ahead he saw her burst into the light. Her hair caught the sun like something rare and golden. She tipped her face skyward, waved both arms, and ran out of view.

When he reached the crest and saw her slumped over with her hands on her knees, he knew that she had been too late. Nina appeared by his side, billing her hand against her brow to search the empty sky. They stood in the glare of midday and listened to the thrum of the engine slowly fade.

CHAPTER 21

NINA WIPED away the perspiration slicked across her forehead. After the cool of the ravine, the sun felt white hot on her head and face. She had left her hat and sunglasses in the Cruiser, as had Griff and Abby, but none of them seemed in a hurry to go back. They stood silently with their eyes on the blank sky, listening in vain for the burr of an engine.

Nina spoke first. "Could they have seen you, Abby? Maybe dipped a wing?"

"I'm afraid not." Abby shook her head. "By the time I got here, the plane was well past me, going south. I'm sorry." She turned and started toward the shade of the trees. "It was a white-bellied Cessna."

The aircraft that flew us here, Nina remembered. Possibly shuttling other guests, not even looking for us. She knew that Griff was thinking this too.

Their strenuous, almost desperate attempt to signal the plane had revealed a new and disturbing reality. Although none of them had shaped the notion into words, their simple mission to drive and fetch the men was beginning to feel like a misadventure requiring rescue.

Nina scowled at the sun. It was fixed like a lantern in the exhausted blue of the afternoon sky. Two o'clock? Three? Impossible to know the time. An exultation of larks burst into the sky and then faded to nothingness. Here, then gone, like everything in that unsettling place.

She turned to follow Abby. Griff's footsteps crackled behind her. They picked their way down the hippo path, lost in thought.

The crocodile was gone too, Nina noticed, scanning the shore as she descended into the chill. The sudden deep shade combined with the disturbing phenomenon of things, people, and wildlife simply vanishing made her shiver.

One evening at the campfire, Bones had told a story about a couple he had known in his youth—neighbors, driving home through the bush in their lorry after dark. The truck's back gate was rattling, so they stopped to securely latch it. The husband got out and walked to the back while the wife sat and waited. And waited. She heard nothing. She called to him. He didn't answer. She got out and went around to look. He wasn't there. She never saw him again.

"A cat must have taken him," Bones had said. "A lion or a leopard. They found drag marks in the dirt, but no sign of the man. Not even a boot."

The story still horrified her, and now she tried not to think about it, or about the dozens of other ways a person could disappear in the bush. This was like trying not to think about the missing men or her thirst or the little stinging cuts on her fingers—impossible. And probably not desirable either, she reminded herself. A person in the African bush needs a firm grip on the here and now, especially without a guide to keep a grip on it for her.

Abby had reached the vehicle first and started to dig sand away from the tires. Nina went to gather material to aid traction. She ventured a few steps up the overgrown bank onto a spongy mass of moss, vines, and voids ready to trap a poorly placed foot. A chameleon roosting on a branch scooted off, inches from her hand.

A few feet away she spotted a twist of wire and realized with a lurch of fear that she had discovered the work of poachers. Nestled among the blameless greenery, the trap looked cunning and malevolent and far more threatening than the natural tangle of plants. The heightened sense of danger she felt at the sight of a manmade object struck her as counterintuitive and, at some level, appalling.

In a tree not far from the snare, she made out the camouflaged platform of a hunting blind—surely illegal. Creatures that come here to drink don't stand a chance, she thought, searching the shadows. She realized that she felt more worried about meeting a poacher with a rifle than about seeing almost any animal. A chill that had nothing to do with the air temperature shuddered through her. She gripped her armload of sticks and hurried away.

Griff staggered in with a sizable collection of branches hugged in his arms. He knelt to help her wedge sticks into the depressions Abby had created in front of each tire. They labored silently accompanied by the sizz of insects.

"A miniature boardwalk," Nina said, sitting back to assess their work. She saw every reason to project a positive attitude, no matter how dire things got.

She had already decided not to mention the snare and the blind. "Sometimes known as a foreshoreway, a riverwalk, or an oceanway."

"So where's the cotton candy?" Abby asked. Her easy demeanor suggested that she had decided to overlook Nina's snarky tone following the mud-splattering incident. A relief.

The women put their shoulders to the job while Griff applied light pressure on the gas pedal. The Cruiser rocked back and forth and suddenly spun ahead at the same moment a chunk of leadwood caught under the rotating tire. The kindling-size plank shot backward, straight into Nina's shin. She doubled over and dropped to the ground.

Oblivious, Griff drove to firmer terrain several feet away while she sat in the sand contorted with pain.

Abby knelt beside her. "My god, Nina. Are you okay?"

Clearly not, Nina thought, trying to hide her irritation. She rolled up her pant leg. There was no blood, but a nasty purplish lump had already formed. She wondered if she could stand. "Help me up, please."

"Shouldn't you wait for the doctor?"

By now Griff had seen them and was treading back through the sand. Abby yielded her spot at Nina's side. Without an X-ray, Nina knew, this would be the touchy-feely school of orthopedics.

"Does this hurt?"

"Um, yes."

"Here?"

"Yesss," she said through clenched teeth. "Yessss!"

The swelling on her shin looked like a hideous special effect, housing for some alien, bone-sucking symbiont. All she could do was watch the distention puff and empurple while she sat there hissing like a reptile. The whole maddening predicament scraped against her idea of herself, her native sufficiency and calm.

The river a few feet away still flowed along, of course, untouched by her bad luck. As a diversion she fixed a stare on the water while Griff completed his exam. She thought about chance, flukes, random events that in an instant change everything for an individual yet alter nothing in the larger scheme of things.

If only she had been standing a few inches to one side when the projectile shot back. If only Griff's palm had landed on flat ground instead of on the piercing thorns. If only the aircraft had flown over a few minutes earlier, when the Cruiser was out in plain sight. If only, if only …

The part that unnerved her, she realized, wincing as Griff pressed a tender spot, was the bland neutrality of it all—the benign indifference. How can people order and control their lives when things just happen? Or don't happen?

We're all delusional, she thought, watching a pair of hamerkops take flight. That's why we cheer when someone says, "Make no little plans." We really think we run things—that we can impose symmetry and order on the unruliness of nature. But our mastery is only temporary. Nature always retakes the upper hand.

Near her a mouse scurried into the underbrush. She spied a bandy-legged gecko creeping along a branch. The leaves rustled as usual in the trees overhead, and the water babbled ceaselessly beside her. An event that might have been catastrophic for her had caused not a blip in the everyday life of the lovely riverine woodland.

"I don't think the bone is fractured," Griff said, helping her to her feet. He looked at Abby. "Although given the patient's aversion to showing the slightest weakness, it is difficult to say for sure."

Nina gave him a look. To her relief she found that she was able to put weight on the leg. "See? I'm still a bipedal ambulator." She proved it by hobbling to the Cruiser with only minimal assistance despite the pain. The habit of emotional concealment can be useful, she thought, stifling a gasp. The last thing she wanted was to be treated like a casualty.

"Ice would be helpful," Griff added. "But under the circumstances, just keep it elevated."

She positioned herself sideways on the middle seat with the bruised leg up across the bench. Abby joined Griff in front. When he said he would drive the rest of the way, she literally crossed her fingers. *Here we go again.*

She was quite sure she was capable of driving and willingly would have given it a try. But the route ahead looked uncomplicated enough for Griff, even with his current disability. She decided to settle back and watch the river slide along by their side.

Chapter 22

THE RIVERBED was an ecosystem unto itself, ripe with lurid algae, darting bugs, and mats of flat, floating leaves that shone as if rinsed for a salad. Sunken glades rippled in the current. Whole companies of winged insects danced across the surface. Nina watched a dragonfly the size of a sparrow spiral in for a landing on a lily pad.

Griff was driving well, if slowly, to avoid shifting to a higher gear. The water fanned and eddied, and occasionally the tires splashed through a shallow runnel that meandered away from the main channel. (At last, a puddle!) Water did not worry her. Bones had forded water so deep it sloshed over the floorboards and obliged everyone to lift their feet to avoid soaking their boots.

The silver slant of a fish caught her eye. She wondered what kind of fish it was. Could she consume it? Could it consume her? She had no idea. The life forms that teemed around her existed almost completely beyond her store of knowledge.

Foreign languages do a fat lot of good out here, she thought, staring at some kind of fungoid ring on an overhanging branch. *What is that?* She was a long way from the world of manmade architecture too; there wasn't a parapet or pilaster for hundreds of miles. It struck her that the entire construct of the place was way beyond her competence and vocabulary. Without a guide she couldn't begin to know the rules.

Unaccustomed to feeling so inadequate, she shifted restlessly in her seat and flexed her florid leg. She was still smarting from her clumsy performance behind the wheel that had sprayed Abby with sand and dug in the tires. In other circumstances, if someone had done that to her, she would have thought them a perfect idiot.

She watched Abby bend over Bones's journal and thumb though the pages—the eager teacher brushing up on her bushcraft. She regretted that she had been dismissive earlier, when Abby had given her an earful about driving in sand. The slight hadn't seemed to cause Abby more than a moment of exasperation, and for that Nina felt grateful.

She knew that she could be bristly when corrected and dubious about the competence of others. She was hard on people, including herself. Too exacting and critical. These were excellent traits in a proofreader or a brain surgeon, she supposed, but not so helpful otherwise.

She unclenched her clamped jaw and made an effort to relax the muscles that pinched in her shoulders. If she could loosen up now, think what a paragon of forbearance she could be at home! She worked her mouth into a smile. Well, maybe not a paragon.

Griff steered the Cruiser around a bend, and a sweet fragrance mingled with the damp perfume of moss. They had entered a dappled glade where the banks on both sides flattened to a mild grade dotted with caper bushes. The sudden beauty of the place lifted her bruised spirits. Date palms leaned over the ravine, and a spreading leadwood tree shaded a wide expanse of sandy shore. A flock of blacksmith plovers pecked in the mud.

Abby was sitting forward now, more than ready to lay eyes on Bones and Todd. The paths that wandered through the bushes and down the bank suggested easy access from the plain. Nina estimated that they had driven far enough south to be in line with the baobab tree. Like Abby, she sensed that this was where the men had come.

The Cruiser rocked and slowed, each tire searching for something to grip. The riverbed had turned dark with moisture. She noticed deep animal tracks and realized with a flutter of apprehension what an exceptionally fine water hole they occupied.

She held on, eyeing the banks for animals approaching to drink as the Cruiser swayed and lunged. Some kind of snake knifed through the shallows in front of them. Griff looked to be heading for drier land beyond the snake's kingdom of water and muck. He gave it some gas and plunged forward.

Without any warning the Cruiser bellied into sucking mud and stayed there, sinking rapidly while Griff frantically turned the wheel. For a few terrible seconds she feared they were being swallowed by quicksand. Griff stalled the engine, and the vehicle came to a resting place, sunk almost to the axels in a pungent clot of muck.

Griff propped his forehead against the steering wheel, clearly riven with frustration. A black-winged stilt scissored its long red legs in rapid retreat. Abby looked at Nina with a face as pale and expressionless as polished stone.

Nina closed her eyes and counted to five. She was aiming for ten but didn't make it. Griff, she knew, felt wretched without any input from her. She turned to Abby and made a point of keeping her voice calm and respectful.

"What does Bones's journal say about getting unstuck from mud?"

Abby swallowed. "Well, unless you have a winch—which we don't—you jack up the front and put logs under the tires." She looked from Nina to Griff and back again. "Are we even capable of that?"

"Of course we are," Nina answered sharply, not at all sure. She took in the rank muck bed around them, the scrappy vegetation on the nearest river bank, and the distance they would have to walk to find and drag back suitable logs—not to mention the strength she imagined it would take to haul those logs and jack up the Cruiser. It was a struggle to contain her dismay.

Griff leaned back in his seat. "I'm sorry. I should have tried to go around."

Nina silently agreed. "We're all sorry, Griff." She tipped her face to gauge the angle of the light beaming through the trees.

Abby followed her gaze. "We don't have much time."

There was a brief hiatus in their remarks, an uncomfortable pause as the significance of Abby's statement settled over them.

Afternoons in the bush were short. Dusk lasted about five minutes. After a dazzling display of color, the sun sank fast and darkness arrived as if by the flick of a switch.

"Can we free the Cruiser before sunset? With just the three of us?" Abby's voice was tremulous.

Nina met Griff's glance. They both knew where this was headed.

Griff cleared his throat. "We need Bones and Todd to help us. One of them, at least."

This line of thought appalled her, but she could not argue differently. The chances were slim that she, Griff, and Abby could free the vehicle before dark, or at all. She could imagine few more dangerous places to spend a night than stuck in the middle of an African watering hole. She managed to nod and say, "They've probably returned to the baobab by now."

Griff reached for his hat. "If I hurry, I can hike over and get them in time to jack us out in daylight."

"No." Abby was rolling down her shirt sleeves. "I'm going."

Nina and Griff stared at her.

"I can run faster than you." She fumbled with the buttons on her cuffs. She was hurrying now, racing against the descending sun to tuck her shirt, shrug into her vest, locate her hat and binoculars. "Would you mind if I took my water bottle?"

"Of course not." Nina had found her voice. "But Abby, are you sure about this?"

The image of Abby alone, on foot, in the bush was almost too awful to contemplate. She didn't like the idea of Griff venturing out there one bit better. She would much prefer to go herself instead of waiting and worrying, but the painful swelling in her leg reminded her that she was not the best-qualified candidate.

"Yes, I'm very sure."

"Then I'll go with you," Griff said.

"Please, no." Abby was firm. "Forgive me, Griff, but you might slow me down. You need to stay here with Nina. If anyone is waiting at the tree, I won't be alone for long."

Nina regarded Abby with enlarged respect. Her budding courage had blossomed in a most impressive way. She loathed the thought of any of them crossing the plain on foot, but she couldn't argue with Abby's reasoning.

"Let's talk about what you will do if the men are not at the tree," she said evenly.

Abby nodded. "I should be able to tell from a distance whether they're there, through the binocs. If I don't see them, I'll come straight back." She paused. "And I'll look for logs along the way. The three of us could still try to get out before dark."

Nina turned to Griff. "What do you think?"

He wore a look that said he didn't like one single thing he had heard. Deep ruts separated his brows.

"Walking through the bush is a risky business." He ran a hand through his hair. "But I do think there's a good chance that either Todd or Bones is at the baobab. Maybe both." He paused. "Whoever is waiting at the tree will see you long before you get there," he continued, using his most reassuring voice. "If you wave at him, or them, to come this way, you won't have to go very far." He glanced at the long shadows. "We probably shouldn't take any more time talking about it."

Abby rose to her feet and turned to face the slick expanse of mush that separated her from solid ground. Griff was rummaging through the books on the front seat. He held up two volumes. "Stepping stones."

He knelt on the seat she had vacated and reached past her to make the drop. *The Birds of Southern Africa* landed with a slosh about three feet from the side of the Cruiser. *Reptile Encyclopedia* ended up halfway between the bird book and shore.

"Good luck, Abby," Nina said, half-standing to embrace her.

"Don't worry about me," Abby said with a little smile. "Worry about Todd. When I see him, he's in for it."

She rested her hips on top of the passenger door, swiveled her legs over the side, and pushed off. Her right foot landed squarely on *The Birds*, causing a goopy splash. She windmilled her arms and struggled for balance as the volume slowly sank under her weight. Mud rose over the sole of her boot. Her left foot waved in the air. It occurred to Nina that the athleticism and control that had kept her upright in the mogul fields of the Rockies were likely to save her now.

She watched Abby fix a stare on the next landing pad. A four-color image of an African python glared back.

Falling in the mud was not the worst thing that could happen, Nina told herself, although she had no idea what microbes or worse might be waiting there. She tried not to think about the snake she had seen. She realized she was holding her breath.

Abby reared back a little before thrusting her arms and swing foot forward, creating enough momentum to propel herself almost like a skipped rock. *The Birds* tilted and sank, muddying her push-off boot to the laces, but she managed to touch down lightly on the python, mid-flight, and scissor the muddy boot smoothly to solid earth.

"Good job," Griff called.

She turned and flashed a triumphant smile.

Something like cheers erupted in the leadwood tree behind her. Nina looked up, astonished to see a troop of vervet monkeys that had come to life in a frenzy of excited chattering. At least a dozen monkeys roosted at various elevations among the branches, chuttering and chirping as they craned their necks to look at the human on the ground below.

At the moment Nina did not fully appreciate the entertainment value of the vervets, and she knew that Abby didn't either. She watched her friend hurry up the grade using footwork as nimble as a young impala's. Occasionally she hesitated, apparently to consider the best route through the bushes. The long-barreled binoculars swung from her neck, and one pumping hand gripped her water bottle. She quickly reached the top, waved again, and stepped out of sight.

CHAPTER 23

ABBY PLANTED her feet in the last patch of shade at the edge of the ravine. A blade of fear scythed through her, and she struggled to control her panic. Inhaling deeply, she vacuumed up an insect that made her gag and cough. The sun was behind her now, beginning its descent. She lifted her water bottle, gulped a mouthful, and noticed that her hand was shaking.

A red-footed falcon described a circle high above her head, and a few feet away, she spotted a quivering shrew that could become the raptor's next meal. The falcon not only knows I'm here, she thought; it knows the thread count in my shirt. Yet she was aware that the sharp-eyed bird of prey didn't frighten her at all. What frightened her was everything she could not see.

It boosted her a little to know that she had put on a brave face for Nina and Griff. Crossing the moat of mud between the Cruiser and solid ground had required focus and a plan—just the sort of challenge that absorbed and strengthened her. Then had come the surprise of the monkeys in the leadwood tree. She had almost laughed when she saw them, more from relief than from amusement.

But once she turned her back on the sanctuary of the vehicle and made her way up the path, a crushing inventory of the dangers ahead worked their way into her quickly overwrought mind. In the absence of an immediate task, a goal to glom onto and conquer, she felt unmoored, vulnerable, in need of focus or maybe myopia—anything to fuzz out paralyzing mental images of the beasts great and small that preside over the African bush.

She looked across the grassland and let herself imagine for a moment the benign Midwestern plains of home. The notion calmed her, even as she took in foreign variations in vegetation and topography, most strikingly the crazily shaped baobab tree that poked its top branches up in the distance like a muscular, outsized animal. That tree was no maple.

She had been correct in her estimation of the baobab's position relative to the embedded Cruiser, but she hadn't factored in the marula woodland—the same grove of trees that had sheltered a herd of elephants earlier in the day. She wedged the water bottle into a pocket to free her hands for the binoculars. Beyond the marulas, she scoped the baobab's highest, pointy limbs. The tree seemed farther away than she remembered, and from her vantage point she could see only its crown.

The shortest distance between herself and the baobab was a route straight through the marulas. She glassed the dusky woodland and wondered what predatory eyes might be staring back. Compared to that inscrutable shade, the wide open plain looked almost inviting. She swept the lenses across the expanse and, in a new twist on the safari experience, hoped to see nothing but grass.

Earlier in the day, when the sun had stared down from its zenith, the nearly treeless plain appeared flat and even. This had been an illusion, she realized, remembering deep depressions that had rocked the Cruiser on the trip from the baobab to the river. Now, in the differently angled light of afternoon, rising rumples of hills were evident, and she knew that soon the shadows would darken even more to bring the slopes and dips into high relief.

Dips deep enough to hide a stray elephant or a lone rhinoceros? Her grip felt clammy on the tubes of the binoculars. The last time she saw the elephants, they had been moving south, well past the marula grove. Griff thought the musth bull that had given them a scare was probably going south too, following the herd.

The amorous rhino, however, had been grazing quietly on the north side of the woods. She swung the lenses left. Although she couldn't spot the rhino now, she guessed that it was less likely to have moved away, being a little slow on the uptake and possibly still longing for a tryst with a passing Land Cruiser.

The safest choice, she knew, would be to stay far from rhino territory by circling south around the woodland to reach its eastern side. There she would gain an unobstructed view of the baobab and, she fervently hoped, at least one of the men.

With a flush of embarrassment, she remembered the last time she had peered through binoculars toward the baobab in search of the men and hoped not to see them. Was it only that morning that she had been so raw to risk? So ensnared by the romance of adventure that she preferred the hunt to its safe and sound conclusion?

A slate-gray comet swooped earthward, extracted the squirming shrew from the grass not ten feet in front of her, and shot back into the sky before she could blink. She stood rooted to the ground, almost numb to the sight of predation but ever more stupefied at the speed with which the killing could occur. The falcon and its heavy burden soared up and out of sight. Poof.

With minutes slipping toward sunset, she knew that she had to get moving. She fixed her sights on a goal, the shade of the nearest edge of the marula grove about two hundred yards away. Three hundred yards? Distances, like measurements of time, seemed irrelevant in that deceptive and changeable environment. When she reached the shade, she would try to stay in it as long as possible by circling the woodland at its edge until the baobab came into full view. She adjusted her hat, pushed up her sunglasses, and stepped into the arena of light.

Jogging with boots on her feet felt clumsy, but she was glad for every molecule of leather, rubber, and cloth between herself and the pushy vegetation. She plowed through a whippy stand of grass, careful to keep her mouth shut tight against the friable earth, botanicals, and bugs. Flying insects were doing their best to breach the khaki stronghold that protected her body. Only the skin on her face and hands was exposed, and that she had thoroughly embalmed in sunscreen and insect repellant.

She entered a small clearing, waved off a simmer of flies, and almost stepped into an impressive heap of dung. It brought her up short. She knew what elephant scat looked like, and this wasn't it. Buffalo? The midden glistened in the sun, and the steamy odor that rose to her nose was as unsettling as a whiff of fresh death. The animal that made this deposit had passed by very recently, perhaps within minutes.

She executed a slow turn. Something shifted inside her, and a sense of calm deliberation settled in to quash her fear. At first glance the grass around the clearing looked uniformly tattered and splayed, but she knew there must be some evidence to indicate which way the animal had gone.

The scat itself suggested a direction. She followed her hunch to the edge of the clearing and found herself bent at the waist, gently probing for spoor with her porcupine quill. A detachment of flies directed her to a fresh midden a yard or so into the underbrush. Beyond the dung she saw a vaguely barrel-shaped tunnel through the grass.

She did not know how to tell whether the animal had come or gone through the parted vegetation. Traveling south or north? A quick inspection of the fringe directly opposite was inconclusive, but she felt she could reasonably assume that the direction of travel was not toward the marula woodland but instead parallel to it, on a north-south line between the trees and the river. This was the closest thing to good news she could hope for.

She let herself dwell for a moment on the interesting art of tracking, even as she tried to banish from her mind the frightening words "dagga boy." Bones would have been able to tell which way the buffalo had gone, how recently it had crossed the clearing, and probably the animal's age, weight, and gender too. Even she was pretty sure this was a lone bull, but she did not have time for the luxury of terror. She drew a bead on the westernmost marula tree and set out on a route perpendicular to the path of the buffalo.

The going was slow. She found herself incapable of simultaneously wrestling aside the exuberant plant life, minding where she placed her feet, and monitoring the world around her. Every few yards, she was forced to stop for a look beyond the tall shag that engulfed her. It was during one of these observations that she spotted a dark rib of granite poking up through the grass on the south side of the trees.

She felt something like a frog leaping in her chest. Was that black shape a buffalo? The view through her binoculars reassured her that the rock was indeed rock, a foothill to a larger, rectangular boulder that stood just beyond it. Her planned route fell between the trees and the outcroppings of stone. She eyed the sinking sun and tried to pick up the pace.

Although the shadows were lengthening, the temperature seemed to hold steady at a punishing degree. Beneath her shirt and vest, her skin felt slimy with sweat. Her stride at times reached a fast, efficient clip that pleased and encouraged her, but the pace never lasted for long on a surface mined with rocks, pits, and treacherous snares of plant life.

As she neared the woodland, two more very large granite formations came into view beyond the trees. Together the three biggest boulders rose from the plain like a string of rail cars. They were striking in appearance, flat on top and stark against the golden grass. Something about the three rocks tweaked a memory, a fragment that she couldn't quite bring to the surface.

But now most of her attention was focused on the shady oasis of marula trees. She pressed forward, feeling less like an unseemly intruder with every disaster-free step through the grass. Emboldened, she kicked aside a shock of weed and was startled to bang her toe against something hard.

CHAPTER 24

THE CANTEEN was what kept Todd going. The sight of it hanging heavily on its canvas strap against the baobab tree gave him the strength to plant the crutch one more time, to swing the good foot forward another few inches, again and again, ever closer to a long drink of water.

The sole of the shoe atop the crutch continued to burn into his armpit. His fair shoulders, chest, and back endured the sting of the sun. Although the shirt wrapped around his head shielded his scalp from direct assault, the heat it trapped was bringing his brain to a slow simmer—or at least that's how it felt.

He had almost stopped thinking about his twisted ankle except as part of a useless stump he was compelled to hold in the air. The quads on that leg screamed from the effort. Some kind of rodent rushed across his path, but he hardly noticed.

When the tree was within reach, he fell forward against the trunk and grabbed at the canteen's canvas strap. His walking stick and the shoe on top of it dropped to the ground. He thought he saw a white butterfly flitting past and then realized it was a falling piece of paper. He unscrewed the cap and drank.

The water tasted warm, stale, and delicious. He fought the urge to guzzle, thinking about electrolyte imbalances and cells that could swell and die. It could take twenty-four hours or more to correct the fluid deficit in his body, he knew, even with an unlimited supply of specially formulated rehydration drinks, which he did not have. But the water in the canteen would be sufficient to keep him going, and already he felt a little better.

Clearly the others had anticipated his return to the tree. He silently thanked them for leaving behind the canteen, even as he felt a growing sense of irritation that they hadn't simply waited for him. Had he been gone *that* long? The fold of paper in the grass caught his eye. He braced himself against the trunk and reached for it.

Bones and Todd:

We have driven to find you. If we are not successful, we will return to this spot before dark. The water in the canteen is for you.

Abby, Nina, and Griff

He recognized Abby's neat penmanship. Even in his weakened condition, the sight of it, the graceful loops and uniform spacing, stirred a twinge of desire. He pictured her slender fingers on the pencil, her golden head bent over the paper. Hey, Ms. Precise, he thought with a surge of affection, who else would the water be for?

He tipped back his head and swallowed another mouthful, enjoying sweet streamlets of sensation and insight. He surprised himself by realizing that he missed Abby acutely, as though they had been separated for weeks instead of hours. Abby of the tidy tendencies, of lotions and doodads and elegant binomials. His longing for her was palpable, a swelling in his chest that radiated random currents almost like pain. He wanted nothing more than to look into her luminous face and tell her she was the most important person in his life. The most important thing.

The paper still rested in his hand. He was gazing at it absently when it hit him that the note was addressed to Bones too. Bones had not come back to the vehicle? The news struck him like a sucker punch. He stared at the name and experienced a moment of indignation that was fraught with self-pity. Weren't his throbbing ankle and his battered and bitten skin enough? Now he had to worry about (and not incidentally, he realized without an iota of shame, share attention with) Bones too?

He squinted at the rope of greenery that marked the river and saw in his mind's eye disturbing images of the dagga boy, the snake, and the drooling hyenas beneath what he had guessed was a baboon in the rain tree. At least Abby, Griff, and Nina are safe inside the Land Cruiser, he reasoned, vividly aware of the greater vulnerability of a person on foot. He considered the possibility that Abby might be driving the vehicle. After witnessing her performance in Europe, he hoped that either Griff or Nina knew how to operate a stick.

It gave him some comfort to know that those three would show up sooner or later, with or without Bones. Abby had said they would return before dark, and he knew that she would follow through even if she had to pilot the Cruiser herself. His cracked lips stretched into something like a smirk. He could hear the gears grinding already.

He tipped the canteen toward his mouth and lowered it again without drinking. Bones had walked off empty-handed except for the rifle and the radio, he remembered. Wasn't this Bones's own canteen? He shook the container, estimating its contents. With a prickle of guilt, he realized that he had drunk water intended for Bones too.

He screwed the cap back on and tucked the bottle in a shady nook formed by the baobab's foot-high surface roots. The temperature in the shade was at least ten or fifteen degrees cooler than out on the plain, he guessed, unwinding his shirt from his head. Sunburn made itself felt as he slipped his arms into the sleeves. He flinched when the cloth brushed against the raw skin in his armpit.

It took several minutes to find a suitable sitting position at the base of the tree, one that enabled him to elevate his injured ankle and keep watch toward the river at the same time. Before he lowered himself to the ground, he retrieved the walking stick and used it to poke around for ants and anything else that looked like an undesirable seat mate. He forced himself to make a thorough inspection even though he wanted nothing more than to sit down and rest. Every part of his body ached or itched or stung, and he longed to be prone and utterly still.

He settled in the shade with his back against the trunk and the bad foot up on a high ridge of root. The walking stick rested across his outstretched legs. He kept the loose shoe close at hand for slapping away insects. Not exactly a day at the beach, but comfortable enough, he thought. He was resting his eyes, maybe even half asleep, when the buzz of an airplane jerked him upright.

He rubbed his eyes and focused on the shape in the sky. A Cessna, flying south along the riverbed. He blinked again, remembering that Bones had intended to deliver them to a plane around noon. At almost the same moment, he registered the fact that twelve o'clock was long gone, and the events of the day swam to the surface.

He sat forward, squinting across the savanna. Had Bones, wherever he was, radioed ahead to say they would be late?

From day one of the safari, Bones had inspired in Todd a brand of masculine awe reserved for other men who combine estimable career status with harebrained adventure. The notion that Bones might still be in charge after all, that he might have engineered the whole disappearing act and arranged a later flight, appealed to Todd's sense of order and hegemony. His opinion of the guide remained sufficiently heroic to make a planned desertion more believable than some ghastly mistake or chance occurrence that had caused him catastrophic harm. Surely Bones had mastered the art of hiking through the bush and could do so on any given day without dire consequences.

But why would Bones subject his guests to uncertainty and fear? Because safaris are all about uncertainty and fear, he told himself. The milder versions at least—suspense and goose-bumpy excitement—come into play every day, on every game drive and often back in camp too. Uncertainty is integral to the thrill of adventure. And maybe, he thought with a smidgen of pride that trumped any anger or resentment he might reasonably feel, Bones had judged that he and the others were ready for a more advanced safari experience—a few hours in the bush on their own.

With narrowed eyes he tracked the aircraft's flight over the jagged marula woodland. The sun was sinking toward the treetops now, and sundown couldn't be more than a couple of hours away. His fingers drummed against his thigh. He was still in command of ordinary facts, and facts (the ones he chose to consider) could be made to support his preferred conclusion.

Bush pilots seldom fly after dusk, he knew. With only fires to light a runway and only if someone can be summoned to light the fires, takeoffs and landings at night are extremely risky. Poor visibility combined with the very real chance that an animal or entire herd could wander onto the airstrip at the worst possible moment make air travel in the bush a daytime pursuit.

But safaris are full of surprises, he reflected, warming to the notion that Bones had masterminded everything. At least some of those surprises are man-made. Already he and the others had been treated to more than one well-orchestrated stunner.

His head was pounding now. He leaned back against the tree trunk, closed his eyes against the wattage of the sun, and brought to mind an evening he would never forget.

It had begun as usual, with their second game drive of the day—the one that concludes in the blackout after sunset. Bones was adept at using a handheld beacon to ferret out a nightscape of glittery eyes. As he swept the light over the land around them, little phosphorous spheres peered from every elevation. They glowed emerald green, yellow-orange, deep amber—carnivore hues that signified a nerve-wracking, life-or-death shift in the balance of power from day to night.

On this particular evening they were shadowing a trio of nine-foot-long female lions with empty bellies stretched high and taut against their ribs. Bones had not needed to mention that those lions were out for blood. Todd remembered the agreeable sense of manly composure he had felt when Abby slid so close to him that she practically sat on his lap.

The three lions slipped silently through the underbrush, breaking trail for four cubs that scrambled after them. The cubs were so clumsy in their efforts to keep up that they must have alerted every species of prey within miles. They were easily distracted by moths and grasshoppers, windblown seeds, their own shadows. They jumped and swiped at the air, crushed leaves, tripped on twigs, and sent nuggets of rock spinning across the gravel. The cubs were charming to watch, but they made such a racket that Todd expected at least one of the females to circle back and exert some discipline.

The hunt did not result in a kill as far as he or any of the others knew. Bones followed the pride to a steep embankment where the females herded their young into the underbrush and vanished. It was an exhilarating chase, yet the best was still to come.

Around the time they normally would have headed back to camp for dinner, Bones swung the Cruiser through a pitch black stretch of broody scrub and out into a remote clearing. Todd still remembered the gasp that had escaped his lips. Abby had let out a little trill of pleasure.

A table covered in white linen and lit by a galaxy of candlesticks sat in the middle of the clearing next to a blazing campfire. Small *bomas* had been erected off to the side: a bush kitchen, a loo, and a hand-washing station, also lit by candles. The guests were greeted with a pulsing African ballad sung by camp staff lined up to form a corridor from the Cruiser to the circle of light.

Drinks by the fire preceded a four-course seated meal that rivaled any in Todd's memory—pea soup with mint; pork tenderloin with curried pumpkin and *nshima*, a local staple resembling polenta; a salad of papaya and greens; warm caramel cake.

He remembered the tinkle and plink of cutlery, china, and wine glasses against the mysterious hum of nighttime in the bush. Bones told captivating safari stories in a low voice that never rose too far above the muttering, whispering, blabbering sounds that drifted in from the blackness beyond their field of vision. Seemingly idle men loitered around the perimeter. Their job, Todd found out from Bones who sat next to him, was to shoo away elephants.

If Bones could engineer an evening of such complete magic, couldn't he also arrange a night flight to the next camp? With airstrips illuminated by fires and guarded by men? A torchlit welcome to their new accommodations? Of course Bones could. He pictured Abby wide-eyed with the thrill of it, squeezing his hand.

A sudden movement caught his eye. He squinted into the light. A long-limbed steenbok streaked past the baobab, and behind the steenbok he saw a flash of yellow and black. He blinked. It was a cheetah, the fastest sprinter in the animal kingdom.

He smiled with half his mouth, a tight, lopsided grin. The region teemed with animal life, but really. Did he have to see every wild creature *today*?

He pressed himself against the tree, hoping that his khaki clothing provided sufficient camouflage should the cheetah's attention wander. It relieved him to observe that the cat appeared locked in a race to the finish and that the steenbok was a worthy competitor in the realm of track and field. This chase could go on for a mile. He hoped it would.

For sheer velocity no animal matches the cheetah. Todd recognized a well-made running machine when he saw one, and even as his heart pounded, watching the cheetah fly across the plain made him want to stand up and salute. The cat possessed a chassis like a greyhound. Its permanently unsheathed claws functioned like the spikes on a sprinter's shoe. Extra-long eyelashes and black weep marks defied the glare of the sun.

The cat rocketed through the grass so fast that it was airborne more often than not, using the rudder of its tail to steer toward the darting antelope. With the precision of a drone, it anticipated every dodge and feint. Then, in a perfectly timed strike, the cheetah hooked the steenbok's hind leg, sank a dewclaw into its flesh, and tripped the bleating animal before a final, fatal lunge for its throat. There was an anguished shriek and then silence.

Sweat coursed down the gully between Todd's shoulder blades, and he realized that he was breathing hard. He surveyed the open expanse. Now the exhausted cat would drag the carcass to cover to hide it from other predators.

But what cover would it choose? The fever berry thicket? The termite mounds? He shifted his elevated leg to a new position and tried to slow his breathing. With a jolt he realized that the cheetah could also be on its way to the sheltering curves and crevices of the baobab tree.

CHAPTER 25

SHE HAD kicked a skull the size of an oil drum. The skull rolled a half turn and sent a brood of iridescent beetles scurrying for cover. She drew back at the surprise of it. The broad jaw and grossly enlarged canines told her this was hippo bone. Every hippo yawn she had seen displayed to full effect the four incurving tusks that even now fit together with the precision of a staple remover.

She stepped quickly around the skull, thinking of the feast this hippo had provided for the animals that had accomplished the difficult job of bringing it down. Where were those animals now? Asleep under a tree, still sated and content? Or looking to feed again?

Hurrying through the heat, she breathed hard through open lips that felt parched in spite of frequent applications of lip balm. Dehydration had begun to work its insidious ways on her body. She felt episodes of light-headedness, and by the time she reached the marula grove, she knew that fainting was a real possibility. The shade of the trees helped some. She crouched there and lowered her head between her knees. When she unscrewed the cap on her water bottle, she had to hold the bottle with both trembling hands to find her mouth.

A startling volume of bird calls erupted a few feet away. More birds than she had ever seen in one tree were squawking loudly, flitting and diving in a fever of agitation. The birds were small, some kind of warbler, she guessed—songbirds. But the noise they made was far from melodious.

She slowly stood, holding her arms close to minimize her movements. Birds mob animals they perceive as a threat. The patchy undergrowth around her provided plenty of cover, and she was not eager to get in the way of a predatory strike. By following the trajectory of the birds' darts and dips, she figured out where to look.

It was a python. A fat coil of muscle a yard from her feet.

Snakes strike at movement, she remembered, trying not to blink. She also knew that pythons are well endowed with teeth, and are as likely to snap up birds or eggs as they are to crush and asphyxiate animals many times their own size—humans, for instance. She still felt a little dizzy, and the possibility of fainting seemed too real to ignore. What if she fell?

She took a tentative step back, guessing that the brouhaha in the tree would be sufficient to hold the python's attention. The creature appeared lethargic and half asleep, but the deception did not fool her.

Even so, she gasped when a great length of snake sprang into the air. The wide-open jaw rose three or four feet toward a bird that had darted too close. She didn't wait to see whether the strike was successful, but turned and ran as the volume of squawks reached a frenzied pitch.

In spite of the heat she dashed toward the sunshine. Pythons weren't the only animals likely to be sheltering in the shade. When she had put some space between herself and the woods, she stopped to splash water in the crown of her hat and take a long drink, measures that helped stave off the incipient wooziness. There would be a welcome drop in temperature after sunset, but the slanted light of late afternoon still radiated almost unbearable heat.

She jogged a good distance along the tree line before seeking cover again, at the southern edge of the woods. This time she paused to inspect the area and listen for birds before venturing into the shade. She saw nothing to fear, and only an occasional tweet broke the silence. Stepping carefully from the shelter of one tree to the next, she worked her way along the eastern edge of the marulas to a position with a clear view of the baobab.

Even without binoculars, it was evident that the patterned tablecloth still hung like a postage stamp against the trunk. But the canteen? She lifted the lenses.

Hope rushed through her as she scoped the gray bark with its familiar knobs and scars and saw nothing of the canvas-covered jug. At least one of the men must have removed it to drink, she surmised, and at least one of them must be waiting there now. Her sudden elation stood in sharp contrast to the worry she had worked so hard to manage.

When she spotted Todd reclined against a fold in the tree trunk, she was already so relieved that the first sight of him seemed almost a neutral experience. Her anger at his foolhardy venture gave way to the calming possibility that the uncertainties of the day would soon come to an orderly conclusion. Was Bones also at the tree? She moved the lenses back and forth, daring to think that both men might be on the scene awaiting the return of the Cruiser, ready to greet the sunset with stories and drink and an expedited transfer to camp.

But a survey of the area brought her hope of seeing Bones to a disappointing end. She did locate his canteen tucked in the shade near Todd's reclining form. Todd himself looked to be asleep.

A long stick lay across his lap, and oddly, she saw a shoe loose by his side. She felt a sinking sensation as she followed the long lines of his legs to the shoeless foot raised up on a root. There were burrs on the sock but no bloody indication that the flesh underneath had met tooth or claw, and for that at least she felt grateful. But one unshod foot elevated in this manner was not a good sign.

His face told more of the story. She fingered the focus and zeroed in on a livid red abrasion cut across the ridge of his jaw. Had he fallen? His sunburned cheeks bore multiple scarlet scratches amid a sparkle of day-old beard. A constellation of telltale swellings suggested insect bites. His curly hair had flattened against his scalp, and his formerly crisp shirt looked wrinkled and sodden.

She stood under the marula tree spying on her man, torn by conflicting emotions. Her eyes traveled over the intimate geometry of his body, up one incline and down another, while she struggled to unravel the tangle of feelings that threatened to trip and disable her.

Overall she felt the simple tug of Todd's gravity. Even through lenses and across many acres of blinding turf, she felt the force of this attractive man, the magnetism that had drawn her to him in the first place and held her firmly there. Life with a partner like Todd was a kind of surrender, she knew, a subsuming. As good as he was to her, as generous and loyal, his high-wattage persona could make her feel as though she had idled back her very soul. And now, aware of this pull, she felt wary.

At the same time she harbored little doubt that Todd was wounded and hurting, and the realization raised in her a natural urge to rush to his side with aid and comfort. To see his face brighten at the sight of her. To smooth back his matted hair and do what she could to soothe his scratches and scrapes.

A first, faint whiff of cool air meandered through the heat and brushed against her face. The afternoon shadows had stretched, and the coming nightfall felt like impending doom. To fall prey to panic now would be easy, she knew. She swallowed hard and forced herself to sort out the complex trigonometry of choices before her.

The muscle power she had been looking for to help free the Cruiser was unlikely to come from a man with a bum foot. Could Todd even walk? She lifted the binoculars and dialed down on his face, trying to get a clearer picture of his condition through the two tight circles of magnification.

Although he still sat back against the tree, he appeared more alert now, and by the rigid camber of his chest and the movements of his eyes, she guessed that he was tracking a bird as it flew low across the plain. She glanced in the direction he was looking but saw only tall, gently stirring waves of grass.

Should she go straight to him in the hope that he was capable of limping back to the Cruiser before dark? Or would it make more sense to turn around and run to help Nina and Griff get out before nightfall and then drive to pick up Todd? Failure at the river would commit Todd to a night alone at the baobab. But failure to escort him quickly to safety could leave both of them out in the open at night, highly exposed and vulnerable.

She stood under the marula tree feeling like a very small speck in a vast, unhelpful universe. She was not unaware that the relatively short distance back to the Cruiser frightened her less than the great expanse of plain before her.

She shifted her weight from one foot to the other, grappling with indecision. Then, from somewhere behind her came a sudden, ominous snort, a low basso profundo so full of menace that her scalp prickled. Without waiting to find out whether the animal behind her was a dagga boy, a rhino, or some other terrifying species of snorter, she took off like a gunshot into deep grass and the general direction of Todd.

CHAPTER 26

THE RECTANGULAR shape of *The Birds of Southern Africa* still pushed up through the mud, Griff noticed. And the African python on the cover of *Reptile Encyclopedia* continued to stare from under Abby's muddy footprint. The books had not sunk nearly as deeply as the tires on the Cruiser. The weight of the vehicle might have pressed the Cruiser farther down into the muck. But it was also possible that the vehicle sat in a depression, and that the mud on the port side, at least, was much shallower.

Behind him, with her contused limb stretched across the middle seat, Nina had rolled up her pant leg to reinspect the damage. The discoloration remained as vivid as an African sunset, but the swelling looked to have stabilized at the dimensions of an egg rising from her shin.

"Uncomfortable but not disabling," she announced. He knew she was as concerned as he about the effort it was going to take to dislodge the Cruiser, with or without help from Bones and Todd. At the very least she would want to step down to lighten the load.

"Keep it elevated as long as you can," he said. "I'm going to go gather wood for under the tires."

She gave him a look he wouldn't soon forget, her face drawn and importuning as if begging him not to go. It frightened him, this crack in his wife's iron composure. But she said nothing and instead handed him his jacket. They both knew they could not give in.

"The mosquitoes will be out in force before long," she said. "You need to cover up."

He put on the jacket and was tucking his pant legs into his socks when he felt the first waver, a dip in energy as abrupt and fleeting as the flicker of a guttering candle. Dehydration and hunger were taking a toll.

"I don't think anyone would mind if we shared a cookie, do you?" He summoned the strength to climb past her to the top seat, under which they had stowed the camp box. The tin of shortbread was about half full. He broke a round in two and felt a stab of shame as he handed Nina the smaller piece.

Loud chuttering from the vervets in the leadwood tree reminded them that they were under close surveillance. They ate the cookie fast and drank a half cup each of tepid coffee fortified with sugar. Griff screwed down the tops on the food containers, returned everything to the box, and securely latched the lid. He suspected that given enough time and space, the monkeys would plunder and carry away every item in the Cruiser.

He wasn't nearly as agile as Abby, but he managed to land his feet on the two books and reach terra firma with only minimal indignity and spattering. A young monkey dashed out in front of him and back to the tree as if on a dare. A chorus of hoots rang out. A big male on a low branch hissed, showing tiny fangs and a shell-pink mouth. It was an easy decision to go the other direction, away from the rowdy bunch in the leadwood limbs.

The mud at the edge of the water shone as if freshly oiled and polished. It had the viscous quality of a bog that could suck the boots off his feet and maybe the socks too. He stayed clear of the damp and made his way higher up through a grove of spreading caper bushes to more promising sources of wood.

He gripped a log stuck in the undergrowth but wasn't able to budge it an inch. A clump of elephant-ravaged acacias a dozen or so yards uphill yielded an easier harvest of shredded bark and broken branches. He lifted the plant debris with care, watchful for thorns and insect life. The work wasn't difficult, but he found himself worn out after only a few minutes. Every movement seemed to require extraordinary effort, even the simple act of lowering himself to rest on a moss-covered rock.

When the first wave of cold rolled through his body, he interpreted the chill as the normal change in temperature that precedes evening in the bush. A moment later, icy fingers gripped and shook him so hard that his teeth began to chatter. He raised a hand to his forehead. Hot.

Even before he examined the wound on his palm, his trained and nimble mind scooted up the clinical decision tree and eliminated malaria (prophylaxis up-to-date), yellow fever (he'd been vaccinated), and dengue fever (no muscle, joint, or back pain). The sudden onset of chills and fever could mean many things, but the trail of red he saw streaking out from under the bandage on his hand, evidence of inflammation in the lymph channels, told him this was the most likely source of his symptoms.

He lifted a corner of the bandage. A foul odor wafted up from the suppurating lesions—clearly, a raging bacterial infection. Necrotizing fasciitis?

The detached, professional demeanor that had become as integral to his being as the bones in his body gave way to a racing heartbeat. Tachycardia, he knew, was a secondary symptom caused not by the wound itself but by the burden of knowing too much. Necrotizing fasciitis produced toxins that destroyed muscles, skin, and fat, and early treatment with antibiotics was critical.

Then, in violation of his own diagnostic guidelines (common things are common! do not multiply entities needlessly!), his mind turned to another, possibly worse scenario. Only a month or two earlier he had read with particular interest a journal article about a rare case of wound mucormycosis. The author was an orthopedic surgeon practicing in sub-Saharan Africa, a location that had caught his attention because of his forthcoming trip.

The patient, a young man with a traumatic injury to the hand, was not immuno-compromised or otherwise particularly vulnerable to infection. Nevertheless, his white blood cell count soared, and studies of wound swabs revealed a mixed growth of pathogens. Intravenous antibiotic therapy did not prevent the rapid spread of infection.

On day seven or so—Griff couldn't remember the exact timing—lab studies uncovered tissue necrosis consistent with mucormycosis, a rare fungal infection. The man was immediately started on antifungal drug therapy, but the infection had already progressed too far. With a shudder Griff recalled that to halt the life-threatening spread of infection, the surgeon performed a forearm amputation.

He had read the study dispassionately, drifting on the sturdy raft of scientific inquiry that had borne him for years. But now, as he considered even a remote possibility that his own case could chart a similar course, from puncture wound to untreated infection to (good god!) amputation, he felt a tightening in his chest. For a moment his heart banged alarmingly. He struggled for calm in the only way he knew, by clamping a lid on his emotions and filling his mind with facts.

Fungi belonging to the order Mucorales are everywhere in the environment, yet they are incapable of penetrating intact skin. Infection requires direct inoculation through a compromised cutaneous barrier, ideally one or more deep puncture wounds. So far, he thought, he was a prime candidate.

But mucormycosis also tends to be opportunistic. The infection is readily suppressed by healthy individuals like himself and more easily established in patients with chronic diseases such as diabetes, or those receiving immunosuppressive drugs. He fell into neither of those susceptible categories.

And, he thought with a mental scrape of Ockham's Razor, wasn't the case in the study characterized as "highly unusual"? Yes, of course it was. Bacterial infections are far more common, even in Africa, and antibiotics, the medicines he carried in his own luggage, are a highly effective remedy.

Furthermore, nothing even close to seven days was going to pass before his infection received proper pathological study and care. Fortifying himself with a needed dose of bravado, he reasoned that if Bones did not show up soon to take him and the others to civilization, he would take them there himself. The solution was quite straightforward, really. Free the Cruiser and drive to a road.

He had been staring blindly toward the gash of the river below his position on the embankment, and now he startled at the sight of a water monitor lizard floating by on a mat of vegetation. The lizard was an equally hefty and prehistoric-looking cousin to the rock monitor they had seen earlier. This one measured at least five feet from its bulbous snout to the tip of its fat, weapons-grade tail.

Through feverish eyes Griff watched the retractile tongue fork in and out over the gently flowing water. Then, without as much as a ripple, a crocodile—a giant of the species—shot up from under the flotilla of plant life and clamped the lizard's entire head in its jaw.

The clawing and flailing that ensued, the terrible life-or-death frenzy, both captivated and repulsed him. Another, smaller crocodile appeared, and in a horror show of cooperative feeding, the second croc sank its teeth in one of the monitor's hind legs and spun like a screwdriver on its long axis until the leg twisted off.

The thrashing, splashing boil in the water ended almost as suddenly as it had begun. The smaller crocodile swam away with the streaming leg in its mouth, like a dog with a fresh bone. The larger croc simply pulled the mortally wounded monitor underwater and disappeared. A moment later the water was still.

Griff rose unsteadily from the rock and made his way through the caper bushes back to the swamped Cruiser. Nina's face floated above the rear rail, as white and staring as a full moon. He managed to cross the muddy shore and haul himself up as far as the middle seat before another round of chills shivered through his body.

Bones's journal was open, face down. Apparently Nina had been acquainting herself with facts of life in the bush. As he fell onto the cushion next to the splayed volume, he realized that he had failed to bring back a single stick of wood.

CHAPTER 27

ABBY SPRINTED away from the sound of the snort like something launched from a slingshot, nearly flying across the plain. She wasn't about to stand still and wait to find out what creature had produced that chilling sound. The prime candidates, rhino and buffalo, were herbivores—hoofed mammals unlikely to come after her unless she managed to annoy them. At least that was her theory. Just get away.

It occurred to her that the rugged boots on her feet had never hoofed it so fast. The ground was less chunky here, the grass a little thinner. She managed to get up some speed and even think about running techniques she had learned from Todd. There were ways to conserve energy while jogging, she knew, and focusing on those helped divert her mind from the frightening animal sound she had fled.

She was fine-tuning the lateral movements of her arms when she ran past the three boxcar-sized boulders she had scoped earlier. Several smaller outcroppings of granite poked up through the grass and forced her to make a course correction. She worked her way around the barriers as fast as the terrain allowed. It pleased her that she managed to keep up a decent pace even while dodging rocks, swatting flies, and swigging water. Soon she forgot all about the lateral movements of her arms.

Beyond the boulders, she paused to reconnoiter. The plain to the south shimmered in the late afternoon sunshine. On it she spotted no elephant or any other terrestrial animal. A pair of circling buzzards appeared to hone in on some hapless prey.

To the north stretched more open grassland dotted with a smattering of acacias and a small herd or two of calmly grazing impalas. Relaxed impalas were a good sign.

Ahead stood a thick stand of bushes. The thicket was not a big one though, and she knew that the baobab and Todd were only a short distance beyond it. She tried to rein in a premature sense of euphoria. The crossing was almost over.

But a scatter of spiked aloe plants turned her forward progress into an awkward, side-stepping dance. When she got to the thicket she chose what she thought was the least difficult way around. About halfway, she ran into another mess of aloes, and a thorn caught her pant leg.

She stooped to undo the snag, and something made her look up. The muscles in her jaw went slack as she stared into the beautiful, amber eyes of a cheetah. It sat in dry underbrush beneath the canopy of shrub and was hunched over the shreds of an antelope, watching her through pupils as round and black as buckshot.

Time seemed to stop—time and movement and breath itself. She stood less than the length of her shadow from one of Africa's most elusive and dazzling hunters, close enough to see every hair on the animal's coat. A tawny ruff framed its elegant, foreshortened face. The characteristic tear streaks, two black swipes, looked like a painter's special flourish. She picked out a short spinal crest and a fluff of pale hair floating over the narrow breast.

She took a slow, tentative step away. The cheetah peeled back its red-stained lips and let out a frightening snarl but did not move to abandon its closely guarded prize. Did it view her as a threat? A challenger for the meal secured between its paws? Every instinct told her that it did not.

Electric blue butterflies the size of polished fingernails hovered over the dead antelope. A whiff of fresh blood rose on a draft of air. The cheetah's amber eyes did not leave her.

She retreated slowly, restraining every movement. Five or six exquisitely placed footfalls were all it took before the cat's tan and black-spotted coloration became one with the surrounding foliage. If she hadn't known the animal was there, she couldn't have picked it out from where she stood now.

But she did know that the cheetah was still watching her, wary, annoyed by the interruption, and eager to get back to feeding before a real challenger showed up to snatch away the kill.

Animal behavior wasn't all that complicated, she told herself, backing away as quickly as she dared. Humans who unthinkingly fear all wild animals in all circumstances, who expect aggressive or hostile behavior at every encounter, do not consider animals' basic agenda or their native intelligence.

The thought reassured her even as she felt the rapid and overly shallow suck of her lungs. Species that have known abuse at the hands of humans— elephants by poachers, for example—could be a threat, and for good reason, she thought protectively, recalling the grandeur of the elephant that had approached and almost touched her while she sat in the Cruiser. She remembered those glorious tusks, as vulnerable to thievery as a pedestrian's swinging necklace of pearls.

She remembered too what Bones had said about elderly lions with missing or rotten teeth. Tormented by hunger, those sorry creatures might hunt down and devour tender human flesh. Random, opportunistic attacks by carnivores out for an easy meal were always possible, she supposed, looking around uneasily. And of course one wouldn't want to startle an animal or come between a mother and her offspring.

She was aware that she had worked her thinking in a complete circle, back to the notion that a person would be crazy not to fear every wild, unpredictable creature in the universe. No, not fear, she amended. Respect.

She picked up the pace and put the thicket well behind her. It heartened her to know that a cheetah consumes up to thirty pounds at a single feeding. That could take a while. And once a cheetah eats its fill, it leaves the skin, bones, and digestive tract of the animal to scavengers and does not return. But the most reassuring fact she remembered was that a well-fed cheetah typically fasts for several days between kills.

When she felt safely distanced from the bushes, she turned and saw with relief that the baobab tree stood in full view only a hundred or so yards away. Todd had already spotted her and was pulling himself to his feet. As she drew closer, he stared in her direction with the intensity of a border guard. He held his back to the tree trunk, leaning against it with the shoeless foot hanging limp above the ground. The stunned sequence of expressions that crossed his face told her he was struggling to understand the implications of her astonishing arrival on foot, alone.

She had forgotten the blue of his eyes. Not *that* his eyes were blue, of course, but the intensity of the color, a hue so deep and saturated it appeared to share DNA with the dome of the sky. He reached out to her with both hands. She sensed the stirring knit of masculine motor works and the flex of toned muscle. Even there, under highly distracting circumstances, a familiar current of sexuality crossed the space between them.

But incredulity ruled the look on his scratched and bitten face. "You walked?"

Their fingers intertwined effortlessly, and she felt the practiced, intimate knowledge of hands that had touched every inch of her body. Piano-playing hands that held the songs "Bulldog, Bulldog, Bow-Wow-Wow" and "Roar, Lion, Roar" in their muscle memory, she suddenly, oddly remembered. Her thoughts turned to his impetuous and—by the looks of him—disastrous departure from the safety of the vehicle.

"The Cruiser is stuck in mud at the river. Nina and Griff are waiting there."

His eyes flitted over her as if searching for damage. "You walked here from the river?"

She watched him study her and could hear the disbelief in his voice. His useless foot still dangled in the air. His face and hands were inflamed with sunburn, abrasions, and the weeping swell of insect bites. In the ravaged housing of his ruined shirt and knee-sprung pants, he looked like an evolutionary cul de sac, nature's most benighted creation.

"You're hurt," she said simply, forgoing the sharper words she had planned. "Sit down and tell me what happened."

She helped him settle with his back to the tree and took a position on a root from where she could both look at him and keep watch on the plain she had crossed, now backlit by the sinking sun. He winced, she noticed, when he brought his damaged foot to rest on a woody knob. She handed him her water bottle and fished in a pocket for insect repellent.

The understanding that they could not make it back to the Cruiser before sunset and that she and Todd would pass the night right there, in the tenuous shelter of the baobab tree, settled gradually in her mind like churned-up waters coming to rest. She felt very calm. Something inside her had loosened and yielded.

Todd was talking excitedly now, about a dagga boy he had met in the ravine, about hyenas beneath a kill in a rain tree, about an elephant and her calf. She noticed that he was watching her face for reactions, signs that she was suitably impressed, and she made the appropriate murmurs and exclamations even as her thoughts threaded forward.

Nina and Griff would be safe overnight in the Cruiser, she believed, stealing a look toward the river, hoping that Griff hadn't gotten it into his head to come after her. Both he and Nina would be very worried, she knew. But they also had the good sense to stay put, especially with the sun diving toward sunset. At first light she would help Todd hobble back. And maybe by then someone from camp would be on the way to find them.

The long oval of Todd's face suggested recent grindings in the dust, and his mangled clothing projected a punishing struggle. But as he related the story of his day in the bush, he leaned easily against the tree trunk with his good foot flat on the ground and one wrist resting casually up on the jackknifed knee. He exuded a clueless bonhomie that made her stare at him with wonder. Did he have any idea what was in store for them after dark? Any thought for Nina and Griff?

"So, Bones brought you here, right?" he said finally.

She looked at him. "Bones?"

There was a pause during which the first pulse of alarm appeared to beep through his brain.

"You know, our guide?" He cast a squint across the plain. "Are you in on it now too?"

"In on what?"

Something in her expression galvanized his attention, and she could see that he was struggling to gain control of their shared information, of reality itself. He was holding himself stiffly now, as though his joints had suddenly fused. She saw confusion in the wide blue eyes and felt something like pity for the man whose unshakable optimism she was about to crush.

"Todd, we did not find Bones. We went looking for both of you, and it turned out badly. Griff's hand is wounded, and Nina is nursing a painful bruise on her shin. The Cruiser is up to its axels in mud. I came back hoping to find at least one of you to help get us out."

He was sitting very still and watching her lips, like a person trying to make sense of a foreign tongue.

"You and I will stay here tonight," she continued, speaking slowly, conscious that a tectonic shift in assumptions had thrown him way off balance. "Nina and Griff are safe in the Cruiser. We'll rejoin them in the morning."

"There was a plane." As he gazed at her, his face was taut with disbelief. "Coming to get us."

"I saw it too. A Cessna flying south. The airstrip is north of here, Todd. That plane was leaving."

In the silence that followed, she heard the first tentative *creek creek creek* of a cricket announcing the onset of dusk. The day's last warm breath touched her face and hands. Somewhere in the distance a baboon called out a sharp *wahoo*. Todd stared wordlessly into the sinking sun.

"Well, screw them," he finally said. He wore a look of weary resignation that suddenly gave way to a smile so brilliant it startled her. The travails of the day had done nothing to narrow the width of his grin or dim the white of his teeth. "Darlin', now we're really camping."

She couldn't help herself; she laughed out loud.

"I was saving some water for Bones," he went on, picking up the canvas-covered canteen. He sloshed the contents as if to prove his magnanimity. "But now I'm not so sure he is worth the trouble."

He unscrewed the cap and tipped the canteen to his lips but only pretended to drink, Abby noticed. He wasn't willing to give up on Bones yet—unlike her. The spill of light had faded to soft focus, and she did not see anyone else making preparations for their long, dark night out in the cold. She pulled the woven cloth from the tree trunk and tore off a long strip. Kneeling next to Todd, she gently lifted and wrapped his swollen appendage and tied the loose ends of the cloth in a knot. He was skilled with an Ace Bandage too, and while he watched and winced, she fully expected him to pipe up and boss her a little. But he literally bit his lip and did not make a sound. Between the scrapes and welts on his face, his sunburn had turned a sickly shade of mauve.

When she had done the best she could for his foot, she used a moistened tissue to clean the sore, scuffed skin on his hands, jaw, and brow. He did not resist or try to help when she buttoned his shirt to the neck and turned up the collar, dabbed insect repellent on his unbroken skin, and sprayed the cuffs of his pants and shirt sleeves. His eyes followed her efficient movements with rapt, slightly amused attention, as though he had discovered an exotic new species that would become the subject of a world lecture tour and make him famous. She found the look on his face mildly belittling and tried to ignore it.

An extravagant sunset was underway that basted his body in peachy light. He was shivering now, and the sudden cold had begun to seep through her clothing too. She gave fleeting thought to the mysterious craft of generating fire without matches and knew enough not to waste her time. When she had made all the preparations she could think of, she sat down with her back to the tree trunk and her body pressed from shoulder to toe against Todd's.

Thinking about heat retention as well as the possible merit of appearing to be one large animal, she hooded the remains of the torn table cloth over her hat and Todd's bare head and layered the two ends across their shoulders.

"Nice. A babushka built for two," he said jauntily enough, but anxiety had lifted the pitch of his voice. He laid his walking stick across their thighs, and they both gripped the pole like a safety bar while they watched the orange globe of the sun fatten and fall. A spray of bats rose from the baobab tree high above them. Abby recognized the haunting, five-note call of a nightjar. In just ten or fifteen minutes, spectacular color rouged and then drained from the sky, and darkness arrived as if someone had pulled a plug.

An expectant silence fell upon them, an awkward pause while each seemed to be considering what to say next.

"Todd."

"What?"

"I want to go back to teaching full-time."

She heard a puff of air that must have forced apart his tightly pursed lips.

"Would you mind if I did?"

For several seconds he said nothing. Was this the extra-wide break before the lie?

"I guess not."

"Good."

CHAPTER 28

WITH THE dying light, crepuscular creatures had begun to stir on the banks of the river. Nina watched a bat-eared fox emerge from a burrow and scoot through the dusk with its nose to the ground. A springhare shot out of nowhere on slender hind legs, hopping like a tiny kangaroo. Color had faded to three shades: black, gray, and white. She almost didn't see the nyala standing motionless next to the leadwood tree. The charcoal gray antelope stepped forward and dipped its head to drink and then melted into the night.

A full-faced moon had risen somewhere behind the trees leaning into the ravine, and now it cast a ghostly light in random patches along the otherwise pitch-dark riverbed. The vervets had gone silent. Griff was stretched out with his head in her lap, feverish and exhausted, wrapped in two of the waterproof, fleece-lined ponchos they had retrieved from under a seat. Her own poncho crackled every time she moved. Inside the voluminous wrap she felt collapsed and vulnerable, as though something invisible had sucked the bones out of her.

Abby had not returned. The litany of possible reasons offered little reassurance. She couldn't escape images of predation and death that she had come to understand as part of the great, never-ending circle of life. But to lose Abby here, now?

Was she guilty of cowardice or worse for not going to look for her friend? Had she been wrong to let Abby go by herself, or at all? The questions, she knew, would haunt her even if Abby turned up unharmed.

Now as night held her in its grip, she tried to think positively, to envision Abby alive and well, hunkered down somewhere hugging herself to stay warm. The crisp air was sharp in her own lungs, and the poncho weighed on her shoulders as heavily as guilt. Wherever she was, Abby would be very cold.

She shifted inside the man-sized wrap, cradling Griff's head in her hands. She knew she could do little until dawn except sit in the Cruiser and try to keep Griff as comfortable as possible. She had never seen him so weak and lethargic, and his depleted condition rubbed against her very sense of him.

If help did not arrive before morning, she would hike out of the ravine at first light and construct some kind of signal to alert a passing plane or vehicle that they were there. Stake down a patchwork of ponchos or hang ponchos from branches. From up on top she could scan the plain for Abby too—for any sign of now *three* missing people.

No matter what she discovered up there, she knew that her top priority must be to get the Cruiser unstuck and drive to find help as soon as possible. Bones had indicated a road somewhere east of the river. She would drive straight into the rising sun.

But first she would have to collect sufficient quantities of wood to shore up the tires and then figure out how to use the jack. The idea of dragging logs around a croc-infested bog and standing in black water to muscle up five thousand pounds of vehicle frightened her to the core. She knew herself capable of rising to physical challenges, but she dared not think too much about the brute strength and extraordinary courage this project was going to require.

Mosquitoes whined around her head. The repellent she and Griff had applied before sunset seemed to be keeping at bay the insects if not her own distressing thoughts. Whole nations of luminescent bugs circled the Cruiser and spun skyward.

She was becoming accustomed to the throb in her shin, and as long as nothing touched the tender area, she could almost ignore it. She waved a hand over Griff's face, white inside his poncho hood. He had closed his eyes and possibly fallen asleep.

When he had wobbled back from his unsuccessful wood-collecting errand with his hand held out like an exhibit, his body quaking with chills, and his face a chalky mask, she had focused all her energies on taking care of him. Bones's journal, she discovered, held quite a lot of useful information. Abby had been way ahead of her in understanding the value of those tattered pages.

In one section she found instructions for treating wounds without the benefit of first aid supplies. Tips for the unprepared? For the Boy Guide underachiever merit badge? She had wondered how frequently professional guides or their clients actually needed that information.

But apparently tea bags steeped in warm water really can draw toxins from wounds, insect bites, and burns. At least that is what Bones had scrawled in his rangy handwriting. He described the treatment as "a transdermal means of delivering herbal antibiotic therapy."

Feeling hopeful and with an energizing sense of purpose, she had rummaged through the camp box and found packets containing both Earl Grey and rooibos, the sweetly fragrant African bush tea. Bones had not mentioned what variety of tea makes the better poultice, so she unwrapped two of each sort, placed the four bags in a metal cup, and added steaming water from a thermos. When the water turned a rich shade of amber she transferred the dripping bags from the mug to Griff's bare, upturned palm.

He accepted the treatment without a sound. His passivity worried her almost as much as the oozing wound and the possibility that she might introduce a new infection or otherwise make things worse. But the tentacles of red snaking up his arm, the fever, and the chills told her this was a risk worth taking.

He had saucered the poultice in his hand with the Earl Grey strings dangling down, their yellow tabs swinging in the air like a pair of moths hired to advertise A Better Cup of Tea. After a few minutes he reported a soothing sensation although he said he was unsure whether the efficacious agent was the moisture, the warmth, or the tea.

Bones's journal did not specify the optimal duration of tea bag treatments, but as long as Griff let her continue, Nina did. When the poultice had cooled, she repeated the process with fresh tea bags, hurrying to extract maximum benefit before the sun vanished. In the last orange light of sunset, she patted the wound dry, applied a new bandage, and helped Griff tuck both arms inside his poncho.

Now, with her patient drifting off and utterly dependent on her, she felt a familiar recalibration of senses—a heightened acuity of smell, hearing, and even sight as the rod cells in her retinas adjusted to the inky darkness. From the muck bed a chaotic stink roiled up that smelled of wet leaves, rotten fish, and trampled fruit and flowers. A green salad odor wafted in from the tender shoots that lined the waterway. Her own poncho enveloped her in a blend of not unpleasant scents she identified as damp pup tent, candle wax, and road dust.

Over the constant chirrup of crickets came the yodel of a distant jackal. The *tu-tu-tuee-tuee* of a pearl-spotted owlet. Highly unsettling drips and sloshes in the water mere feet from where she sat. A sibilant she couldn't place.

A vervet sentry sounded a warning, and she heard a flurry of relocation in the branches of the leadwood tree. She watched a low-slung animal creep through the tracery of the moon. A serval? Or civet?

The patchy lunar light offered no ambient illumination, and the creature passed silently from moon glow to blackness. She felt its presence and held herself still. Sensed the whisper and scurry of a hundred busy lives on her left and her right, in front of the Cruiser and behind it, even in the water lapping under the floorboards and in the branches overhead. Wild dogs yammered somewhere far away. Then something splashed through the muck bed so close to her that water landed on her face and the backs of her hands. She felt droplets run down her neck and under the cover of her poncho like small creatures heading for shelter.

Panic knifed up inside her, a new and distracting sensation for a cool cucumber such as herself. She recognized the signs not from personal experience but because panic was everywhere in fiction—the racing heart, the clammy skin, the sense of impending doom. Where would Shakespeare be without a good panic scene in the fourth or fifth act?

For some reason, this ridiculous thought reassured her even as she strained to listen through the darkness and her breathing turned rapid and shallow. Field work undertaken to gain a fuller understanding of Macbeth! she thought (as though she had chosen to sweat and willed her pulse to pound). Panting, she rubbed her damp hands together and told herself somewhat unhelpfully that panic was entirely proportional to her current situation.

She heard another splash and then the lapping of water against the shore. Or was that an animal drinking? There was a trickle, a gargle, another splash. And it came to her that the Cruiser would be an excellent resting place for night-roving creatures looking to roost.

CHAPTER 29

THE MOON and the stars shone with stunning clarity. Thousands, millions of stars wheeled so vividly against the sky that Todd could have been viewing the universe from a rocket ship lost in deep space. He picked out the four bright lights of the south-pointing Southern Cross, guide to centuries of navigators. At the foot of the cross, Musca, the arrow-shaped Fly, aimed southeast. A dark spot in the nearly solid sparkle of the Milky Way marked the Coalsack nebula, a dust cloud fifty light-years wide. There were more shooting stars than he could count.

With such a splendid view and Abby pressed up against him, the night would have been promisingly romantic were it not for the rock-hard earth bruising his butt, the baobab trunk pressing dents in his back, and the mind-numbing cold. The ridiculous tablecloth tented over their heads and the occasional yowl of a not-so-distant animal didn't help his mood much either.

At least his injured foot and ankle felt more secure cocooned in Abby's makeshift bandage. She had done a decent job of wrapping his wrecked appendage halfway to the knee and with impressive composure too. Now he turned to study her profile in the moonlight.

She was resting her head back against the baobab, and the one eye visible to him appeared closed, but he couldn't tell for sure. In the cold he could see her breath, steady and even. Had she actually fallen asleep?

Her weird demeanor, this unprecedented *sang-froid* or whatever it was, confused him. She had sat by his side under that tree and watched the African night close in without a whimper, as though ice water coursed through her veins. And not just then, either. Ever since he had first spotted her picking her way around the fever berry bushes (on foot, alone in the African bush!), she had seemed as cool and collected as—well, as he usually was.

He went on in that mode for a while, wondering what had come over her and how he felt about it. He searched his memory for clues that this steely side of Abby, this surprising "I want to work full-time" decisiveness, had always been there. Her insistence on returning to the classroom had come as a big surprise.

But the images that still held fast in his mind evoked her excessive caution and fear—the wrinkle in her lovely brow when she was uncertain or scared and a particularly memorable episode of fright when she had fallen into his arms and gone limp with the relief of being there.

As he ruminated on the pleasures of sheltering her, he shifted his weight against the unyielding earth and couldn't help noticing that heat had flooded his face. Was he blushing? In the dark he couldn't care less. But he possessed enough insight to understand that something about the relish he took in Abby's frailty was making him squirm.

What had popped into his admittedly twisted psyche was Bones's commentary on the sex life of the topi antelope. When Bones first told the story, Todd had chuckled along with everyone else, but he remembered feeling certain twinges. The gist of the matter was that during mating season, a male topi would try to keep females in heat inside his territory by making them afraid to leave.

If a female started to walk away, the male would run ahead of her and assume a rigid stance while staring and snorting in the direction she was headed. Typically the behavior meant that the male had spotted a predatory lion or cheetah and hurried (valiantly, Todd would add) to the forefront to sound an alert. Upon hearing the warning, the female topi almost always retreated back inside the male's presumably safer domain where he wasted no time in mating with her.

While Todd tried to marshal the implications of this (clever!) self-serving male behavior, a particularly brilliant comet with a luminous tail shot across the Milky Way. The distraction came as something of a relief. "Wow! Did you see that?"

"Mmm, no," Abby finally answered after a long pause. "I was resting my eyes."

"Oh. Sorry."

An interesting new thought sidled into his head. He groped for her hand, cool and limp on her thigh, and closed his fingers around it. Maybe the great stresses of the day—the shock of the separation from Bones, his own defection, and who knew what else that had gone on since he last saw her—had pushed Abby into an entirely new and emotionally depleted state, catatonic but functional, like a reptile.

Feeling more comfortable with this formulation, he stroked her fingers tenderly. She sat forward and pulled her hand away. "Look!"

The force of her voice startled him. "Uh, where?"

"Beyond the river. Follow it south."

He cast a squint. A patch of sky beyond the riverine woodland glowed orange, like a giant hearth.

"Wildfire."

There was a pause while they both took in the frightening dimensions of the blaze.

"Do you think it could burn all the way to the water?" A familiar tremor had entered her voice.

Neither of them needed to spell out the implications of a fire cornering frantic creatures in the same ravine that trapped Nina and Griff. Todd sat forward, matching the angle of his body to hers while he beheld the flaring sky. The scrim of trees formed a lacey silhouette against the firelight. In the middle distance he made out the outline of the rectangular boulders he had passed on his way across the plain. The glow in the background made the rest of the savanna seem even blacker.

An eruption of cackles, whoops, and yelps in the darkness very near the baobab seized his attention. He found himself gripping both of Abby's hands. He did not know which of them had reached out first, but he was aware that the demented sounds ripping through the air terrified him.

"Hyenas," Abby whispered. "Maybe wild dogs too. Fighting over the remains of the antelope in the bushes."

"Remains?"

"A cheetah was there, feeding."

Todd recalled the chase through the grass and the steenbok's final moments. Abby had seen the cheetah?

A new round of yowls and snarls suggested a fierce contest. He heard the crunch of bones and imagined the scavengers' hunched and bristling backs;

their twitching, dripping nostrils; their bloody, obscene jaws. He tried to swallow and failed. This was a total nightmare, a feeding frenzy a few dozen yards from where he and Abby sat like two helpings of fresh meat.

He struggled to clear his constricted throat. A movement against the firelight caught his eye, something at the three large boulders. Abby had seen it too. She lifted one of his hands and used it to point in the direction he was already looking. They watched the motion become a shape, an unmistakable silhouette atop the nearest rock. And then came a bone-chilling roar.

"Lions." Abby made a strangled sound. "Now I remember."

The fear in her tone scared Todd almost as much as the roar. For the first time since she had arrived at the baobab, Abby sounded afraid. Swallowing hard, he realized that he needed her to be strong. The stuck vehicle, the fiendish animals, his own humiliating disability—suddenly all of it seemed more than he could manage.

"Remember what?" he croaked.

"Threeflat Rocks." Her whisper in his ear was like a rasp drilling for nerves. "Bones finds lions there. It's in his journal. The Asooni or Asani Pride, something like that. A lot of lions."

Before he could respond, he felt her pull the cloth from their heads. She lifted his arm and laid it across her shoulders. Her voice took on new urgency. "Let me help you up. We're moving."

CHAPTER 30

NINA PULLED Griff closer and leaned protectively over his upturned face. The thorny branch he had saved was stowed under their seat. She touched it with her foot, considering its potential as a weapon. No, too treacherous to human hands. The shovel they had used to dig out of the sand was stored in the rear hold, but she wouldn't think of stepping into the water and slogging back there to get it now.

She guessed that Bones would advise her to forget about weapons altogether and simply be silent and still in the company of animals that happened to jump on board. Could she and Griff do that? Sit quietly while some wild thing lounged on the front seat? In the dark, how would they even know one was there?

She remembered that Bones's handheld beacon, the light he used to find animals during night drives, sat somewhere beneath the dashboard. He had mentioned that he spotlighted night-roving species only briefly to avoid distracting predators or targeting their prey. She noticed that he also directed the beam away from the animals' light-sensitive eyes. Would a sudden blast of wattage scare off an unwelcome stowaway? She had no way of knowing, but using the beacon as a deterrent seemed plausible and worth the preparation.

She gently repositioned Griff, climbed across the driver's seat, and felt her way forward. She tried not to think about the riverine residents that might already have stolen onto the cushions. To her relief the chilly expanse of leather felt unoccupied. Her fingers found the lamp about where she thought it would be, attached to a coiled wire that spiraled to a connection under the hood. With the engine off she would have to rely on the starter battery and use the lamp very sparingly.

She managed to climb back and resettle herself and Griff up on the middle seat with the unlit beacon gripped in her hand. She felt the tug of the stretched wire and the heft of the bulb. In her palm the lamp stem felt as comforting as a pistol, even though she had never fired a gun or thought of weaponry as particularly comforting. She touched the on/off switch, moved her finger away, and touched the trigger again to memorize its location.

"My hand feels a little better." Griff's voice rising from her lap startled her. His poncho crackled as he sat up. She noted another muffled snuffle that drifted in from somewhere upriver.

"How about the rest of you?" she whispered.

"Can't tell yet. About the same I think." His voice sounded hollow, reduced.

"I'm holding Bones's spotlight in case we need to scare something away."

"Good. Have you tested it?"

"No, but I will."

She aimed into the night and flicked the switch. The beam fell on the backside of a very broad hippopotamus making haste up the river bank. The tail was a flat paddle that flung water with every jouncy step.

"Goodness," she said in a low voice, shaken, and quickly turned off the light. "Did you know that a hippo just went past us?"

"Uh, no."

They fell silent, listening. A faint snap of twigs up on the ridge might have been caused by the departing hippo, but otherwise they heard nothing that resembled the footfall of a three-ton mammal. Nina was reminded again how excessively humans rely on sight alone and how poorly, by animal standards, humans rank in hearing and smell.

Hippos forage individually, she remembered. She guessed that the one they had seen commutes solo to its private pasture and returns at dawn to rejoin the pod upstream. Human deaths from hippo attacks occur most often when people come between a grazing hippo and the water it calls home. With a shudder she added hippo attack to her inventory of things to worry about when she started out in the morning.

Just as she was getting her head around the disturbing idea of hippos on the loose, a lion somewhere up on the savanna voiced a mighty, full-throated roar. The sound must have reverberated for miles. The chilling reminder that lions own the crowded and lethal night inflated her anxiety to monstrous proportions. Griff winged out his poncho and drew her to him. She leaned into his chest and for the first time in years felt tears spill unchecked from her eyes.

As hard as she tried to think otherwise, she could not believe that persons as sparely equipped as Abby and Todd could survive a night alone on foot in the African bush. How could they? If they hadn't already met some violent end, now they faced twelve hours of darkness ruled by superbly equipped carnivores that were surfacing from their hideouts by the hundreds to stalk, kill, and feed. Bones stood a decent chance with a rifle, a radio, and a lifetime of bush camp experience. But her friends?

Even in the relative safety of the vehicle, she herself felt powerless and vulnerable. The unending rustles and tinkles and trills coming from every direction had ramped up her fear and crushed her already dwindling sense of control. Hunger sank its jaw into her stomach. Thirst gummed her mouth. Her back was beginning to relay its displeasure, and her shin continued to throb. Tears dripped from her chin.

Griff's breath was warm against her ear. She turned her face toward his. Her voice came out thin and unrecognizable. "'Tiger! Tiger! burning bright, in the forests of the night.'"

"There are no tigers in Africa," he whispered.

"I know, but I can't think of a lion poem."

Another roar echoed across the plain. From the same lion or another one? She tried to keep her mind on the verse: "'What immortal hand or eye could frame thy fearful symmetry?'" She paused and whispered, "It's about the origin of good and evil ... 'Did he smile his work to see? Did he who made the lamb make thee?'"

"But the animals that frighten us, the lions and tigers and bears, aren't evil. They're just hungry," Griff replied.

It was not lost on her that as ill as he was, Griff understood her attempt at a diversion. Grateful, she pressed closer to him. "Well, yes. 'Murder, murder burning bright' or 'arson, arson burning bright' would be more literal. The tiger and the lamb are just symbols."

Griff put his lips to her ear. "Animals aren't evil, but they can still scare you to death."

She swallowed and managed to whisper, "Let's hope not."

They watched a gauzy moon edge into the ribbon of sky above the ravine.

Falling stars streaked through the tree limbs. Dark shapes along the shores appeared to shift and recede. In normal circumstances she would think the African night magical, a captivating world imbued with beauty and expectation. Now she just wanted the darkness to end.

Time in that place seemed more linked to the eternal than to watches and clocks, yet her inability to fix the hour continued to unnerve her. The transit of the moon and the stars told her nothing. Crying had wrung her dry. With the passage of the long, dark night, fatigue and habituation wore away the sharp edges of her fear, and in the warmth of Griff's embrace she felt herself nod off.

She must have been dozing when a thump on the hood of the Cruiser went through her like an electric jolt. She sat up at full alert. There was movement against the vanished background, a flurry of activity behind and in front of the vehicle that she sensed more than saw. The chassis rocked under a sudden new weight. She felt Griff stiffen and press back against their seat.

She groped for the beacon that had slipped from her grasp and now rested somewhere in the folds of her poncho. Her fingers trembled against the cold metal. She fumbled for a handhold and flicked the switch.

An emaciated man with yellow eyes and rusted teeth stared into the light. He was standing on the passenger side running board holding a shiny machete. Nina saw two or three other figures stream through the light beam behind him. They were a raggedy bunch of men, angular and lean. At least one of them carried a rifle slung by a strap from his shoulder. She gripped the beacon in both hands and held it like a gun on the machete wielder's watery eyes. No animal could frighten her more than this armed and calculating man.

He raised a hand to shield his face from the light. Then in one stroke he lifted the machete over his head and swung the blade with force onto the electric cord stretched across the front seat. There was a thwack of sliced leather as the steel edge cut into the seat cushion, and the light went black.

Nina dropped the dead spotlight and wrapped both arms around Griff, braced for a body blow. Instead she felt the Cruiser rock and settle and then heard the slosh and suck of footsteps in the mud. There was a murmur of low voices. The sigh of crushed grass. Something being pushed or dragged through the underbrush.

"Who's there?" Griff called in a sharp voice. "Who are you?"

Whoever they were, they didn't want to be seen—or to talk. Someone opened the rear hold. Nina heard the clank of metal, possibly the shovel. Were they looking for the camp box and the first aid kit? The men seemed to know their way around the vehicle. Surely they would guess that the provisions had been moved aboard, under the seats.

There was a clacking sound she couldn't place, the ping of metal. The Cruiser rocked again, and she realized the men must be trying to strip or dismantle the vehicle. Griff tightened his arms around her. This was it, she thought. The last straw.

CHAPTER 31

THE SHAFT of moonlight that fell through an opening high above their heads bathed the walls in a milky glow. Abby ducked through the split in the baobab trunk and listened for movement, for animal sounds, for any indication that the hollow in the tree might be occupied. Todd stood next to her teetering on one foot.

"Geez, what is this?"

"Shelter, I hope."

The shrill chorus on the far side of the tree had reached a rabid pitch, as though the feed had turned into a fight to the death. She felt prickles on her arms and knew that the fine hairs under her sleeves were trying to stand straight up. Then, for the second time that night, she heard the deep baritone of a lion.

Todd's walking stick felt lame in her hand, a feeble excuse for the tools they badly needed now. She leaned into the dim interior of the tree and used the stick to poke a semicircle on the floor in front of her. Not surprisingly this was a room of uncertain dimension.

A second step forward brought her closer to deep, inaccessible recesses. Her frayed nerves seemed to lay bare her senses, and even as she worried about what might be hiding in the tree, she detected a power in the embrace of the ancient baobab, a potency that evoked a tiny chapel—or a tomb. She waved the stick in the air, poised to jump back at the sound of a snarl or hiss. There was more darkness than light, yet the moon glow was sufficient for her body to cast a faint shadow on the wall.

Todd hopped to her side. "Let me," he said, taking the stick in his hand. "My reach is longer."

She yielded the implement willingly and supported him with both arms while he sprang forward, tapping right and left. It crossed her mind that this was the way a partnership was supposed to function, two people working together to accomplish something more effectively than either one of them could do alone. She adjusted her movements to his as they moved across the soft surface into the center of the chamber. In her hands his body felt as hard and lean as a sapling.

Something scooted up the wall near her ear. Only a gecko, she hoped, hunching in her head and shoulders to minimize the risk of touching the trunk and whatever might cling to it. Surely all the bats had left.

Even with her help, Todd needed every bit of his natural coordination to balance on one foot, crouch low, and probe through the dark with the stick. Her vision had adjusted, and she could make out the shape of his bent waist and crooked knees. They both knew the risk involved in disturbing a natural shelter. Watching him now, she felt a profound gratitude for the crannies of his soul that housed fortitude, courage, and even chivalry.

"If an animal is in here, it wants to stay hidden," he said in a quiet voice. "I'm guessing we can coexist."

This was not her preferred conclusion, but she understood that without a flashlight or the sensory gifts of a shrew, it was the best they could do. She cleared her throat. "Right. Let's sit on the cloth."

Although the cushiony floor would provide a more comfortable resting place than the roots outside, she did not want to think too hard about what composed the cushion. The loamy, not unpleasant scent reassured her that at least they were not settling down on a bed of bat guano or a place where animals went to die.

They spread the former tablecloth and lowered themselves onto it—like the food at a feast, she couldn't help thinking. It also occurred to her that earth-dwelling creatures might reside beneath the woven fabric. A drawing in Bones's journal came to mind, the crescent-shaped hole that scorpions dig to accommodate their pincers. She fingered the contents of a pocket.

"I'm going to spray repellent in a circle around us, like a moat," she announced, not knowing whether the precaution would have any effect at all on a venomous arachnid.

"Excellent. Then we can relax and get a good night's sleep."

The faint chemical scent of the spray rode up their noses as they sat side by side, wide awake, facing the triangular opening in the trunk. A wedge of starry sky was visible above the sweep of plain outside. The snarls and barks had become intermittent, as though the feed might be nearing an end. Abby stared at the moonlit grassland and wondered uneasily where the hyenas would go next.

The air inside the tree did not feel much warmer than the air outside. When Todd put an arm around her, she leaned gratefully into the heat of his body. Looking out into the night, she thought about Nina and Griff huddled together against the chill. Even if they were unaware of the flames west of the river, she knew they would be worried about her and no doubt afraid that now they could be alone for good.

"Do you think Nina and Griff can see the fire from down in the ravine?" she asked.

"They might smell the smoke." He was silent for a moment. "Would they try to leave? Maybe come here?"

"I doubt they would move until the flames were almost on them. Even then Griff wouldn't cross the plain at night."

"I wish they would come here. And bring the edibles."

The mention of edibles made her stomach pulse and contract. She was famished, and she was an entire calorie-rich shortbread ahead of Todd, who hadn't eaten since their predawn breakfast. Hunger moved inside her like something alive. Another snarl rose above the fight outside, and at that moment it seemed to her that all distress must be food-related.

"Would you kill for a cookie?" This arresting thought had come upon her suddenly, like an ambush.

"Only for chocolate chip."

"I'm serious. Food is the great imperative, you know. In the end food drives all behavior."

"Food and sex." He pulled her closer. "I have it on good authority that sex is the greater imperative."

"That fact is widely disputed among the world's leading experts."

He started to opine about a world of competing appetites when a loud, full-chested moan sounded outside the tree. With speed that impressed her, he seized the walking stick and brandished it at the split in the trunk. They heard a smothered cough.

She folded up her legs, knees to chest, and hugged her shins to make herself into a tight bundle. Todd was gripping the stick with both hands, visibly trembling. Somewhere a bird let out an inelegant screech. A baboon yakked from a lookout post. There was another cough and a menacing, fricative *pfff-pfff,* along with the unmistakable crackle of footfall in the grass just outside.

A dark, shaggy shape eclipsed the doorway. The silhouette blacked out the stars and seemed to obliterate all life beyond the tree. Abby looked up at the lion's whiskered muzzle and watched the great predator sniff the air not five feet from where she and Todd sat.

The stench was overpowering, an amalgam of cat urine, halitosis, and carrion. A corona of buzzing flies circled the thickly maned head. In the moonlight the supersized profile looked both monstrous and magnificent, and even as the blood pounded in her veins, Abby felt a terrified reverence for the undisputed king of beasts.

Forepaws the size of dinner plates rested on the ground in front of her. From where she sat she could look under the lion's sagging belly and see the grassland beyond. She was sure this animal knew that she and Todd were there. With one lunge, one casual swipe of a paw, he could reach inside the tree and scrape out either one of them.

She watched the belly contract, the head lift. Then came a roar that must have carried for miles. The effect within the tree trunk was a deafening, reverberant concussion. Abby had the presence of mind to appreciate that any animal hiding inside the baobab would not dare come out now.

With his ears up and twitching, the lion stared into the distance. A duet of answering roars sounded not far away. They were communicating, Abby realized—a coalition of males, or maybe this male and the pride he dominates.

With a terrible sense of foreboding, she guessed that the lion was calling others to the tree. Which posed the greater threat, a gang of males or a pride of females? She found herself stuck on this disheartening question, painfully aware that both groups cooperatively hunt and kill.

Males leave their natal pride at adolescence, form coalitions of three or four, and live a nomadic life until they mature and are ready to compete for reproductive rights. If they are to have any chance of dominating a new pride, the young males must bulk up by eating well. It didn't take an expert to figure out that this tautly muscled male was an excellent hunter.

Now he turned and dipped his head to peer through the opening in the tree. Africa's mightiest carnivore trained his acute night vision on her and Todd. A detachment of flies dove in for a look. Abby let them buzz around her face without a blink. The stick wavered only slightly in Todd's grip. He held it with the pointed end hovering like the snout of a viper inches from the lion's inscrutable, forward-facing eyes.

The lion coughed. *Huh.* Then, just as abruptly as he had arrived, he turned around and picked his way over the tangle of roots that braided out to the grass. His lean haunches pumped like oiled pistons, and in a moment the swaying backside sank into deep scrub and disappeared.

"Okay," she whispered, not relaxing one bit. "Bring on the others."

Soon there were two more—males, both heavily maned and at least nine feet long. *Pfff-pfff pfff-pfff.* The sound of their greeting carried clearly from where they came into view about ten yards from the entrance to the baobab.

"Just go away. Follow the other one," Abby whispered. Her knotted stomach weighed in with an impressive growl. She clenched her gut, not wanting to find out how a lion might react to the gurgle of soft, edible flesh.

The two lions stood for a moment with their noses raised. One of them turned his gaze on the baobab and then started toward the tree.

"Here he comes," Todd said. "Get back."

She scooted her bunched-up body until she felt the farthest wall press against her ribs. Todd moved a little to the side. She could not avoid thinking about their resemblance to the fatty marrow inside a bone—tender, nutritious, there for the taking.

At the edge of the root structure the lion halted. She was sure he was glaring directly at her through the split in the trunk. Then he lowered his rump and raked his back feet over the ground, tearing up the turf with his claws while he dribbled urine onto the soil. This was scent marking—planting an olfactory and visual signpost that announced to every lion in the vicinity that his coalition owns the tree, the inhabitants of the tree, and all the territory around it.

When he finished, he cast one final stare in her direction. *Huh.* He coughed, turned, and slunk into the grass. She watched the two partners come together. *Pfff-pfff pfff-pfff.* They're high-fiving, she thought. *Pfff-pfff.* Masculine knuckle bumps.

Then the pair moved away with a loose-limbed arrogance that suggested full awareness of their dominion over the land and all of its residents, including her and Todd. There was a flurry of leaping and snorting as a small herd of impalas fled to make way. The two lions ignored the commotion and shagged off in rough file. In a moment they were gone.

The silence seemed absolute. The hyenas and wild dogs had either scrammed or gone mute. Abby herself felt too used up to utter a sound. Todd remained wordless, still keeping watch at the door.

Before long the wild things in their vicinity grew tired of wariness, and normal life slowly resumed. She heard the mewling cry of a gray lourie, the scratching song of a butcher bird, a hoot she couldn't identify, and finally, Todd.

"Your repellent works pretty well."

Instead of replying, she scooted over and laid her head on his shoulder. He hugged her to him, and in minutes she managed to achieve at least a fugue state between wakefulness and sleep. Todd might have dozed too. She didn't know for sure because the next thing she heard was his voice in her ear.

"Abby, wake up."

CHAPTER 32

THE SPECTER of the wraith in the spotlight—the wild hair, gaunt face, and rotten teeth—swam through Griff's fevered head. Whoever the assailant with the machete and his companions were, they were long gone now. The moon had rolled down behind the tree tops since the clanging and heaving of the Cruiser finally ceased, and he and Nina had sat limp with fear and exhaustion listening to the suck of the men's footsteps fade downstream.

Now Nina was curled up next to him, wrapped in two ponchos, not talking much. Not crying anymore, at least as far as he could tell. The glimpse of armed men and the terrifying whack of the silvery blade that plunged them in darkness had unraveled her more than anything else they had encountered in the bush. *Poacher, poacher burning bright, in the forests of the night.*

It was even darker now that the moon had descended. The lions had gone silent. In the hush of the men's absence, the nocturnal animals in the ravine had piped up again. Unnerving hisses and mutters and whoops sounded from every direction, and even the water next to him churned with life. He thought he caught a whiff of wood smoke. He sniffed again and decided no.

He had no idea what the looters had done to the vehicle. As much as he wanted (in theory, at least) to feel his way forward to assess the damage, he rationalized that the risk of injury in the dark was too great. He and Nina had decided to sit tight in the protection of their ponchos. Or more accurately, they had defaulted to inaction. Shock and fatigue had enervated both of them, and they had readily agreed that sunup would be soon enough to discover whether the Cruiser still had bumpers, doors, a windshield, or even tires and wheels.

Griff actually welcomed a few hours of rest before learning the worst. There had been sufficient ratcheting and splashing to suggest ruinous pillage.

The Cruiser tilted at an alarming new angle. For some reason the men had not touched the food box or the first aid kit stowed right behind him, even though he had plainly seen that they could use the contents of both.

He raised his left arm and flexed the useless parts at its tip. Every one of the twenty-seven bones in his infected hand and wrist and all the ligaments, tendons, and muscles there felt invaded and abused. Nina's poultice had helped for a while, but as he suspected, tea bags were no match for the pathogens that were busy setting up camp in his palm and sending out scouts to investigate the rest of his body.

The possibility that in the morning they would have to walk instead of drive consumed him less than the idea of ending up with only one good hand—or maybe one hand, period. Amputation was an extreme, over-the-top, highly implausible outcome. But any impairment of his fine motor skills could be catastrophic.

An attending surgeon with only one fully functional hand? Even as the prospect staggered him, deep in his meticulous, deliberative psyche, he knew that he had to consider the possibility. Contrary to the nomenclature, patients expected their attending surgeons to do more than simply attend their operations.

Nina moved inside her poncho. He was aware that to mull over his career while they sat stuck in the dark on a wrecked vehicle in the middle of a African water hole served as an escape, a little mental break, even if he was feeling less than sanguine about his work. It was not lost on him that for years, surgery had been an all-consuming diversion from the good things in his life too, from Nina and their kids.

He tucked the poncho under his legs and raised the hood. The coldest, darkest part of the night was closing in. The first ray of light would turn his warm breath to white vapor. He felt disturbingly hot and chilled at the same time, and he did not want to dwell on what the morning would bring.

He closed his eyes. His thoughts turned to the sense of accomplishment he had felt as a resident when he performed his first hip replacement, skin to skin. In training the big thrills had come from technical achievements, especially the firsts—his first rotator cuff repair, his first joint realignment. But his deepest satisfaction even then had derived from patients who returned to say how much better they functioned and how happy they were with the outcome.

Now that he thought about it, his most rewarding connections had always been side by side, with his patients, his peers, and his family. Yet he had lived most of his days on the vertical, striving ever upward in the iron-clad hierarchy of medicine. Was being chief so much better than all the steps that preceded it?

His mind ranged over the tools of his trade, the rongeurs, cutting jigs, bone saws, and chisels. He shaped his right hand as if to grip each instrument and mimicked the role of his left hand in its use. On a ski trip years earlier, he had sprained his left thumb. He still remembered the nuisance that injury had caused, an uncomfortable reminder that every finger played a part. Now his entire left hand felt ossified with pain and swelling.

He stared into the darkness and dared to imagine an alternate future. Research maybe. Orthopedics was flush with foundation funding for academic research. Biomechanics, tissue engineering, gene therapy—all the hot fields interested him. If his hand failed to recover, could he change course entirely?

The idea that his days and nights might revolve around something other than the demands of a well-established orthopedics practice struck him as exotic and intriguing. Family-friendly too, if it wasn't too late. It occurred to him that he hadn't imagined a different path for himself since high school. Even then, he had been an ardent bone-setter with a sharp eye for injured robins and sparrows.

He closed his eyes again and sank into himself. At the moment, just rising from his seat seemed almost impossible. He lacked the motivation to swat insects from his face. He understood that infection was sapping his will as well as his strength, but understanding did not fortify him at all.

A scops owl hooted. *Doo-doo-doo-doo-hohoo.* Movement sounded in the leadwood tree. He heard the rhythmic splashes of some large animal lapping water a few feet from where he sat and wondered absently what animal that might be.

The minutes dragged forward. He slipped into a febrile sleep and sometime later jerked his chin up from his chest. The air was acrid with smoke. Yes, this time definitely smoke.

"What's burning?" Nina asked, apparently just coming to full alert too.

"A bushfire, probably. It's so dry up there." He blinked his smarting eyes. Although a wildfire seemed more benign than anything involving armed poachers, he knew that flames east of the river could be the *coup de grâce* for Abby and Todd. For Bones too, wherever he was. He turned his head toward the left bank and sniffed the air.

"It's west of here," Nina said, one step ahead of him. "The smoke is coming from the west."

He hoped she was right, that the fire was across the river from their friends. He licked his forefinger and held it up to check the direction of the wind, glad that she couldn't see him. Did that old trick really work? All sides of the finger felt equally cold and uninformative.

The *pop pop pop* of gunfire startled him, and for a confused second he wondered why anyone would hunt at night. Then it came together—the poachers, the fire. This was not a random fire at all but grass ignited on purpose to flush out game. He pictured white-eyed animals dashing for safety, straight into the bullets.

Nina touched his leg. "Listen," she whispered.

Something cracked through the bushes up on the western ridge. The footfall sounded too skittery and disorganized to be human or even that of a single animal. It came crashing toward the water like a small stampede.

"Some kind of antelope running from the flames," he said.

"Some kind of animal, you mean. It could be anything. A bunch of them." Her voice had taken on new strength, as though she had already seen and survived the worst. "By morning the ravine will look like Noah's Ark."

"Noah's Cruiser," he amended. "We might have to share our seats."

Neither of them spoke while the truth of that took hold.

The smoke billowed thick in the air, but the cascade of footfalls did not lead to a great migration into the river, at least not that Griff could tell. Activity on the fire side of the embankment was difficult to judge. He heard the occasional snap of a branch and the sigh of matted leaves as some animal light-footed it down a trail. Earlier arrivals must be milling about at the edge of the water or making their way up the opposite bank, he thought. So far he was pretty sure nothing had jumped aboard the Cruiser.

He guessed that the men he and Nina had seen were hunting to feed themselves and their families, not to poach ivory or horn. Commercial hunters would be a sharper-looking lot, better dressed and fed, and they probably wouldn't stop to loot a passenger vehicle. He hadn't gotten a good look at the men's rifles, but he would bet they were smaller gauge than the weapons needed to bring down an elephant or rhino. Fire would root out all sorts of game that was relatively easy to pick off and carry home for food.

The difficulty of convincing hungry people that wildlife was worth more to them alive than dead had been the subject of an impassioned conversation with Bones. Safari camps provide jobs for thousands of Africans, Bones had pointed out—builders, mechanics, managers; guides and trackers; food service, laundry, and maintenance workers; and many more. In this way revenue from game-viewing tourism flows directly to the villages.

But the industry does not benefit everyone yet, and most locals understandably still think of wild animals as sources of meat. In Bones's opinion, hunters who kill for the pot could eliminate all the game in the region even faster than large-scale poachers. For that reason, he said, subsistence poaching has to be controlled as stringently as poaching for commercial gain. Both activities destroy a valuable, renewable resource that could raise the living standard for all.

The frightening, snaggle-toothed grin on the man with the machete swam before Griff's stinging eyes. Those poachers hadn't done themselves any favors by looting a safari vehicle. Feeding families was one thing; attacking tourists another.

Fatigue shuddered through him. He felt worse than helpless just sitting there in the housing of his poncho waiting for dawn, for an onslaught of frantic animals, for the first lick of flames up on the ridge. Fever had drained him to an increasingly depressed and listless state. He had come to accept that something unimaginable had happened to Bones. He thought about Abby and Todd with an even heavier heart.

A crystalline birdsong rose above the hum of the riverway. *Hoet hoet hoet. Hoet hoet hoet.* A warbler. It was almost morning.

161

CHAPTER 33

TODD WATCHED Abby's eyelids flutter and settle. She was an accomplished sleeper who never woke up easily, even, apparently, when she was sprawled on lumpy ground inside a tree. He, on the other hand, had been awake for most of the night, too wound-up and wary to drift off for long.

Now the sky was pink with the coming of dawn. Abby lay across the kente cloth with her head resting on his good leg. She seemed lost in slumber, and he decided to let her sleep a little longer. He told himself that she could use the rest after the exertions of the previous day, which was probably correct, but in truth he needed a few more minutes to sort out new and complicated feelings about the woman at his knee. He, the master of avoidance, wanted more time to think.

He tried to shift his weight without disturbing her. He felt cramped and sore, dying to move his limbs. His face was raw with itching bites. Sunburn flared under his shirt. Even secure in Abby's bandage, his foot and ankle hurt like hell. Hunger was doing handsprings in his stomach.

In the faint light, Abby, however, looked amazingly together. He wasn't sure how he felt about that, about her clear, pale face and the way her hair streamed neatly into its ponytail, even now. Her clothes were hardly wrinkled. He doubted that she bore a single insect bite or the faintest tan line on her well-tended neck and wrists.

He did notice scratches on the hand resting next to her cheek. Her usual tidy manicure had taken a ration of abuse. For some reason this reassured him, even as he knew what a jerk he was for wanting her frailty to match his, or rather, for fearing that he would seem inadequate by comparison. Inadequate and needy.

He saw things differently now that the hours of greatest danger had passed. In the precarious night, her strength had come as a welcome surprise. But he wondered how this unexpected persona would play out in the light of an ordinary day—at home, for instance. Were their comfy, familiar roles irretrievably altered? Or was this unflappable, take-charge side of Abby something she saved for extraordinary circumstances—armor that she could put on and remove like her multipocketed travel vest?

A reservoir of fortitude was an admirable quality in a person, and he admired her for it, he truly did. But even with a bum foot and dark, lame weeks ahead, he rejected the notion that a man wanted a woman to take care of him. He liked to think of things the other way around, that he would always take care of Abby.

He scratched a needy place on his scalp. There could be a middle ground, he imagined, a give-and-take sort of thing. He could not envision a future apart from her. And of course, he thought without a trace of irony, he would always be the alpha male, wouldn't he?

He cast a glance at her lovely profile. The "always" wasn't going to happen by itself. Maybe it was time to make things official, pull a Plan B—if she would have him. This sudden thought caught him up short. He watched a beetle scuttle out from under the kente cloth and rush away on some urgent mission. *Would* she marry him? With his chewed face and livid skin and his useless foot and ankle, he wasn't in the best shape to woo and win a spectacular woman like Abby.

And today, how would she feel about hauling him across the plain to a stranded vehicle he was too banged up to help free? Should he stay at the baobab and let her go by herself? (Abby, alone in the bush *again*?)

His current enfeebled status, especially compared to the ineffable woman at his side, had mashed his sense of self to a pulp. He struggled to tamp down the latent dorkiness in his soul, the awkward self-consciousness he thought he had long ago outgrown. He was too positive by nature, though, to overlook the bonds that already united them. Pascal's Triangle, for cripes sake! Working out! The list would have been much longer, but he got stuck on the memory of his tongue traveling down the river of her spine like a slow-moving canoe.

He jiggled his good foot and tapped all ten fingers against his thighs. Her honey-colored eyelashes rested becomingly against her cheeks. He heard her innards growl and knew how hungry she must be.

When they got home (he never entertained the notion that they wouldn't),

163

he would cook for her, a dinner with champagne and candlelight and all the rest. She was so lean that most people never guessed she ate like a lumberjack. His long bachelorhood had made him reasonably handy in the kitchen, and Abby had an eight-lane expressway from her stomach to her heart. Over dessert, something gooey and chocolate, he would ask her to marry him.

He turned his face to the pale sky and grinned. She herself had said it: in the end, food drives all behavior. He swallowed hard. It was an excellent plan, and of course she would marry him, especially if he presented the ring inside a new backpack she could carry with her to school every day.

He smoothed and tucked his shirt, knuckled the gritty corners of his eyes, and took a deep breath. "Abby, wake up."

She blinked and stirred and blinked again. Then, with only a few seconds' transition from sleep to action, she sat up and said, "What time is it?"

"Time to rise and shine."

He reached for the canteen and unscrewed the top. "Juice or coffee?"

Her expression told him she would commit mayhem for either.

"Perhaps you would prefer water," he said, handing over the container.

In the half-light of predawn, he watched her sip and swish the water around her mouth before swallowing. Abby would keep herself clean and neat in a mudslide, he thought. He ran a hand through his matted hair. "I'm going to go kick a tire."

"I'll help you walk."

"No, thanks. I can manage." There was no way he was going to let her hold him up while he peed. He crawled through the opening in the tree trunk with his loose shoe in one hand and the stick in the other. Once he got outside, he would reconstruct his crutch and do just fine on his own, thank you very much.

A dog's-eye view of the world was an interesting thing, he noticed. A circle of ants had crowded around a feeding trough formed by the upturned body of a beetle. The beetle he had seen moments before perhaps? Even up close, the ants looked like a boiling mass, but he knew that magnification would expose a gang of ruthless predators armed with razor-sharp ant mandibles.

He crawled out of Abby's view, away from the dark scent mark that brought to mind the lion encounter of the previous night, a trauma he did not wish to dwell on just yet. Instead he studied the topography of the baobab roots—the ridges, valleys, and desiccated flats. There was no greenery on the miniature landscape, but there was a multitude of ants, spiders, beetles, and countless deceptive little insect nothings.

A hole the shape of a nail clipping caught his eye. No, what caught his eye was the thing emerging from the hole, starting with a pair of pincers. Before he could even think the word "scorpion," the entire venomous, lobster-like creature had popped out of its lair. Relative to the other inhabitants of that microworld, it was a monster: three inches long. The giant did not move far from its burrow but waited in place while a fat spider sauntered within range. In a blink the scorpion caught and secured the spider between two grasping pedipalps.

Todd considered whether to squash the scorpion with his shoe and decided not to. He had come to Africa to observe animals, not kill them, and he had just seen some interesting arachnid behavior. As he rose on his good foot, he kept an eye on the scorpion that was now absorbed in the complicated process of consuming a body with eight long legs. He turned away. In a minute, vastly relieved, he was zipping up when a dark shape dove from a branch in the baobab and plucked the scorpion from the earth. There was a flap of wings, and the bird—an owl—rose to the sky with the scorpion swimming in the pinch of its talons. *Hu-hoo hu-hoo.*

Hoo hoo, joke's on you, Todd thought, unnerved by the sudden turn of events: two living things, vanished before his eyes.

It did not escape his increasingly sober mind that people could disappear almost as suddenly. He and Abby, for instance. Nina and Griff. Even a man as well defended as Bones. He had been an idiot to chase after Bones on foot. It wasn't lost on him that Abby had spared him a scolding and that he might not be so lucky with Nina and Griff.

With a stab of guilt, he realized that he hadn't thought about Nina and Griff for hours. Both of them were injured, Abby had said. He hadn't thought much about the bush fire, either, or how three banged-up people plus Abby could possibly free the Cruiser. He rubbed his itchy face and noticed that the ants had almost obliterated the dead beetle.

At the moment the problem that weighed on him most heavily was the terrible risk he and Abby would face if they tried to walk back to the river together, with him supported on one foot, a crutch, and her slender shoulders. Hobbled together they would be easy pickings for an opportunistic hyena or one of the lions that hung out around Threeflat Rocks. Sheer luck had gotten him past those dangers as he crutched his way to the baobab. He realized that now. Although he loathed the idea of sending Abby out alone, he had to admit that she would be safer without him.

She had emerged from the tree and was shaking the former tablecloth like a busy housewife. In the gilded dawn she looked more golden than usual, if that was possible. He braced himself against the baobab to compensate for the possible collapse of his one good leg. Although he would admit it to no one, the sight of her could still turn his knees to jelly.

The sky pinked and reddened. A suffusion of light spilled like mist over the savanna. He used his crutch to step-stick to her side. When he reached for her hand, he was rewarded with a look so loaded and intimate he would never forget it. Not a smile, exactly, but a fleeting evocation of a life shared, for better or worse. Together they turned to face the horizon and wait for Africa's most dazzling moment, the break of day.

CHAPTER 34

BIRDS HAD begun to reestablish their territories and status in the predawn gloom. *Fee-yoo fee-yoo fee-yoo.* Soon the river was alive with the full chorus of runs and trills that heralds a new day. *Trrp-trrrr. Kay-waaaaay. Thweeloo. Tleeoo.*

A faint outline of branches became visible against the eastern sky. Nina huddled against Griff and watched the stars in the thin strip above the river disappear. As the heavens brightened, she felt relief and dread in equal measure. Daylight would restore vision and clarity and also bring into sharp focus the full extent of their peril.

The trees up on the western ridge formed a starker border against the glow of the approaching fire. Threads of smoke twisted through the branches. A slender antelope raced across the horizon. She spotted a great black bulk heading down to the water.

"Nina."

"What?"

"We'll have to walk out of here, you know."

Yes, she knew. Even if the looters had spared the Cruiser's essential working parts, Griff in his weakened condition did not possess the muscle power to help her haul logs, and they would be hard pressed to collect enough lightweight wood to brace the jack, shore up the tires, and free the two-ton vehicle from sucking, viscous mud. Not in a riverbed crowded with frightened and skittish animals, where fire was closing in and maybe poachers too.

"Are you strong enough to walk?" she asked, knowing the answer.

"Of course."

"I'm not so sure."

"We don't have any choice, Neener." He sounded used up, spent. "How's your leg?"

"Fine. Good enough to hike into the open and signal the next passing airplane. You can stay here."

"To manage the ark? Toast in the fire? I don't think so."

She swallowed. All of her airways felt the sting of the smoke. She suspected that the large, dark animal she had seen heading down the embankment was a buffalo, a dagga boy, and if it was, neither she nor Griff would be walking out anytime soon. Their options narrowed with every passing minute.

The sky had whitened. Shapes began to emerge—a column of tree, a claw of scrub, the outline of the Cruiser itself: windshield, doors, hood. So far nothing on the vehicle seemed amiss.

She blinked and sucked in air. Not ten feet from where they sat stood a leopard, a gorgeous, low-slung animal, tan with black spots grouped in rosettes that blended almost seamlessly with the mottled colors of the sand. A potent blend of fear and awe overcame her as she took in the rare, close-up view of the shyest African cat. The leopard seemed unaware of her and Griff as it crouched to lap water. Their ponchos had evidently turned into cover as effective as a hunting blind.

A leopard can kill and eat almost anything, and in the growing daylight every animal in the vicinity had taken notice. Nina spied a spectacular sable antelope with back-curving horns at least three feet long moving downriver, putting distance between itself and the superb hunter on the shore. Three warthogs knelt to drink while a fourth kept watch. An Ethiopian snipe stepped steadily away as it foraged in a muddy pool. Even the monkeys in the leadwood tree were on the lookout and vocal about it too. Their warning chirps and chatter sounded like percussion instruments against the morning chorus.

Something made her turn in her seat. A grizzled old Cape buffalo was standing in the water upstream behind the vehicle. He rocked his horns at her and snorted. Or was he looking past her at the leopard? The crackle of her poncho had given her away, and now the leopard was poised at full attention, with its hazel eyes trained on her. Or was the leopard looking past her at the buffalo? A bead of sweat coursed down her back.

Griff had turned and taken in the situation too. He gave her a troubling glance that said he had just about had enough. His face was drained of color.

He closed his eyes. She put an arm around his shoulders, keeping watch on the leopard while trying to look as lumpish and uninteresting as possible.

The leopard seemed frozen in place. It was still staring at her or past her, she couldn't tell which, and in her exhaustion she almost didn't care. Behind her the dagga boy snorted again. He was the boss of this menagerie, and he was letting every creature know.

A brace of helmeted guinea fowl clattered down the embankment calling, *Kek-kek-kek-kek*. Small, flapping birds and more rodents than she could count poured over the ridge ahead of the fire. The smell of smoke had intensified. She spotted a lick of flame. Sparks climbed into the sky. Two black-backed jackals ran into view and made their way down through the bushes.

The leopard blinked and looked away, feigning disinterest. About then, the jackals appeared on the shore. They were handsome animals, a male and a female, and they were panting from fright and exertion, apparently unaware of the leopard.

Nina watched the cat fix its sights on the unsuspecting male a few yards downstream. The jackal dipped his head to drink, and the leopard sank fluidly to stalking position. With its head and belly almost touching the sand, the prince of stealth crept silently forward. The knit and glide of powerful muscles, the laser-like, life-or-death focus, captivated her even as her heart hammered. In the leadwood tree, the vervets were watching too, but neither the cat nor the two canids seemed to pay any attention to their excited chattering.

The attack was over in a few seconds. There were two short yelps. The female jackal sprang back—horrified, Nina imagined—as the leopard clamped its jaw on her mate's hairy neck. Without so much as a glance at the female, the leopard dragged the carcass past her, scattering a small flock of red-chested flufftails. In a minute the cat and its burden were gone.

Nina followed the drama with a pounding pulse and smoke-stung eyes. Or was she weeping again? In the last several hours, her ponded emotions had spilled their normally unbreachable banks. Until that day she had almost forgotten what tears felt like, the gushing and streaming. She sniffed loudly and swiped her nose with the back of her hand.

The bereaved jackal stared downstream, raising and lowering her head as if stunned by the loss of her partner. Even as Nina understood the harsh imperatives of the food chain, she found the scene almost unbearable.

She laid a hand on Griff's burning forehead. He was in no condition to walk out of the ravine. She admitted that now, and her spirits sank further. Despite her earlier bravado, she knew that to abandon Griff even temporarily would be most difficult thing she had ever done. Yet for each minute of daylight that she lingered in the ravine, she ran the risk of missing the only airplane that might (or might not, she reminded herself) pass overhead that day.

The buffalo had gone to dry land and was feeding, seemingly oblivious of the smoke and fire across the river. As he ripped and chewed, the bull drifted away from the Cruiser, apparently unconcerned about her and Griff too. She listened to the crunch of working molars and felt a ray of hope that the animal would simply move out of sight.

She put aside her ponchos and rose cautiously from the seat. A spiderweb brushed against her face. She sprang back, waving away the sticky silk. Bones would call the web "the morning news," just one story of many in the a.m. edition of excretions, tracks, and trampled foliage that reported on the previous night's activity. Bones had introduced her to the morning news early one day while pointing out large, round tracks a few yards from her tent, the same tent in which she and Griff had slept soundly, unaware that an elephant had paid them a visit.

As for this morning's news, she would call the slashed front seat the lead story. Unlike the elephant that had ambled through their camp, the man with the machete was a night visitor she wished she had not seen. Her eyes fell on the gaping leather and then on something else.

A papery, translucent tube stretched almost the entire length of the seat cushions. One end was rounded and flared on the sides, with two slitty eye holes staring vacantly ahead. The other end tapered to a point, like the snake that left it there. The skin had been severed in half.

She caught her breath. A cobra? The six-foot-long reptile must have shed its skin while she and Griff sat on the middle seat just a foot or two away, before the man with the machete showed up and hacked the already vacated membrane in two, along with the electrical cord. With slightly different timing, she could have met that snake in the dark when she crawled forward to fetch the spotlight. The thought stunned her even as she felt a profound sense of good luck. This time the fates had been on her side.

She pictured a cobra winding its way into the Cruiser, over the floorboards, across the leather cushion. This was morning news indeed. A six-foot snake lounging on the front seat must have been a powerful deterrent to any other night-roaming predator with an inclination to jump on deck. She almost smiled. Noah would never let the cobras board first.

She tossed the tissue-light tubes of snakeskin into the river. Other than the gash in the seat cushion and the useless spotlight on the floor, the Cruiser appeared unchanged. The key still hung in the ignition. Bones's journal was right where she had left it.

She leaned over the side, fully expecting to see river water coursing through an empty wheel well where the left front tire should be. She stared and blinked.

Her comprehension entered a numbing antechamber where emotions like despair and joy go to wait until conclusive evidence calls them forth. She scissored her legs over to the driver's side, so distracted that she moved clumsily and banged her bruised shin hard against the center console. She gasped with pain and the understanding that she had compounded her injury. An excruciating few moments passed while the torment in her shin slowly subsided and her mouth went dry. She rubbed her stinging eyes and swallowed hard.

Steeling herself, she leaned over the driver's side to inspect the Cruiser's right front tire. An exquisite, standstill second passed while her observations coalesced into understanding.

Like the left tire, the right one sat high and dry, and even through the smoke, she could see that it rested on a hefty log that was partially submerged. Other logs lay parallel to the one bracing up the front tires. Water lapped gently over their rounded surfaces. She moved her eyes from log to log. There were enough of them lined up side by side to form a crude but sturdy track all the way to shore.

CHAPTER 35

SHE ALMOST reflexively turned to Griff, but he had covered his face with his hat and appeared to be asleep. On the shore, the dagga boy was busy ripping apart a caper bush. Flames that had once rimmed the western bank had begun to make their way down the ridge. In front of the flames, a mob of terrorized animals was rushing toward the water. The yipping, screeching horde included at least a dozen wild dogs, ferocious pack animals that she feared would splash across the mud and jump aboard.

Without taking time to alert Griff, she slid into the driver's seat and turned the key in the ignition. Instead of rolling forward, the front tires spun against the first log and sent up plumes of water. She kept both hands tight on the steering wheel, and tried easing up on the accelerator to coax the vehicle ahead. When the tires finally found purchase, the Cruiser lurched forward, tipping so violently from side to side that she feared she might dump Griff in the river.

At each new bump in the partially submerged roadway, the front tires rose and thudded down hard, and she worried that they might drop through a gap between the logs and stay there. Her palms were clammy with sweat. Her clenched jaw ached, and her lower back felt the impact of every thump.

The going was slow, rocky, terrifying. Sparks from the fire drifted down and landed on the hood of the vehicle, the seat next to her, her sleeve. She heard creatures splash into the water behind her. Ahead, some kind of vulture swooped in for a look and took off again.

The heat and smoke had intensified. Sweat filmed her eyes. She coughed and blinked and hoped that Griff was holding on tight. She dared not turn around to look at him while the Cruiser bucked and juddered.

When the front tires finally met the shore, water sloshed loudly off the undercarriage, assuring her that at least there would be no vehicle fire any time soon. She rolled the Cruiser onto solid ground and almost collapsed with relief.

But her relief was premature. The Cape buffalo had planted the blockade of his body smack in the middle of the only possible egress from the ravine. He stood in the gap between the trees with his front legs wide apart, glaring in her direction. There was no question that this fighter expected to take on the Cruiser.

With heat, smoke, and frantic creatures closing in behind her, Nina knew that she had little choice but to go forward. The Cruiser was bigger than the bull by half. Could she call the animal's bluff? Forcing a lower-ranked individual to move aside by advancing toward it was common buffalo behavior. "Supplanting," this was called. She decided to try.

She shifted into third, stepped on the accelerator, and drove straight at him.

Apparently, though, the dagga boy was set on his own ideas about who held the higher rank. He turned broadside to the Cruiser and locked his legs. With a terrifying bellow, he announced that he did not plan to budge.

Nina jerked the steering wheel toward the narrow space between the animal's buttress-like rear end and a battered torchwood tree. With speed that surprised her, the buffalo spun around in time to catch the tip of one hooking horn in the vehicle's already mangled front grill. The engine raced, the floorboards groaned, and the engine died. She found herself staring into the wide, yellow-ringed eyes of an angry, snared, bellowing adversary that could easily roll the vehicle and stomp it flat.

The Cruiser bucked with the force of the buffalo's furious effort to unsnag himself. Nina was fumbling with the ignition key when Griff yelled, "Duck!" He leaned over her and threw a poncho across the animal's wild eyes and foaming mouth. The fabric caught on the point of the one free horn and settled like a veil.

Nina had no idea whether a blindfold would enflame the bull or calm him. She suspected that Griff did not know either but had made a quick and risky guess. The alacrity of his response only later struck her as uncommon. He had risen from a feverish stupor to take in the situation, think up a strategy, and act—all within seconds.

For a few moments the bull stood unmoving, caught by his horn and shrouded in darkness. Nina flicked the ignition and heard the sweet suck of the engine followed by the grind of a less than perfect shift into reverse. The bull dug in his hooves. There was a shriek of torn metal, and what was left of the front grill ripped free of the chassis.

Now the dagga boy found himself with a twist of automotive wreckage hanging from one horn and a poncho swinging from the other. He stood with his legs wide apart, bellowing while the black block of his head tossed and shook with the fury of a creature pushed to the limit.

Nina gunned the Cruiser past the bull and into the caper bushes. As she sped up the slope, she feared that the dagga boy might give chase even before he shook off his new accoutrements. She had almost reached the top when she was forced to stomp on the brake, nose-to-nose with the huge, gray-purple snout of a hippopotamus, likely the same one they had seen going to pasture the night before. Hippos returning to water are like trains on a track, she remembered. You must not get in their way.

For an awful moment the affronted hippo seemed ready to head-butt the impediment in its path. Nina endured a vision of the Cruiser pancaked between the hippo in front and the buffalo in back. But the hippo nosed the great inflation of its body to the side and lumbered by with a less-than-friendly *wheeze-honk wheeze-honk*. She stepped on the gas and did not look back or even slow down until the deep grass of the plain engulfed the vehicle, and the hippo, the dagga boy, the dogs, and the fire were well behind her.

CHAPTER 36

THE HUM of the engine combined with the fever ransacking his body made Griff almost immune to the jostle of the Land Cruiser. He was stretched across the uppermost seat with his hat secured over his face and his head pillowed on a bunched-up poncho, half-asleep. Even in his depleted state, he had thought to tuck his camera between his waist and the seatback, hoping he would have the energy to take photos if something of interest came into view. At present, though, all he could see was an indeterminate future and the inside of his hat.

He had entered the calmer waters of acceptance regarding the disappearance of Bones. Whatever had happened to the guide, he knew now that Bones was as good as dead and gone to him and his friends. Nothing they did was going to bring him back. The message of that long day and night in the bush, he realized, the difficult reality a fully functioning person must prepare for, was that there were limits to one's knowledge and understanding. Events are unpredictable. People are surprising. What had happened to Bones might never be known.

As for his own future, the hoof beats coming at him could be horses, or they could be zebras. He harbored hope, at least, of receiving proper medical attention before his hand was lost and maybe before permanent damage to his motor skills too. Whatever the outcome of the infection, he knew that he would weigh his options, consult his family (yes, the kids too), make a plan, and move forward.

Nina sat on the middle seat facing sideways, with her bad leg extended across the cushion. From her central vantage point, she was able to keep watch over Griff on the upper seat and also look at Todd and Abby, who were blessedly alive, well enough, and seated in front. Todd held the cookie tin in his lap and was feeding Abby morsels of shortbread while she drove the Land Cruiser with one hand on the wheel and the other quite capably manipulating the stick shift.

That she and Griff had escaped the inferno of the riverbed with the help of poachers took some time to process. Men who had wanted them gone could have arranged the disappearance of two unarmed people far more easily than by assembling a virtual freeway in the dark out of logs. She felt ashamed of her instant assumption that the men's intentions toward her and Griff had been evil.

The men very likely were husbands and fathers doing their best to feed the people who depended on them. Perhaps they understood the value of wildlife tourism even if they were not prepared to let their families go hungry for it. Or maybe they were simply desperate but decent men who wanted to remove obstacles and witnesses to their illegal hunting with the least possible damage. After having glimpsed their ragged clothing and emaciated bodies, she herself felt conflicted about the subject of subsistence poaching.

She flexed her throbbing leg and felt the gnaw of hunger. Though she would not wish the calamities and deprivations of the preceding twenty-four hours on any other traveler, she knew that stepping out of one's comfort zone even a little was an opportunity to learn and grow. A person who shies from inconvenience, ill ease, or the slightest challenge to accepted truths would be unlikely to benefit from travel, or to go at all. A pity, she thought as she watched a reedbuck bound through the grass.

Before coming to Africa, she had thought an antelope was, well, an antelope—not seventy-two different species in Africa alone. She had always known that travel teaches facts, but it had come home to her more starkly than ever that travel can also be fatal to prejudice and narrow-mindedness. Contents do shift during flight. The most fortunate travelers return less blinkered and selfish human beings, more ample-hearted and aware.

Which wasn't the same as lowering one's standards! She pursed her lips against a smile. She knew a thing or two about herself. She knew, for instance, that she would always keep one toe firmly planted in the penthouse of good manners. Her nose would never fail to wrinkle at people, adults in particular, who careen around the world oblivious to the eyes, ears, possessions, and personal space of everyone else. This was a matter of consideration, she felt, of functioning outside a myopic little sphere of self-absorption.

Nor would she relinquish her tight grip on the preferred passenger credentials that gave her and Griff respite from the more public, less savory aspects of going to and fro. She much preferred to save whatever discomfort a destination required for after she got there. Besides, a calm interval in which to decompress between work and adventure was important for Griff.

She regarded him fondly. Even asleep, he looked solid and reliable, and she knew that he would carry on with distinction no matter what adjustments the damage to his hand might require. He had surprised her by suggesting another safari, with their kids. She loved the idea.

She glanced at Todd, whom she still wanted to smack for his reckless foray into the bush, and allowed herself a small smile. There are, after all, limits to even the amplest of hearts. But she had taken her cue from Abby, who had been given plenty of time to unload on Todd before she and Griff rescued them at the baobab tree, and who now appeared to treat her man with equanimity, if not exactly warmth.

The Cruiser hit a bump, and her binoculars banged against her chest. She had become the designated observer since surrendering her place in the driver's seat to Abby. Her young friend had surprised her yet again by girding herself to take the wheel so that Nina could rest her painful leg. Seeing Abby mine hidden lodes of strength had been an unexpected bonus of their journey. She would always remember the joy she had felt when she steered the mud-caked Cruiser across the plain and spotted Abby standing in the grass waving the tablecloth like a flag.

Now, resting on the middle seat in the relative luxury of generalized rather than imminent peril, she raised her sunglasses to the top of her head and lifted the binoculars. Abby was driving straight toward the newly risen sun. They had entered unfamiliar territory east of the baobab, a vast mopane bushveld. She twirled the focus and fingered the zoom. At any moment anything could happen, and she was their lookout now.

In the front passenger seat, not at all bothered by the gash in the cushion under his butt, Todd swallowed a final crumb of shortbread and pressed the cover on the tin. Abby had signaled that she did not want more, though of course she did; they both did. But now that they were even with Nina and Griff in cookie consumption, they agreed to conserve the remaining supplies of food and beverage, just in case.

Hunger was nothing compared to the agony he and Abby would have faced if they had been forced to walk across the plain. The relief he felt when he first heard the Cruiser, long before he saw it barreling toward the baobab tree, was still fresh in his mind. Abby had gotten him so stuck on the idea that their own vehicle was mired in mud that he had imagined a rescue plane, a truck from camp, or even Bones coming back to get them—not Nina and Griff in the Land Cruiser. When he first spotted the filthy, half-demolished wreck rattling through the grass, he spent an uneasy moment wondering if it carried friend or foe.

Fortunately, the occupants still appeared to be his friends. Whatever ill feelings had sprouted from his run to find Bones, Nina and Griff must have decided to let them lie dormant at least until he recovered from his injuries. He suspected that at present the sight of his roughed-up body elicited more sympathy than anger.

With Abby's help, Griff had made a cursory examination of his foot and ankle. Watching Griff probe the swollen flesh using one hand only, he had felt worse than wretched and not just because the attention hurt. The magnitude of loss a hand injury signified for a physician—a surgeon no less—was achingly apparent to both Griff and himself. He would never forget the anxious expression Griff tried to hide as he fumbled through the exam with the useless hand dead in his lap. The consequences of his rash behavior would stay with Todd for a very long time.

He watched Abby downshift and circle a thicket and then steer the Cruiser back on course and climb smoothly into fourth gear. "Where did you learn to drive like that?" he shouted over the burr of the engine.

She threw him a look that she might have used on a pupil who flubbed his times-two tables. "With you, in Germany."

This surprised him, but he nodded and signaled thumbs up. Even hobbled by his injuries (a badly sprained ankle and at least one fractured bone in his foot, Griff had said) and chafed by the repercussions of his recent conduct, he felt unaccountably happy. He glanced at Abby's lovely profile, enjoying the view across the few feet that separated them. She was smiling too. She looked as radiant as a bride, and he hadn't even asked her to marry him yet.

He drummed his fingers against his thighs, wondering again at this newly hatched version of his girlfriend. A booted eagle soared high above the plain, calling, *Kee-keeee kee-keeee*. He eyed the bird and thought what a lame name the "booted eagles" would be for a college team. There were teams called the

Screaming Eagles, Running Eagles, and Marauding Eagles. Also the more familiar Purple, Golden, and Bald Eagles. His favorite genre of trivia occupied him for the next several minutes while he tried to think of more.

In the seat next to him, Abby leaned back and sucked in a lungful of fresh morning air. She had discovered that she could drive the Cruiser rather well, although she kept to herself the immensity of her relief at this finding. Apparently on the autobahn she had learned the fundamentals of using a stick shift better than she thought. The traffic there must have rattled her—the trucks and Mercedes roaring past and the impatient (she had imagined) drivers she could see glaring in her rearview mirrors. She remembered being nervous about Todd's approval too.

Behind her now were only the rapidly receding baobab tree and two of her three injured passengers. She was most worried about Griff, who seemed weaker than he had been when she left him and Nina at the river. Nina had held up better, although the goose egg on her shin had fattened to grotesque proportions and turned a livid purple.

Sitting in front, Todd was now angling his long body to prop his broken foot on the dashboard. The multiple abrasions on his face and hands, further complicated by sunburn, looked as though they would take weeks to heal, and the foot and ankle even longer. She hoped he would be back on his feet before she returned to school in the fall.

With three people in need of medical attention, the plan now was to make a beeline for civilization, for any trace of human life that could lead to help. There would be no unnecessary turning, no circuitous, fuel-wasting detours, just a straight shot due east until they used up their last fumes of gas. Some hopeful sign was bound to turn up sooner or later, and in the meantime, a search plane or vehicle could easily spot the Cruiser now that they were in the open.

A gray hump of elephant came into view next to a distant acacia. She wondered whether it might be the matriarch that had practically kissed her the day before, or the rogue male that had scared her senseless. By safari standards, it had been an excellent day. The species count would come close to the longest list in Bones's journal.

She and the others had experienced enough up-close animal encounters to make a documentarian swoon. Yet, she realized, none of the patients riding in her ambulance had been injured by animals. The most dangerous species in Africa had left them unharmed.

Luck had played a part, to be sure, as had vigilance. But so had respect for creatures that were simply living their lives on their own turf according to their individual natures. Bones had done a good job of demonstrating how to slow dance in synch with the environment—which more often than not meant to back off immediately.

She had come face to face with the realities of life and death in the bush and could name a dozen ways in which an ordinary person might vanish. Yet it still mystified her that Bones could simply disappear on land he knew so well. She half-expected an explanation once she and the others reconnected with the camps. Maybe the story of this safari wasn't over yet. The notion of an unimagined twist appealed to her, especially if it meant a happier ending for the guide she admired so much.

On the other hand, the very fact that Bones functioned so capably in the bush gave credence to the notion that some catastrophic occurrence had overwhelmed him. A man on foot would be easy pickings for any number of stalking predators—terrestrial or amphibious—and clean-up crews from the bird and insect kingdoms would make fast work of the leavings. Bones's rifle and radio, useless in an ambush, might now rest in deep grass or at the bottom of the river or in the possession of a curious vervet monkey. Like the man himself, his belongings might never be recovered.

At one time the thought of a man killed and eaten by animals would have horrified and disgusted her. The near equanimity with which she now, sadly, considered this possibility struck her as notable, as though she were observing her own reaction from a distant, neutral vantage point. She had learned that life in the wild follows straightforward rules, and rules, no matter how harsh and uncompromising, were something she understood.

Her gaze lifted to a magnificent booted eagle cruising on a high current of air. *Kee-keeee kee-keeee.* A slant of morning sun produced a dazzle on the bird's snowy feathers. The bird wheeled like a kite, and as she watched, she experienced a sudden flush of feeling that was close to exhilaration.

Her own life seemed as boundless and free as the big and bluing sky. She felt a tingly sense of expansiveness, as though she had outgrown and shed a confining exoskeleton. She actually looked forward to the spin and frazzle of the civilized world, the clutter and choice. She couldn't wait to teach again, to guide and encourage her students. A flash of inspiration lit her face. She would honor Bones by working to emulate his calm assurance and the way he led so effectively by example.

Bones's journal was still tucked between the front seats, she noticed. What would become of it? The volume held a wealth of wisdom and information, and it occurred to her that she would gladly trade her own missing luggage for those instructive, closely written pages.

The heat of a blush flooded her cheeks. Abby, without her gear? The swap would have been unimaginable only a day or two earlier when she had clung to her stuff like a kid to a blanket. It came to her that she had lost her luggage and unpacked herself instead.

She steered into a shallow depression and almost absently downshifted to climb out again. Driving the Cruiser would have been unthinkable a day ago too. Todd had done a poor job of hiding his amazement when she offered to replace Nina behind the wheel. This had been in part an act of kindness on her part, but mostly, she admitted, she wanted to test her wobbly but rising confidence that she was capable of driving a stick.

She threw a sideways glance at Todd. More than once in the past several hours she had caught him observing her with puzzlement, this woman he thought he knew. She couldn't blame him for being confused.

"Abby, look." Nina laid a hand on her shoulder.

Abby tugged her visor against the stare of the sun. They had entered a great flank of floodplain frothy with grass. She recognized the white of a calcrete shoal and areas of hardpan pitted with corrugations and ruts. A thin woodland bordered a growth of scrub that bloomed with dust.

A sprinkling of impalas colored the flats. In the distance she noted several grazing zebras and the familiar sight of a giraffe looming above the zebras' psychedelic bodies. Birds rode on the animals' backs and heads. And then she saw it: a worked strip of earth. Todd had seen it too and raised his binoculars. Even Griff had taken notice; she heard the rapid click of his camera.

She felt a shiver of anticipation that unexpectedly bordered on regret. A sense of impending loss seemed to fall over all four of them. As sorely as they needed the amenities of civilization, everyone on board fell silent and still, subdued by the knowledge that something rare was coming to an end.

Abby shifted into fourth gear and headed for the road.

─────── # AUTHOR'S NOTE ───────

I wish to thank our friends Pat and Wesley Moore for introducing my husband and me to Africa by leading safaris in Zambia, Botswana, and South Africa. We will never forget the welcoming outposts of Kapani, Tena Tena, Sausage Tree, Tongabezi, Vumbura Plains, Sandibe, Selinda, Chitabe, or Leopard Hills. Leora Rothschild of Rothschild Safaris has been a much-appreciated partner in planning our trips.

Special thanks to the guides and camp staffs who make every day in the African bush a rare and enriching experience. We particularly remember Abraham, Arlene, Aubrey, Basha, BB, Boyce, Dawson, Dukes, Duncan, Ella, Frank, Janelle, Lettie, Levi, Marius, Marks, Newman, Nick, Oates, OP, Roger, Rudy, Sanford, ST, Steve, Teaspoon, and Zara.

I am happy to report that we never lost a guide. *Waiting for Bones* is a work of fiction, one that benefited from contributions by a number of people. Novelist Mitch Engel, a master of characterization and backstory, gave generously of his time, enthusiasm, and insights. Dr. Daniel A. Handel helped me stay on track regarding medical matters. Christina Bates and Susan Garrett were thoughtful early readers whose suggestions helped guide the final cut and polish. I greatly appreciate their help.

For his endless support as well as the answer to every question about wheels, transmissions, axels, and mud, I am deeply grateful to John Cousins.

Last and best thanks to my husband, Dirk Vos, for his wisdom and encouragement every step of the way.

CPSIA information can be obtained at www.ICGtesting.com
Printed in the USA
LVOW101314211211

260497LV00001B/323/P